**He had been fulfilling the last request of his dead friend, and now it looked as if he would joining him in death...**

With little to observe and lulled by the steady movement of his horse, Daniel's mind drifted and his thoughts turned to Nellie. In his mind she always appeared just as she had that day they'd talked on the river, her long skirt rippling from the vigor of her movement as she walked back to the boat, her white blouse tightly buttoned around her neck.

As Daniel approached the rim of a minor coulee, the sudden movement of a man standing up shattered this pleasant image. Looks Beyond had been observing Daniel from a distance for much of the morning. He was waiting for the right time to kill a man who symbolized all that had become wrong in his rapidly changing world. Daniel had a sickening recognition that this was the man he had come to fear. Before Daniel could move, Looks Beyond dropped him with a single shot to the torso. He then walked up and looked at Daniel closely, satisfied that the wound would be mortal and that without any assistance likely he would die a slow, lingering death. While telling Daniel that such a death would be his fate, Looks Beyond took Daniel's rifle and the small box in his saddlebag.

Daniel lay sprawled on the grass, his blood staining the ground, for most of the day. He couldn't have known for how long, for he was unconscious much of the time, but he later remembered how dried out he felt and how he had dreamed of lying in a forest with a soft mist in the air. While having this dream, Daniel felt the presence of someone.

In 1882, Daniel McHarg travels up the Missouri River aboard a steamboat bound for Montana. On the trip upriver, he meets Nellie Sage, a woman who will change his life. But they are separated after arriving and face an uncertain future. With few prospects, Daniel struggles to find his way on the frontier, nearly losing his life in the process.

After a few false starts, Daniel and Nellie settle on the Teton River and build a ranch. It's a time of rapid change and they witness the passing of a way of life, including the slaughter of the buffalo and the winter of starvation for the Blackfoot. In their struggle to build Raven Ranch, Daniel and Nellie endure wolf attacks, cattle thieves, and droughts. Nothing prepares them, however, for the severe winter of 1886-87, an event known as the "Great Die Up."

KUDOS for *Beneath A Towering Sky*

In *Beneath a Towering Sky* by Tom Keith, Daniel McHarg is traveling up the Missouri River on a steamboat in 1882 when he meets Nellie Sage. But Nellie belongs to an upper-middle-class family and Daniel is down on his luck. Still, they are determined to be together, even over the objections of Nellie's father. Daniel homesteads land in Montana and struggles to build the Raven Ranch. He faces Indian attacks, hard winters, and summer droughts, and nearly loses his life trying to do a favor for a friend. Nellie and Daniel eventually marry and settle on the ranch, but life is hard, and they have no one to rely on except themselves and an occasional close friend. The story is a well-written account of what life was like in the Montana Territory in the 1880s and has a ring of truth that is rare in historical fiction today. A thoroughly enjoyable read. ~ *Taylor Jones, The Review Team of Taylor Jones & Regan Murphy*

*Beneath a Towering Sky* by Tom Keith is the story of Daniel McHarg and Nellie Sage who meet on the *Red Cloud* steamboat in 1882. Nellie is from a wealthy family and is traveling with her mother and sister to Helena, Montana. Daniel has little money and even fewer prospects, but he is traveling west to find his fortune. The attraction between Nellie and Daniel is strong and immediate, but Nellie's father whisks the family away soon after the boat docks in Fort Benton. Daniel takes up with a prospector and heads into the badlands searching for gold. When his friend takes ill, he asks Daniel to collect a package he left with a friend. Daniel agrees and his friend dies, but Daniel is attacked by Indians trying to carry out his friend's last request and he nearly dies too. Daniel and Nellie eventually marry and settle on the Teton River where Daniel has homesteaded a ranch. They struggle to protect their meager herd of cattle from drought, winter starvation, wolves, and cattle rustlers, but nothing prepares them for the devastating winter of 1886. *Beneath a Towering Sky* is a moving and poignant tale of one man's courage and determination to make a better life for himself and the woman he loves. Well written, fast paced, and authentic, it is one that historical fiction fans should love. ~ *Regan Murphy, The Review Team of Taylor Jones & Regan Murphy*

# BENEATH
# A
# TOWERING
# SKY

A story of love, death, and survival
in Montana Territory

## TOM KEITH

*A Black Opal Books Publication*

Black Opal Books

BECAUSE SOME STORIES JUST HAVE TO BE TOLD

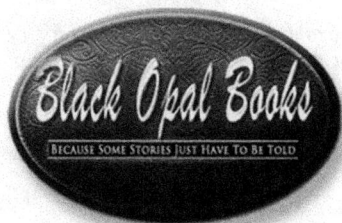

# DEDICATION

*Dedicated to the Keiths who left New Brunswick in the 1880's to build new lives in Montana Territory.*

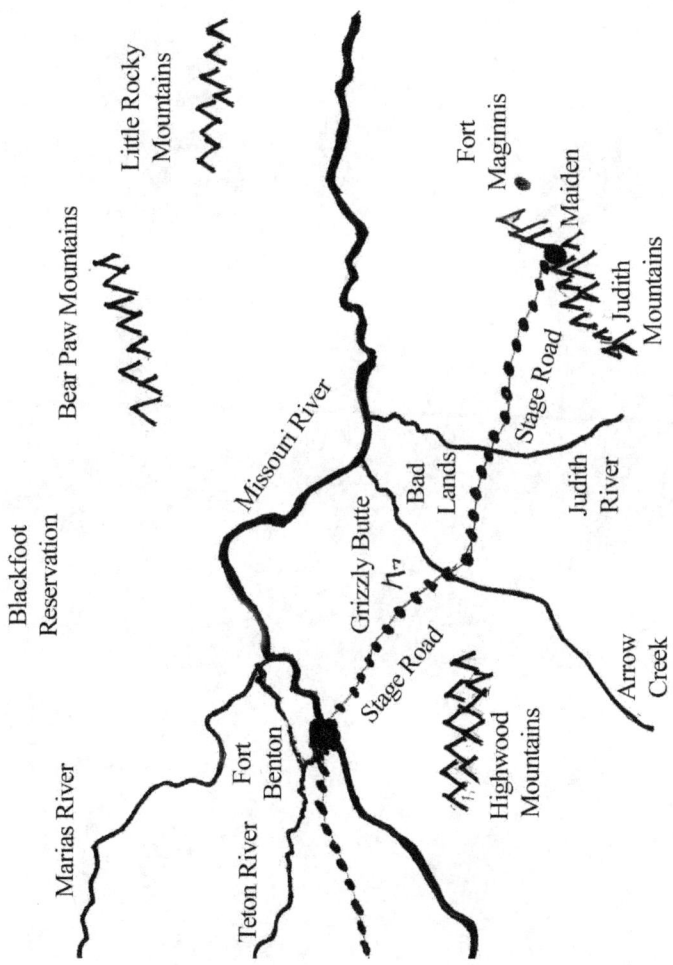

# PART 1

What is life? It is the flash of a firefly in the night. It is
the breath of a buffalo in the wintertime.
It is the little shadow which runs across the grass
and loses itself in the sunset.
~ Crowfoot, Blackfoot chief, ca 1830-1890

# CHAPTER 1

*1882*:

In the early summer of 1882, the steamboat *Red Cloud* slowly beat its way up the Missouri River, nearly two months into a journey that had begun in St. Louis. On a flawless day full of the promise of June, Daniel McHarg stood on a deck piled high with wood and other clutter, idly leaning against the rail, mesmerized by the play of water against the hull. Where Daniel stood, the only sound was the steady slapping of the paddle wheel, a sound that had faded into the background after several weeks of travel.

In his relaxed state, Daniel was startled when a few buffalo appeared, swimming toward the boat, their great collective bulk appearing like a small moving island. As the distance between the buffalo and the boat closed, a rifle shot, followed by several more, rang out from the deck above.

Daniel was shaken and instinctively turned and yelled in the direction of the shots. "You son of a bitch, there's people down here!" Though he felt his anger rising, Daniel kept his attention on the buffalo. One of the shooter's targets was a cow that swam with her two calves. The shots seemed to have no effect initially, but as the boat approached the beast stopped lateral movement and began a slow drift downriver. She passed close to where Daniel stood, her life reduced to a few last twitches, the blood flowing through her nostrils adding its color to the already dark water.

Daniel watched the carcass drift for a moment until a scuffle on the upper deck grabbed his attention. The *Red Cloud*'s captain, a thick man with brawny hands, had one of the passengers in his grip. After several weeks of travel on the confined spaces of the boat, the captain had shown himself to be a calm man, but now his blood was up. He jerked the rifle from the shooter and hurled it into the river, his powerful voice carrying to where Daniel stood well below:

"By God, if another fool tries this, I'll throw his ass overboard and keep the rifle!"

The captain immediately apologized for his language to the several women standing nearby but continued to handle the shooter roughly. Only with difficulty was he able to restrain himself from seriously hurting the man. The captain didn't give a damn about the buffalo; his concern was the safety of his passengers. He had decreed to all onboard that shooting would be allowed only from the lower deck, a commitment he had made after a similar incident had maimed a child on one of his trips downriver. He had vowed to never let it happen again. The shooter, whose clothes marked him as a city man, walked away shakily, showing the good sense not to make a fuss about his rough treatment or the loss of his rifle.

After the captain returned to the pilothouse, most of the passengers resumed their routines, but Daniel remained distracted. Shortly after boarding at Sioux City, he had noticed a young woman traveling with her mother and younger sister. Though he didn't know it during those first weeks, he later found out that her name was Nellie Sage. Nellie was a bit too sturdy to fit the prevailing Victorian ideal, but even from afar she had a beauty and a glow that drew him in. She always dressed elegantly. The broad-brimmed hats she often wore didn't fully conceal her long hair, which she wore loose, allowing the sun to bring out the reddish highlights Daniel found so appealing. Despite his interest in this woman and the weeks that had passed since they'd left Iowa, Daniel and Nellie hadn't met or exchanged any words. Daniel's ticket bought him little more than a space to sleep on the deck, while Nellie was a cabin passenger, which meant a private cabin and meals in a dining room with white linen and waiters. The two groups didn't easily mix, especially when a group of unaccompanied women was involved.

So, when Daniel looked up to see who had fired the shots, he was astonished to see Nellie looking in his direction, showing no interest in the unfolding events. She simply smiled and held her gaze long enough to convey that it wasn't accidental.

Nellie had also taken note of Daniel early on the voyage. She'd found him handsome enough. His even features and bright blue eyes caught her attention first, but they weren't what had drawn her to him. It was the laughter. On the lower deck that had become Daniel's world, he could usually be found amid a little knot of men he had only come to know since Sioux City. Often, when Nellie allowed herself to look down, Daniel had captured the group's interest. The laughter was never far behind.

Their silent encounter was broken when Nellie's mother approached and looked down toward Daniel. She took little note of him but made clear her intention of taking Nellie to the other side of the deck.

Daniel reluctantly returned his attention to the river. To no one in particular he recited a few lines from Robert Burns, a poet his father had regularly recited, especially when the whiskey was flowing.

> "'Twas na her bonnie blue e'e was my ruin;
> Fair tho' she be, that ne'er my undoin';
> 'Twas the dear smile when naebody did mind us,
> 'Twas the bewitching, sweet, stown glance o' kindness.'"

Daniel's little performance was noted by one of his traveling companions, John Campbell, a bear of a man who had befriended Daniel almost immediately.

"That's a fine one you've got there," John yelled toward Daniel. "And what's she doing making eyes at the likes of you!"

"I don't know." Daniel said with a look of bemusement, "but I do aim to find out."

# CHAPTER 2

Daniel had begun his journey in New Brunswick, a stingy place where the little wealth that could be scraped from the land had been taken decades ago when the last of the big trees had been felled. Daniel left Canada in 1879, briefly stopping in western Minnesota, where the black prairie soils produced fat yields and new towns were prospering. Like so many before him, Daniel headed west not just to seek what was new, but also to leave a part of his life behind. When asked, he'd say it was a letter from a cousin that had put him on this path. But it went deeper than that. New Brunswick had become too painful a place. The previous year he had lost his wife, a sweet woman named Katie, who died in childbirth. He lost them both. Despite the passage of more than a year, the pain seemed inescapable, often arising in unpredictable ways, triggered by random events woven into daily life. After a day of intense grief, this time brought on by the fragrance of newly cut hay and memories of working their small fields together, Daniel knew he had to leave.

The letter from Daniel's cousin was filled with references to cheap land and good wages, and they were all true. Though the money was good in Montevideo, a town platted on the Minnesota prairie just a few years before Daniel's arrival, he soon realized that these flatlands offered just another version of an ordinary life filled with hard work—something he had vowed to leave behind. More than that, though, were the stories. Farther west, in the mountains and prairies of Montana, the frontier persisted and fortunes were being built on the minerals and other resources that awaited discovery. Those who had been there said the opportunity to be a part of it wouldn't last much longer.

A heavily laden steamboat forcing its way upriver consumed an immense amount of wood, requiring regular stops to load a resource that had become increasingly scarce with the increase in river traffic. As she approached a little island where the valley widened, the *Red Cloud* stopped to take on wood. It was an opportunity for the passengers to get off and walk on solid ground. Daniel joined the small procession, which consisted mostly of deck passengers who were expected to assist in loading the wood on board. Daniel went to it, returning with armloads of cottonwood and pine scraped from the surrounding breaks.

A group of wood cutters, who were known as woodhawks along the upper Missouri, slouched in the shade and watched, enjoying a chance to see others work and perhaps to catch a glimpse of a woman. They were rough-looking men, hardened by years of difficult and dangerous work. Yet they weren't unlike other men Daniel had known in the woods of New Brunswick, a place where the thirty cords a day needed to keep a river boat running could be readily found. Here, Daniel thought, the work required to gather that much wood for the several boats plying the Upper Missouri was unimaginable.

Daniel paused between loads to talk with the woodhawks. "I hope you fellows are paid well. A lumberman could find himself a hell of a better place to work than this." The woodhawks ignored him at first, conveying the mild contempt they held for anyone who had just entered the territory. Eager to talk with someone new, Daniel persisted. "Maybe, then, you've forgotten the mother tongue way out here. Or is it that your throats are too dry to get the words out?"

Daniel offered up a small flask of whiskey, which the men quickly drained. The oldest of them, a man who was missing two fingers, responded while the others continued to gaze toward the boat. "A pilgrim like you wouldn't know it, but one of them scrawny yellow pines is as valuable here as oak wood in Boston, or whatever Yankee place you come from."

"Ah, you're confused about that, my friend," chided Daniel. "I'm not an American Yankee. That's Canada you hear, maybe with a bit of my family's beginnings in Scotland mixed in."

One of the men recalled his own Scottish ancestry and softened a little. "There used to be more trees down here by the river," he said. "Now we spend more time haulin' 'em down here than we do cutting trees. If it weren't decent money, we'd be damned fools. Look at me. How old do you think I am?"

Before Daniel could respond, the woodhawk declared that he was only twenty-two.

The others roared at this obvious falsehood, and one of them added, "Caleb was twenty-two before the war for southern independence. It's not just the hard work. Fear of the Blackfoot will age a man. Many of us have died along this river, and many have taken their last breath with the burn of a Blackfoot arrow lodged in his guts."

Another woodhawk joked that they were getting kind

of lonely now that the Blackfoot usually stayed north of the Missouri. In the early 1880s, the vast Blackfoot lands stretched most of the way from the Missouri north to Canada. A few more years of pressure and clamoring by the politicians of Montana Territory would shrink it to a mere fragment before the decade was over.

Daniel bantered with the group for a few more minutes before one of them waved his hand toward the *Red Cloud* and urged Daniel to make haste. "Unless you want to walk from here to Fort Benton, you'd better get your ass back on the boat."

Daniel shrugged and urged the woodhawks to watch their backs before hustling back to the *Red Cloud*. The crew was already making ready to push off; clouds of thick black smoke filled the air as the boilers built up a head of steam.

The *Red Cloud* continued upriver for the remainder of the day, until it finally reached a suitable bank to tie up for the night. Daniel and the rest of the passengers hoped this would be one of their last nights on the river. On most nights, if the weather was clear, Daniel preferred to sleep on land. He held no affection for the crowded boat and was glad he'd soon be done with her. He was rolling out his bedding and intently kicking away a few prickly pears when he looked up.

"I didn't want to leave this boat without knowing your name. I'm Nellie Sage." The young woman smiled awkwardly, trying to cover her embarrassment about having approached him.

Daniel was jolted by the recognition that she was the woman he'd been admiring from afar since boarding the *Red Cloud*. He knew it could be dangerous to fully acknowledge the attraction he felt for a young woman he'd likely never meet, but here was his chance. "And I'm Daniel McHarg," was all he could manage initially.

He doffed his hat and nodded toward Nellie, all the while thinking that he had to do better than that. A brief silence ensued. Neither knew what to say next—especially Daniel, who normally had an ability to find the right words for any occasion.

"What will you do in Montana?" Nellie asked after an awkward pause. Before Daniel could answer, she added, "My father sent for us from Helena. He owns one of the mines in the area. We'll be in Fort Benton only a short while. Once we get settled in Helena, I'll probably help my sister with the school."

"Well, that's more of a plan than I have." Daniel thought further. "They say this land isn't all used up yet. I'm planning to look for some gold. Or maybe something else, something I haven't even thought of yet." He smiled broadly before adding, "If nothing else turns up, I can always get by banging on some nails. But I didn't come all this way for that."

Nellie glanced back at the boat. Her mother and sister would be looking for her soon. "Well, I've done what I can do. I hope you prosper in this new land of yours, Mr. McHarg." She turned and began walking briskly to the boat.

Daniel savored the sight of her movement before adding, "I hope to prosper, Miss Nellie Sage, but I'll settle for a chance to see you again."

Nellie paused to look back at Daniel, and that look changed Daniel's world.

# CHAPTER 3

Not long after the *Red Cloud* had entered Montana Territory, the landscape seemed to announce that they were entering a different sort of place. The grassy, rounded bluffs along the lower river had gradually shed their mantle of soil, ultimately emerging as a series of stark white spires and castle-like outcrops. Though they weren't visible from the river yet, Daniel sensed that the Rockies couldn't be much farther ahead, the sight of which would mark their arrival in the West. More importantly, Daniel felt, the mountains would signal an imminent end to a long and often tedious voyage. Inspired by this possibility, Daniel looked forward to the boat's next stop for wood and an opportunity to scramble up a bluff and view the far horizon.

On the next day the *Red Cloud* reached Coal Banks Landing. Aboard the *Red Cloud* were more than a hundred Canadian Mounted Police recruits on their way to the still mostly lawless plains, where the northern tribes and a few reservation holdouts lived off the last of the buffalo herds. A great herd of horses had been assembled onshore to take the Mounted Police north to Fort Macleod. Daniel watched with amusement as his countrymen, who had enjoyed a temporary relaxing of military discipline on the trip upriver, resumed a stiff formality.

They were greeted by a Captain Kincaide, who remained mounted as he addressed the crowd of newly arrived recruits. "May I remind you, gentlemen that you are here in the service of the queen." The captain looked over the carefully arranged rows of men intently, silently assessing the caliber of his new recruits and looking for any signs of resistance to the rigid discipline that was expected of them. After a long pause he continued. "Your primary responsibility is quite simple. We are here to keep American whiskey out of Canada. Secondarily, we are here to keep the Cree and other Canadian tribes north of the border."

For centuries the border had meant little to the tribes that inhabited the northern plains, but in time they had learned that US troops would not pursue their raiding parties past an imaginary line, which they began calling the Medicine Line. To the cattlemen of Montana Territory, the raiding parties from the north were "British Indians," and despite the efforts of the Mounted Police, some of them continued to cross the border with a regularity that outraged the cattlemen in Montana Territory well into the 1880s.

It took longer than planned to unload the troops and the gear and supplies that had been shipped with them. By the time the boat moved on, the light was beginning to fade. The *Red Cloud* made only a few more miles before the captain decided to tie up again for the night.

Daniel was disappointed by the delay and brooded over it as he finished up his meager dinner, all of which came from a can heated over a smoky fire. Before bedding down, he took a walk along the lower deck, hoping to catch another glimpse of Nellie. She wasn't anywhere to be seen. Indeed, though literally only a short distance away, Nellie was in a world apart. She was ensconced with her family in the dining room, a long narrow room with high ceilings and a row of chandeliers that brightly lit the space.

"What shall we have for dinner tonight?" Nellie asked her mother. "I'm growing weary of this menu. I believe we've had everything on offer."

"Well, it's been a few days since you've had the roast pork," Nellie's mother said. "Why don't you have that? I'm going to have the tenderloin of beef with mushrooms. We can share if you like."

Stewards in white jackets stood by each table, awaiting any sign their services were needed. When Nellie's group had made their decisions, she signaled to the steward and ordered the roast pork, which was served with potatoes au gratin and green beans. They ordered a raspberry sorbet for dessert.

Meanwhile, Daniel walked the length of the *Red Cloud*, a distance of over 225 feet, and took the time to observe some of his fellow passengers more closely. He saw some of them up close for the first time and noted that it was an eclectic group he was traveling with. Although the rush to break the Montana prairies with a plow was still decades away, a few cattlemen were on board. They were men with a clear purpose. Daniel overheard some of their conversation, which was dominated by talk of cattle prices and strategies for getting cattle to the market. One of the cattlemen spoke most loudly, drawing Daniel's attention as he exclaimed:

"It all comes down to one thing, gentlemen. Are you willing to bet on the proposition that the grass of Montana will produce more beef cattle than will be lost to rustlers and wolves? I, for one, am willing to take that bet."

The other men nodded in agreement and each of them took another swig of whiskey from a flask being passed around. To his surprise, Daniel was saddened by this encounter. For in contrast to himself, here was a group of men who knew what they planned to do next. Daniel felt a gnawing doubt emerge, something that had only begun the last few days before the *Red Cloud*'s arrival in Fort Benton.

Later that evening, just before bedding down on the lower deck, Daniel shared his thoughts with John Campbell.

"What if all of this is for naught, John? What if..." Daniel grew silent, allowing John to finish his thoughts.

"Right, Daniel. I've had those thoughts myself. What if we're just keeping up a slow drift to a place where things won't turn out any better than what we've left behind."

It had begun to rain, forcing Daniel and John to lie close to each other. Cargo and other deck passengers occupied the interior spaces of the lower deck, which required the two men to bed down near the rail at the edge of the deck, a location where rain drifted in occasionally when the wind picked up. John rolled himself up in a canvas tarp and ended their conversation abruptly. "I just hope this won't be the biggest mistake I've ever made."

On the final day of their passage, Daniel and the other passengers who were on their first trip to Montana Territory spent the morning looking expectantly upriver. Daniel was sure that each new bend in the river would be the last, but the *Red Cloud*'s passage would only reveal another wild landscape lacking any suggestion of a town.

Just below Fort Benton, the river made a big bend, following a course through a series of narrow channels studded with islands and sandbars. In most places, the Upper Missouri was a river that seemed mild mannered. But it was a hard river to read and often deceptively treacherous. Most often, the river was wide and deep enough for a steamboat's easy passage. Sometimes, though, unseen until nearly upon it, the channel would split and force a hard choice. One channel brought safe passage, while the other could rip open a hull with a cottonwood snag lurking just below the waterline. The good river men had an instinct for these hazards but even the best of them were not infallible. The multiple wrecks Daniel had observed on the trip upriver provided stark evidence of the risks.

The *Red Cloud* was one of the larger boats that worked the Upper Missouri and she was tantalizingly close to Fort Benton when she hit a sandbar. The soft sand provided a gentle stop but the *Red Cloud* was stuck fast. The captain bellowed a series of orders from the pilot house, which prompted the crew to shift some of the cargo. But the *Red Cloud*'s powerful engine couldn't budge her from the river's grip. It wasn't the first time this had happened, so there wasn't a general panic. Instead, the passengers clustered where they could get a good view of the crew's vigorous efforts to free the boat, wary of evoking their wrath by getting in the way. Like all the boats plying the Upper Missouri, the *Red Cloud* was equipped with an odd-looking apparatus that allowed her to "walk" over a bar using an elaborate series of wooden spars and pulleys to lift the boat off the river bottom. It was an ingenious system when it worked well, but on this day the crew's initial efforts only succeeded in swinging the *Red Cloud*'s massive hull a slight distance and embedding her farther into the mire.

Amid the commotion, Daniel found himself standing close to Nellie. He was gladdened by an unexpected chance to see her again but burdened by the knowledge that their time together on the *Red Cloud* was running short. With increasing alarm, he began to realize that any chance of seeing her again might depend on what transpired over the next few minutes.

"Well, it looks like that bribe I paid the pilot might have worked," Daniel offered, hoping to lighten the mood.

Nellie looked at him quizzically before laughing aloud. She quickly covered her mouth with a hand lest anyone think she was amused at the *Red Cloud*'s misfortune.

"Assuming we make it to Fort Benton, how will I find you?"

Nellie didn't have an easy answer. "I don't know where we're staying," she replied. "My father made all the arrangements." She reiterated that the family planned to be in Fort Benton for a few days before leaving for Helena and added a mild warning: "My father will be there as well. He can be a formidable man."

Feigning a grimace, Daniel replied, "It's not your father I'm looking to see, Nellie." 'His crack lightened Nellie's increasingly serious expression, which reflected her worry that events would intercede before they even had a chance to begin a proper acquaintance. Now grinning, Daniel added, "Might we meet in Fort Benton, somewhere along the riverbank like we did before? Or will you always be surrounded by a phalanx of family?"

Nellie's seriousness returned. "You'll have to be resourceful, Daniel. I can't offer you more than that."

Just then, Nellie spotted her mother waving from the upper deck. Nellie forced a smile in return, but it barely masked her sadness. She said goodbye to Daniel and turned to rejoin her family. Daniel immediately began to think about how he'd manage to see her again.

When the crew finally sensed that the *Red Cloud* might break free, one of the spars snapped into pieces, sending a few large splinters into the air and evoking the wrath of the captain. "You men are useless," he yelled in frustration.

After his outburst, the captain turned to the passengers gathered below and softened his tone. "We'll be in Fort Benton before the day is over, folks. Please don't be worried. I very much appreciate your patience."

Daniel's patience would be needed that day, for it took over an hour to mount a new spar onto the rig and the crew's initial efforts to get enough leverage to lift the hull fell short again.

"I think we might have to spend another night on the river," Daniel said to a man standing nearby. "This damned river must have it out for us."

The man shrugged. "It's not just us, friend. This cussed river is no man's friend."

At last, when he thought the hull had moved into the proper position, the captain reversed the engine, a procedure that effectively dammed water near the hull and sometimes allowed a boat to float free. It worked this time, and the *Red Cloud* moved back into the main channel amid a chorus of cheers.

After just a few hours of travel, the *Red Cloud* finally pushed through a bend that brought Fort Benton into view. The captain let loose a series of whistle blasts and a rousing cheer came up from the decks. The *Red Cloud* pulled past two other boats that were tied up along the levee and tied up near the town's new hotel, a soaring structure still under construction.

Fort Benton edged up to the Missouri's north bank and marked the head of navigation on this remarkable river. Its location so far inland and utter isolation prompted more than one traveler to think it an apparition. In the early days, like much of the western frontier, Fort Benton was a place where community builders and outlaws, preachers and ruffians, lived side by side. It wasn't always clear which side would win out. Even so, the town had long been a vital place. Before the arrival of the railroads, steamboats transported nearly everything that entered or exited the interior Northwest—and none of the boats could make it farther upriver than Fort Benton.

Even with the heavy river traffic of the past decade, the arrival of a steamer was a major event. Long-awaited shipments, friends not seen for months or even years, new people to gawk at, and news from the outside world combined to stir up the town. Many of Fort Benton's inhabitants stood along Front Street as the Red Cloud pulled up to the levee and set out its lines.

Daniel was traveling lighter than most passengers and was among the first to leave the boat. He knew Nellie would be engaged with her family and was confident that he'd have time to seek her out the following day, after she settled into her hotel. As he shouldered his bag, John Campbell hailed him.

"It's the saloon I'm headed for, Daniel," said John. "We deserve a snoot-full tonight, I'm thinking."

Daniel had been practically bred to the taste of whiskey, but at the moment he had other things on his mind and felt a need to get away from the crowd. "I'll find you in a while, Johnny," he called to his friend. "Try to pick out a place where we won't get shot."

Daniel set off along Front Street, determined to get a feel for this Montana, a place he hoped would be his last stop. Along with the curious and those waiting to greet family and friends, the levee was crowded with porters and hustlers for all manner of services. Daniel pushed past them all and seized the first opportunity to climb out of the confined river valley and see the country beyond. As he walked briskly through town, he noted all the construction underway and felt some relief from the knowledge that he could always find work here if nothing else panned out.

North of Fort Benton, the land slopes gently up a ridge that rises more than two hundred feet above the river. Daniel pointed himself in that direction and followed a swale that meandered through the treeless grasslands. From the heights, he looked out on a vast landscape, one dominated by short grass in every direction. The land was irregular, rising and falling with no apparent pattern, except where the river had cut down through it and exposed a series of stark, barren cliffs. Isolated ranges rose from the plains here and there, the closest of which were the Highwoods to the south. Daniel lingered on a high spot and tried to see some glimmer of destiny, a hint of a new life beyond the distant hills. It wasn't to be seen that day. Instead, as he looked out over a vast and completely unfamiliar landscape, he felt out of place. Worse, he felt the pain of losing his wife and child return. Before the pain could sink in too far, he forced himself to remember that this was a special day and it was time to join the boys and celebrate their arrival in Fort Benton.

Daniel found John Campbell in the Antlers, one of the numerous saloons that lined the levee along the riverfront. Many of them were rough looking places but a few were graced with a touch of civility, such as an upright piano or a portrait of Lincoln. The Antlers had both of these touches, along with an ornate wooden bar brought upriver from St. Louis. John was with a small group of men, most of whom wore an expression of wonderment that made them look out of place. The expressions were genuine, for the group largely consisted of newcomers just arrived on the *Red Cloud*. Among them, however, was a man Daniel had not seen before, an older man who dominated the conversation. He wore a bright red shirt and a gold pendant, items chosen to announce that he was no ordinary man. The stranger winced from time to time, especially when he rose from his chair. His wincing, Daniel would soon learn, resulted from the pain of a terrible old wound.

Daniel greeted John and the others warmly. "Glad you could join us, Daniel," John said, "but you'll have to drink fast if you want to catch up to the rest of us!" Amid general laughter, the older stranger ignored Daniel's arrival and resumed the tale that had been interrupted.

"It was in sixty-five, I think, when we started to crack down on the bad sort that had moved into Last Chance Gulch. They called us vigilantes, but we were decent citizens who were trying to create some semblance of the law. Of course, we did so by decorating trees in a particular way." He paused, sure that questions would follow.

As if on cue, one of the younger men posed a question. "What do you mean by that?"

"Well, I mean we hung those scoundrels from a tall tree and left them there to hang for a while. Sometimes we did it two at a time. It had the desired effect!"

Later, the man moved on to other tales and held the floor nearly continuously. He occasionally paused the story at a suspenseful moment, usually involving a narrow escape from claim jumpers or some other peril. The newcomers learned they would be required to purchase another whiskey for the story to resume.

Daniel listened patiently for a while, but this wasn't the celebration he expected at the end of a long voyage. By the next break in the story, Daniel had reached his limit. "I don't know about the rest of you, but I'm tired of such seriousness," he said, and began to lay out a drinking wager. The prospector, loathe to give up the group's full attention, began to interrupt, but Daniel waved him off. "Let's have a little wager," Daniel continued. "I'll buy any man a drink if he can do a simple exercise. Any man who tries it but fails buys me one. Do I have any takers?"

There were murmurs of agreement. The prospector, however, uttered a few cusses in Daniel's direction.

"Now hold on there, pal," John Campbell interjected. "You've got no cause to insult my friend Daniel." John loomed over the prospector, holding a grin while making his loyalty to Daniel clear. John had become protective of Daniel after an incident in Bismarck during an unplanned stop for repairs. Daniel had used his wits to get them out of an encounter with an angry drunk. Still, it was a close call and an encounter John could not easily forget.

Daniel could see that despite John's efforts, there would be no celebration as long as the prospector's dominance persisted. He tried to deter the stranger with an offer. "Here's a proposition, my friend—"

"Call me Limestone," the prospector cut in.

"Very well, Limestone. You'll get an equal share of my winnings, which I assure you will be considerable. All you have to do is enjoy the free whiskey."

Sensing that he had nothing to lose, the prospector finally nodded.

Daniel moved to the center of the room and made a small show of taking off his jacket. "We can all bend our knees, squat, and get up again," he began. "It's a familiar act. But try it on one leg." With that, Daniel extended his left leg horizontally and lowered himself to the floor. After holding that position for a few seconds, he smoothly rose back to full height. "Now, who wants a free drink for doing such a simple thing?"

There were plenty of takers. Men of all sizes, each confident in his ability to match Daniel's maneuver, made the effort, and all of them failed. Some made it halfway up before falling back on their haunches. Others crumpled to the floor before they could make it to a crouching position. Every attempt provoked much anticipation from the man up next and many of them boasted about how easy they would make it look. Neither Daniel nor the hard-drinking prospector could keep up with the free drinks that kept coming his way. After a few rounds, both men put their winnings back on the table for any takers.

After the action slowed and the liquor settled in, Limestone sensed another opportunity to hold the group's attention. He pulled a piece of dark metal from his pocket and dropped it onto the table without comment, once again confident that questions would soon follow. In response to the first, Limestone said only one word: "Shiloh." Then, after a pause, he went on. "It was a brutal fight. Both sides threw everything they had at each other. The surgeons pulled this chunk of metal out of my hip but another piece was buried deep. They said they could get it out, but it might kill me on the spot. I decided to take my chances and leave it in." Limestone paused then added, "If this thing kills me tomorrow, I figure I won that bet!"

More questions followed and Limestone was happy to resume his tale. "On the last day of the fight, the man next to me was split open, and I went down too. At first I thought I was the lucky one, but I had no feeling in my legs and couldn't crawl without an unbearable pain somewhere in my gut. No one came for us. I lay there all night and listened to the others beg for help. By morning there were no other sounds. With a swollen tongue and the belief that my own death was just a matter of time, I began to envy my friend's quick death."

When Daniel thought Limestone's tales of the war might have run their course, he brought up gold prospecting again. "How long ago did you find that gold piece hanging off your neck?" he began. "Did you find it near Fort Benton?"

Limestone brightened at the chance to talk about gold again and extended his arms broadly, as if embracing the whole room. "All we've got around here is mud and grass. If you want to find gold, you've got to head into the mountains."

He looked at Daniel more closely, noting that he wasn't a tall man but had the broad chest and shoulders of someone who wasn't a stranger to hard work. *I could use a man like that*, he thought. Limestone was now past fifty and the years of hard living and old wounds had sapped much of his strength. Still, he dreamed of another chance to make a big strike and knew he'd need help from someone younger and stronger than himself. Maybe Daniel was the man he was looking for.

"Have you come to Montana to look for gold?" Limestone asked casually.

"Not particularly," Daniel replied, "but I wouldn't turn down a chance to strike it rich if I thought it had some chance of success." He thought for a moment before adding, "After listening to some of your stories, I'd also want to know that we'd have some chance of making it back alive."

Limestone laughed loudly at Daniel's crack and urged him to move into a quiet corner of the room where they could talk further.

"Daniel, I need a partner. And not just anyone. I need someone I can trust and someone who can dig and crack rock for me. This isn't an offer you'll ever get again. I know how to find gold and I'll split anything we find with you fifty-fifty."

"What makes you think you can trust me?" was Daniel's first response.

"I don't know that I can, but there's something about you I like, and when I like someone, they usually turn out to be trustworthy. What do you say? Are you interested?"

Daniel replied that he was and they should talk more later. They returned to the group and resumed the whiskey drinking. By the end of the night, the whole group had bonded deeply—but the biggest winner was the house, which realized twice the sales of a normal Tuesday night. Finally, after a few men had slumped into their chairs, the group broke up. Glad that there were only a few streets to choose from, Daniel drifted back up the hill, slipped into the boardinghouse where he had dropped his gear, and collapsed into the oblivion that always followed the whiskey.

# CHAPTER 4

Daniel awoke from a vigorous shaking, grimaced at the bright light of midday, and looked up to see Limestone, who urged him to gather his gear and head out to the mountains. Daniel was about to lash out when Limestone reminded him of the arrangements they had made the previous night.

Daniel responded, "I recall agreeing to go with you, old man, but I didn't say anything about when."

"Daniel, the time is right. I've got a good feeling about this, something I haven't had for a while. So let's get started, and we'll find that lode I told you about."

Daniel forced himself into a greater awareness and was immediately struck by the realization that he didn't know where Nellie was staying and wasn't even sure when she would be leaving for Helena. Ignoring Limestone's plea, Daniel decided that his only option was a direct approach. "Where's a rich man's daughter likely to stay in this town?"

Limestone was tempted to have some fun with Daniel, but hesitated when he saw how serious his new friend had become. "Just head down Front Street, and you'll see it. Most of the other places…well, let's just say that a rich man wouldn't put his family in any of them."

Now more aware of the pounding in his head, Daniel splashed some water on his face, told Limestone he'd be back later, and left abruptly. He headed straight for the riverfront and entered the lobby of the hotel Limestone had described. A uniformed bellman eyed Daniel disapprovingly as he pushed past the front door. Daniel moved briskly across the lobby and stood at the front desk for a moment before he was noticed by the clerk. Alarmed by the bellman's reaction, Daniel used the time to brush himself off and wiped his dusty shoes against the back of his trousers.

"Good morning," Daniel said with as much confidence as he could muster. "I'm here to see Miss Nellie Sage. Is the Sage family still in residence?"

"They were here last night," the clerk responded, "but they all took the morning stage to Helena." The clerk saw a look of great disappointment descend on Daniel's face. "I'm sorry, but that was more than three hours ago."

Daniel turned to leave. As he neared the front door he heard the deskman call his name.

"Might you be Mr. Daniel McHarg? I have a note for someone by that name."

Daniel nodded and took the note from the deskman. Though he feared the worst, the sight of a woman's fine hand writing on the envelope brought a sliver of hope, just enough to allow himself to imagine the possibility that Nellie's departure was not an abrupt ending to something that had become very important to him. Despite his eagerness to read the note, he first walked across Front Street to the river and sat on one of the many crates that lined the levee, most of which were awaiting shipment to the mines.

The note was addressed to Mr. Daniel McHarg in a flowing script. He opened the envelope carefully and read its contents:

*Dear Mr. McHarg:*

*I regret that we had to leave Fort Benton sooner than anticipated. We had intended to visit with my aunt who resides here, but my father unexpectedly learned he had urgent business back in Helena. He insisted we all leave with him the day following our arrival.*

*I don't know how this may occur, but my hope is that Montana is not so large as to prevent our meeting again.*

*Yours very truly,*
*Nellie Sage*

Daniel slowly walked back to the boardinghouse. He was so preoccupied with thoughts of Nellie that he was almost surprised to see Limestone sitting on the porch, obscured by a cloud of smoke rising from an oddly shaped pipe. He looked older in the morning light—his face was marked by creases and a few scars but his eyes shone with an eagerness for life.

"Well, Daniel," said Limestone, "looks like you've come to your senses and decided to make yourself rich."

Daniel was far from ready to let go of Nellie, but he knew that chasing her to Helena might not do any good. No, he'd have to figure out the right approach, which would be easier to do if this expedition of Limestone's paid off. Daniel knew full well that Nellie lived in a world different from his and that anything he could do to narrow the economic gap separating them might enhance his prospects. He returned his attention to the prospector. "All right, Limestone, where's this gold you've been talking about? Where are we going?"

"The Judith Mountains," Limestone replied. "I've

got a good hunch about a particular place I saw last year. I don't know if it's got a name, but I call it Jackass Gulch on account of the carcass I saw there last time."

Though Jackass Gulch didn't sound like an auspicious name, Daniel let it go. Instead, he pursued his curiosity about the Judith Mountains, an unfamiliar range that also, he thought, bore a peculiar name. "Who was this Judith, Limestone?" he asked. "Why'd someone name those mountains after her?"

Limestone was happy to point out that as with many places in Montana, the name of the Judith Mountains originated with the Lewis and Clark expedition. "Judith was Clark's sweetheart, and a special one she must have been," he informed Daniel. "Anyway, we'll start near Jackass Gulch, but I've seen traces of gold throughout that country. Besides, Daniel, a man could do a lot worse with his time than wander through the Judith Mountains in summer. It's beautiful country."

Daniel was thinking of a different kind of beauty, but he nodded before adding, "One more thing. I just got here. Whatever gold is lying in those mountains will still be there in a few days. I've been sitting on a damn boat for the past month, and I've hardly seen this town."

"There's nothing more you need to see in this town," Limestone protested. "Unless you want a job working for someone else. Come with me now and your days of earning a wage will be over."

Despite Limestone's persistence, Daniel wasn't easily deterred. In the end, they agreed to take the stage to Maiden, a town that had recently sprouted up near the base of the Judith Mountains, at the beginning of the following week.

For the next few days, Daniel watched the comings and goings on the waterfront and listened to the talk in the bars. In addition to the usual rumors of where gold was being found, there was talk of another type of boom: the imminent cattle boom. Though the local market for beef remained small, the railroad was coming, and its arrival would change everything. The vast grasslands of Montana were there for the taking, the talk went, and would bring riches to those who took a chance on the land.

Inspired partly by the local commentary, but perhaps more by an immediate desire to wander outside the town, Daniel and John Campbell rode north one afternoon. John's horse was too small for his bulk but it was the best option available that day at the livery. Along the way, the two men talked of Daniel's plans.

"Come with us," Daniel urged John. "You'll never get another chance like this."

"Maybe not, but I can't see myself going on a wild goose chase with that fellow Limestone. Too risky for me. I'm happy to take a job here in town."

They soon came upon the wide valley of the Teton River, which rose far to the west among the great peaks of the Continental Divide. Near Fort Benton the Teton is a plains river, richly lined with cottonwoods and hemmed in by low bluffs. Amid the cottonwoods the valley seemed almost lush, offering deep soils and shelter from the harsh Montana winds. Daniel was moved by the setting.

"There's something special about this place, John. I can't put it very well. It sure looks different from where we come from, but I feel at home here. It's almost like I've been here before."

John thought about Daniel's comment for a moment before responding. He liked the Teton Valley well enough, but what caught his attention was the water. "A man can't do much in this country without water. There may be a lot of grass out there, but this is a place where you can work with the land and grow something."

Daniel wasn't thinking very far ahead that day. He had enough on his mind with Nellie and a pending trip with Limestone. He was more interested in casually wandering through the valley and enjoying the sunshine. When it was time to go, Daniel urged his horse up the bluff, pausing from time to time to savor the views of the Teton Valley. Those images of the land would stay with Daniel in the days to come.

# CHAPTER 5

Three Blackfoot men were riding south and had almost reached the Missouri River when they saw a group of vultures circling overhead, effortlessly gliding in the afternoon updrafts, gathering their numbers in a series of tightening concentric circles. The object of their interest was a dead buffalo that had washed up on the shore and become stranded by the quickly lowering river flows that followed the June rise. Despite the stench, the men closely inspected the carcass and noted that the animal had been shot and not simply drowned. Two of the men wondered how such a thing could happen, but the oldest of the group, Follows Bear, said he had heard that the white men sometimes shot animals from their "fire boats" and let the bodies drift away with the current.

One of Follows Bear's companions, a fierce-looking man known as Looks Beyond, became quiet, his anger deepening as he contemplated how much had been lost. He broke the silence forcefully: "They do not belong here. The white men do not belong here!"

Earlier that year, the buffalo hunt had been successful. Expecting the same result on the next hunt, the three

Blackfoot men had set off to scout the locations of the herds. They had traveled many days without sighting any buffalo, all the way to the standing rocks that marked the descent to the Big River. They had become more anxious with each passing day.

Until the very end, few Blackfoot—especially those who shunned the government handouts and clung to traditional ways—could imagine the possibility that the 1881-1882 hunt would be the last successful hunt. It was inconceivable that something so ingrained in life itself and abundant beyond counting, could vanish forever. It was no more likely than the grass ceasing to grow or the stars ceasing to glow in the sky.

After discovering the dead buffalo, Follows Bear led the little group across the Big River at a ford that had been used by the Blackfoot for centuries. Though dropping quickly, the river still had a substantial flow, enough to push the men's horses downstream and momentarily divert their thoughts from a growing sense of the futility of their quest. Once across the river, they were no longer on Blackfoot land. What had been part of their homeland was now a forbidden place. This reality hadn't fully set in. In fact, many Blackfoot refused to acknowledge that land could be bought and sold or made to belong to someone else. Certainly not Looks Beyond, who continued to roam beyond the reservation boundaries at will.

Still, they saw no buffalo. The white man's cattle had yet to take their place, which made the land seem empty, nearly devoid of life. The three men felt empty as well. As they continued to the east, Follows Bear stated what had become obvious. "There are no buffalo here. We need to look elsewhere. I've heard reports that buffalo have been seen up near the Medicine Line. I say we go there directly."

Looks Beyond agreed but had a request. "The day is late. I say we camp at the kill site and go north tomorrow."

The kill site, a place where ancestral people had driven buffalo over a cliff, was nearby. There, where the bones of long-dead buffalo still littered the ground, Looks Beyond had often meditated. Follows Bear knew it was a powerful place and agreed they would camp there that night. This would prove to be a fateful decision.

# CHAPTER 6

As planned, Daniel met Limestone at the upper ferry, where the river flowed past a dark cliff nearly black where it met the floodplain. The gloomy setting added a sense of foreboding to the venture they were about to undertake. The ferry was a simple affair, just large enough to hold the stage and its team. A system of cables pulled them across the river.

It felt odd to be on the water again. "Damn, Limestone, I thought I wouldn't have to be on this blasted river again so soon."

"It's only a small part of the trip," Limestone replied. "And it sure beats having to swim."

Soon, as the stage crept up a tight little cleft in the bluffs, scarcely faster than a man could walk, Daniel was reminded of the advantages of river travel. These advantages would become even more evident as the day wore on. Daniel and the others endured hours at a stretch in a cramped cabin, jolted by a rough road. The stiff springs of the carriage did little to soften the ride. Daniel was in a pensive mood, brought on by the knowledge that he was heading mostly east, a direction that would take him even farther from Nellie.

In addition to Daniel and Limestone, the stage held two other passengers and the driver, who, like most everyone else in town, was acquainted with Limestone. Now and again, when the ride was quiet and the road smooth, Limestone and the driver would yell back and forth. Their conversation came in little bursts followed by periods of silence. In one exchange, the driver mocked Limestone's ability to find anything of value, much less gold: "The only gold Limestone's ever been close to was in someone else's pocket."

Limestone quickly retorted to the group. "Has anyone noticed that we're in the company of the ugliest stage driver in Montana Territory? He's so ugly that he has to put blinders on his horses to keep them from bolting when he walks by."

It went on like that most of the morning.

Just when the travelers were reaching the limit of their endurance, a prominent landmark came into view. "There she is: Grizzly Butte!" Limestone proclaimed. The butte was a welcome signal of a station ahead, a place that offered rest and a meal and a chance to get out of the little box that had confined them since leaving Fort Benton.

The station stood just off the road and presented a rude appearance. It consisted of a few sheds, some corrals, and a low log building with a sod roof. They were greeted by a stout woman named Anna, who dressed plainly and spoke with a German accent. She had a Teutonic formality that gave her personality an edge, one honed by the need for a woman who was often alone or greatly outnumbered by men to keep them at a certain distance. Limestone and the stage driver knew of her no-nonsense reputation and remained unusually subdued.

"Welcome to my little palace," she said with a slight smile. Anna gestured toward Limestone and the stage driver. "Even you two old scoundrels. Folks, don't believe anything these two tell you."

Limestone objected, though mildly and with good humor. "Now what kind of a thing is that to say in front of my new partner? Are you trying to scare him off before we even get to Maiden?"

Anna took a closer look at Daniel and was tempted to offer her pity in jest. Instead, she observed that Daniel was a fresh-faced newcomer who was probably already wondering what the devil he'd gotten himself into. She decided to leave things where they were and concentrate on serving the meal, which she preceded with an announcement. "I hope none of you travelers think you're at the Delmonico's of the West. I've got limited fare, so I hope you like what you get."

Anna proceeded to serve up a meal of cold meats, bread, and warm beer. As she went about her work, she noted that one of the passengers was carrying a small case. "Ah, that's something I haven't seen for a while. Mister, is that a violin you're carrying?"

The passenger, who was on his way to Chicago, pronounced that it was indeed and, to Anna's delight, opened the case. She moved closer and admired the violin for a moment. "Oh my, that's a beautiful instrument. Would you mind playing a piece for us?"

The man, who was a professional musician and engaged to play with an orchestra that summer, initially declined. He dressed formally and probably thought the rough bunch he found himself with wouldn't appreciate the music. But Anna persisted. "I've got some good whiskey on the shelf. Have some on the house. All I ask is that you play."

The musician glanced at the shelf. "Is that a bottle of Stark's I see on the top shelf?"

"St. Louis's finest," Anna replied. "I'll pour you a tall one if you play a piece for us."

Thus persuaded, the man carefully removed the instrument from its case and performed a little ritual to limber the bow while making a few adjustments to the strings. Once ready to play, he began with a series of vigorous strokes, producing an intensity of sound that startled his little audience in the confined space of the stage stop.

The music settled into a melodic sequence. Daniel and the other travelers recognized none of it but were drawn into its elegance and the clarity with which the man played. Focused intently on the violinist, the group was distracted only by a suppressed sob from Anna, who wiped a tear from her cheek in apparent embarrassment.

By the time the piece was over, Daniel and the others were also moved. They hesitated before applauding, not sure if he was finished. But Anna knew the piece and led them on, clapping enthusiastically and complimenting his performance of a difficult piece, which she pronounced Bach's "Air on a G String."

Then, because she had a reputation to maintain—especially in front of the stage driver—Anna felt compelled to explain her sentimentality. "When I was a child in Munich, we attended a concert nearly every Sunday. I haven't heard this music for many, many years. When I listen, I'm a girl again and my family is still close." She gestured with open arms to the dimly lit space and the primitive furniture before adding, "Now I have only this."

Though Anna didn't speak of it, Limestone and the stage driver knew that she was still waiting for her husband, who had never returned from a solo hunting trip the previous year. Everyone but Anna assumed he was dead. Anna clung to a hope. On some days, she felt it was the only thing she had left.

When the stage driver announced that he had a schedule to keep, Anna embraced the musician and thanked him again for his performance. Her spirits buoyed by the occasion, she even thought to reassure Daniel. "Limestone is a good man. Pay no mind to what I said earlier."

It took another full day of travel and an overnight stop to reach Maiden, a newly risen town at the edge of the Judith Mountains. It was nearly dark when they arrived and the group was weary. Still, Limestone insisted on going to a saloon, where the talk was about who had come and gone, new claims, and feuds. Daniel felt like an outsider and soon tired of it. As he headed to the hotel, Limestone called out, "Now, Daniel, remember this night and what it feels like to go to bed a poor man. You haven't many of these nights left."

"We'll see. But I'm afraid that kind of luck just doesn't run in the McHarg family."

The next day was clear and brilliant. Daniel awoke early and walked along the town's main street. Maiden was a beehive of activity, with heavy freight wagons moving equipment up the mountain to the mines. Though many buildings had sprung up, the town retained a raw appearance. Everything was new but roughly constructed with minimal ornamentation. The main street was rutted and muddy with an occasional plank thrown across some of the larger depressions. Still, there were stores with nearly everything you'd want to buy and more than enough saloons. Before turning back to roust Limestone, Daniel paused and looked up, past a devastated forest, to the spoil piles and scars on the mountain. *Maybe Limestone is right*, he thought. *Someone like us probably stumbled onto that ore body. Maybe it'll happen again.*

For the remainder of the morning, Daniel and Limestone acquired the necessities for their expedition. They bought supplies and a few basic items, like a shovel and a pick for Daniel to carry. Limestone already had a gold pan and rock hammer, but he insisted that Daniel get a gold pan to join him when they worked the placer deposits. But their biggest purchase was the horses. Limestone insisted that a breeder named Brooks, who lived along Warm Springs Creek, raised horses that were better suited for the mountains than any of the stock they could get in Fort Benton. After much discussion and some bargaining, they purchased two saddle horses and a larger pack animal. Daniel's anticipation grew, but even though Limestone paid his share of the costs, Daniel's excitement was tempered by the knowledge that the money he had saved wouldn't last long at this rate.

Once the transactions were completed, Limestone led them farther north. Limestone, who knew the country well and exulted to be in the mountains again, pointed out an occasional landmark to Daniel. They traveled slowly, for Limestone took time to observe the land intently. They stopped occasionally and at each stop Limestone directed Daniel to dig a small pit or use his pick to break off some rock from an outcrop he judged to have potential. It was hard work, often conducted on a steep slope with loose rock. Limestone carefully examined the rocks Daniel uncovered but was particularly interested in the limestone formations they came across.

"Now you know where my nickname comes from, Daniel. Some think I'm crazy looking for gold in limestone, but I'm going to prove them wrong."

Daniel knew nothing of prospecting but didn't like hearing that Limestone's theory was unproven. "You might have told me before that no one has found gold in limestone."

"Don't worry about that. The others didn't know where to look. Besides, I guarantee we'll at least fill our pockets with placer gold. You'll see."

They made only a few miles that first day and camped by a small stream. Limestone chose the campsite carefully, looking for a place where larger boulders had lodged in the stream bed. Before the light faded, he pulled a gold pan from his pack and urged Daniel to do the same. Daniel reluctantly agreed, for he was tired out from the day's activity.

"I didn't know you were going to work me like a mule," Daniel groused. "And now you want me to get my feet wet?"

"Watch me, Daniel. Pick a place next to a boulder where the gold flakes can settle out. Then swish around some gravel in a little water and look for the color of gold. It's a beautiful thing to behold."

Almost immediately, Daniel found a few gold flakes and whooped at the discovery. Limestone delighted in Daniel's enthusiasm, remembering the feeling of finding his first gold back in the 1860s. Of course, these flakes wouldn't make them rich, but it was good fun and covered some of their expenses. They both stayed in the stream until the light faded to full darkness.

Over the next several days, their routine didn't vary. They arose early but lingered in camp and drank coffee as they waited for the sun to rise above the ridge and bring more warmth to the land. A trace of placer gold here and there kept them motivated, but in those first days there were no signs of the major ore body Limestone had targeted. By evening they were tired and stiff but happy to settle by the fire and feast on elk steaks cut from a cow Limestone had shot earlier in the day. Limestone enhanced the meat with a gravy of flour, grease from the pan, stream water, salt, and a few herbs plucked from the shrubs they passed on their daily travels. Before drifting off to sleep, they'd talk on a wide range of subjects. Limestone had a repertoire of stories from the wild years he'd spent in places like Bannock and Virginia City, where, lured west by news of gold strikes and a determination to leave behind the bloody mess of the war, he had arrived in late 1862. He also spoke of more practical matters, introducing Daniel to the people, geography, and ways of this new land. Limestone delivered all his tales with the usual braggadocio and humor, yet Daniel realized he was getting a serious education not easily acquired in any other way.

"What if we make a big gold find?" Daniel asked one evening. "What happens then?"

"That's when the real work begins," Limestone responded. "First, we need to file a claim and establish ownership. There's a lot of paperwork in that. Then we can either work the claim ourselves or sell it to someone else. Someone with enough funds to make us rich!" He went on to explain the whole process in detail, including how they'd need to take ore samples and have them assayed.

Daniel listened patiently, bored with some of the details. "I like the idea of selling. I don't fancy myself a miner, spending all my time underground."

"All right then. We're agreed. Let's just strike it rich and leave the work to someone else!"

Although Limestone dominated most conversations, he often prompted Daniel to talk about his life in faraway New Brunswick. "Tell me about your beginnings, Daniel. What was it like where you come from?"

"For starters, it couldn't be much more different from here. It rains a lot and the forests are dense and a lot of the ground is too wet to farm. Not much happens there, really. Most families have small farms and work hard to scrape out a living. They've all been there for three or four generations. But we all got along, maybe because nearly all of us are somehow related through marriage. I guess there just weren't enough families to go around."

"Ha, that doesn't sound much different than where I come from," Limestone pointed out.

"Maybe not," Daniel replied, "but it goes deeper. We all descend from Loyalists."

Limestone hadn't heard the term before. "What the hell is a Loyalist?"

"We all remained loyal to the king during the war, I guess is what it boils down to. My great-grandfather fought in the British Army and surrendered with Cornwallis at Yorktown. For that service, he got some land in the wilderness, along with the rest of the families that still live there."

"Goddamn, Daniel. Isn't that something! My grandfather and your ancestor may have fought against each other. But I guess enough time has passed that I won't hold it against you!"

Limestone laughed at his own jest and added, "I'm providing you with a great service, you know. You stick close to me, Daniel. You've got a lot to learn about this country, and you'll do well to listen closely to the bountiful wisdom that flows from your partner."

"Oh, I plan to do that," Daniel said with a smile. "But, I've had enough of you for one day. I'm turning in."

Near the end of the week, following a fine breakfast of trout fried in bacon grease and flour, they moved farther north to try another ridge. Limestone's mood was buoyed by the fine weather and his delight at being back in the Judith country. "Far as I'm concerned," he remarked, "just the chance of being in a place like this makes a man rich. I've found a bit of gold in my time.

But even if I never found anything, I'd still be doing this."

After they set out that day, Limestone maintained his usual chatter. He pointed out unconformities and other geologic features that might give some clues about the minerals below. Daniel, who was less experienced at riding on steep terrain, held the reins tight and moved cautiously as his horse picked its way across the stony ground.

Soon after they started down an unremarkable slope, Limestone's horse slipped and put him on the ground. At first it seemed like a minor mishap. The horse stood up quickly, and Limestone did the same. He brushed himself off and was ready with a quip.

"I told you we'd need sure-footed horses," he said through a muted laughter.

Within moments, though, the color began to leave Limestone's face. He declared that he hadn't broken any bones but was feeling a little squishy inside. After he sat back down, both men began to suspect that the jarring had moved the shrapnel buried in his body.

Their suspicions were confirmed when Limestone spat up some blood. By late morning he became very weak. Daniel moved him carefully into the shade of a pine and comforted him for the remainder of the day. Occasionally Daniel suggested that he head back to Maiden for help, but Limestone would have none of it. He maintained a calm that likely came from a belief that he was destined to die in this manner.

Even in his weakened condition, Limestone remained talkative. He spoke more slowly and had to pause for breath a few times, but told Daniel of his fondness for the days when the range held only buffalo and no roads scarred the prairie. Now the cattle were here, and soon there would be more towns and even farmers. "I'm not sure I want to live long enough to see it," Limestone pronounced before drifting off into a fitful sleep.

By nightfall they both knew he was dying. Though the evening was warm, Limestone began to shiver. Even after Daniel built a fire and wrapped him in his bedding, the prospector's shivering continued.

"I may not make it through this night, Daniel," said Limestone, "and there's something I want to give you before I'm gone." With discomfort, he reached into the small pouch he always carried and handed Daniel the metal fragment pulled from his body twenty years earlier at Shiloh.

Daniel hesitated and then joked, "If I'd known you were going to give me this, I'd have tripped you myself."

Even in his grave condition, Limestone saw the humor in Daniel's remark. "You're catching on, Daniel, but listen now. This is important." Limestone went on to describe how to get to the home of an old and trusted friend, a man who lived along the Judith River just a few miles above the Missouri. "Give him this, Daniel. Jean Baptiste will know it's from me. If he's still alive, he'll give you a package, something I've had him hold for me."

Daniel felt a burden being placed upon him. He doubted that a man who worked so hard to get others to pick up his bar bills could have anything of value hidden away. "Why not let Jean Baptiste keep it?" Daniel asked.

"LaValle? Well, I've never known a man who cared so little for possessions. You take it. I want you to have something from me."

Daniel promised he'd go to visit LaValle, mostly because Limestone wanted him to. Any expectation of personal gain was secondary.

By morning, Limestone was gone. Daniel carefully secured the man's body to the pack horse and made his way back to Maiden. While he was there, someone sent for the sheriff, who took Daniel's statement. The sheriff knew Limestone well and had no reason to doubt Daniel's account. He asked to see the body and quickly concluded that there were no obvious wounds or other evidence of foul play. But the sight of Limestone's body, laid out on a table and eerily white, shook Daniel from the determination he had mustered to focus on getting his companion to Maiden. Now the finality of Limestone's death fully sank in, and Daniel realized that he had lost a great friend and mentor.

A reporter from Fort Benton's River Press, who regularly sent a dispatch from the region's biggest boomtown, had heard the buzz around Maiden. He made sure to get an interview with both Daniel and the sheriff. The whole experience left Daniel shaken. He was no longer eager to prospect, at least not in the mountains where Limestone had just died.

# CHAPTER 7

Helena had settled in to her glory days. The once-rambunctious mining camp was becoming respectable and comfortably wealthy. Rather than focusing only on mineral wealth, the townspeople had turned their energy to the business of mining, and the mine owners and bankers had built dozens of impressive homes at the foot of Mount Helena. Among them, on Dearborn Avenue was the Sage residence, a two-story Victorian with a sweeping porch and graceful lines. Following a late breakfast, Nellie and her sister Helen, a schoolteacher, sat in a sunny room to consider their day. Nellie stared idly out the window while Helen read the local newspaper. They sat together quietly, the silence broken by Helen's occasional comment on an article she thought might also interest Nellie.

"Hey, Nellie, here's something. A poor man died, and the article mentions a Mr. Daniel McHarg, who came up on the *Red Cloud*. I don't believe we met him, but—"

Nellie cut her off in alarm. "Oh, my god, Helen, is he dead?"

Puzzled by Nellie's reaction, Helen responded, "No, it's not Mr. McHarg who died. Let me read it to you.

"'We were saddened to learn this week of the unfortunate death of Limestone Smith. Mr. Smith, who was known throughout much of Montana Territory, died while prospecting in the mountains north of Maiden. The immediate cause of death was a fall from his horse. In a real sense, though, he was a casualty of the civil war. The wound he suffered at Shiloh finally killed him. He served the cause of the Union admirably and will be remembered fondly by all who knew him. Limestone's body was brought into town by his partner, Mr. Daniel McHarg, a newcomer to this country who came up river this season on the *Red Cloud*. Mr. McHarg plans to return to Fort Benton.'"

Eager to learn more about her sister's reaction, Helen continued, "Who is this Mr. McHarg, Nellie, and why are you so interested in him?"

Nellie tried to explain, though she herself was unsure how to answer Helen's second question. All in all, she concluded, it didn't really matter why. It was more important just to acknowledge that she was interested and that she had thought of Daniel often since leaving Fort Benton.

By the end of their conversation that morning, Nellie had convinced Helen to accompany her to Fort Benton. "Even if nothing comes of it," Nellie said, "I need some time away from this house. I can't stand another day of Father needing to know about everything I do. Come with me, Helen. You don't start school for another month, and we can stay with Aunt Betsy. If you agree to come, I know Father will let us go."

# CHAPTER 8

It took a few days to make all the arrangements for Limestone and to put him in the ground with dignity. Daniel left Maiden the day after the burial. He was still focused on following Limestone's final wish: to seek out Limestone's friend Jean Baptiste LaValle, a reclusive man who lived far from anywhere along the lower Judith River. As Daniel descended from the mountains, the views opened up to the spreading plains, their vastness streaked by the long shadows painted by the low morning sun. For the rest of the morning he kept to the northwest as he rode across the broken grasslands. The light air had a luminous clarity that compressed distances, making it possible to see individual trees on mountain slopes miles away. From a low ridge Daniel spotted a wispy plume of dust that marked the movement of a herd of cattle, one of the arrivals from Texas, still thin from the journey across a thousand miles of the more arid lands to the south.

He made it to the lower reaches of the Judith River in the fading light of a long summer day and continued downstream toward the Missouri, hoping he hadn't missed LaValle's place and that he'd reach it before full dark. Finally, a cabin appeared among a grove of cottonwoods, a smoky cooking fire betraying its presence from the distance.

Daniel approached cautiously and hailed at regular intervals, no doubt long before his voice could be heard. First he heard the dogs, and then a voice emerged from the near darkness. The voice sounded strangely familiar. "Hello, I am Jean Baptiste. Who are you?"

In a sense it was familiar, for Jean Baptiste retained a French accent that reflected his youth in Quebec. It was an accent often heard in the Canada Daniel had left behind.

"My name is Daniel McHarg. You don't know me, but I'm a friend of Limestone's."

"*Eh, bien.* Come up to the house and join me for supper."

Jean Baptiste had come upriver the hard way, pulling a flat boat laden with supplies for Choteau's company. The work was brutal, and the years working the towropes had left his thick shoulders scarred. For the first few years he had tried to be a company man, but he soon felt too confined by even their limited direction on where to go and what to do. He adopted the life of a free trader, roaming the northern plains and keeping to himself much of the time. But living in the land of the Blackfoot required their tolerance and a certain amount of interaction with them, which he achieved by marrying a young Blackfoot woman. Through it all, he developed a fearlessness and a fierce independence shared by few other men.

For such a man, Daniel's arrival near dark caused no immediate concern. LaValle was now well over sixty years of age, with a slight stoop that exaggerated his already short stature. Still, his broad chest and thick shoulders marked him as a man of great physical strength. Like many who took to the mountains, he had little need for company but enjoyed it when an occasional opportunity arose.

Jean Baptiste inquired as to Limestone's whereabouts.

Daniel felt an unexpected dread in bringing the bad news. "I buried him near Maiden yesterday morning," he said softly.

Jean Baptiste winced and turned away toward the cabin. He paused for a moment before urging Daniel to join him on one of the hewed logs that served as an outdoor bench. After they sat, Jean Baptiste stated simply, "Tell me more."

Daniel told the whole story, going back to his first encounter with Limestone at the Antlers. Jean Baptiste listened intently. When Daniel finished, Jean Baptiste nodded and finally broke his silence. "Limestone always expected he'd go like this. 'I'm living on borrowed time,' he'd say, and he lived like that too. There's only one thing to do now."

Jean Baptiste headed into the cabin and returned with a ceramic jug of whiskey. The lack of glasses prevented them from toasting their friend formally, but Jean Baptiste seemed to know of no other way to drink. They drank to a man who had cheated death for many years and had led a life worth living. When Jean Baptiste ran out of tributes, he told Daniel more about his life as a free trader and his marriage to a beautiful Blackfoot woman, who had died several years earlier. A few hours of this was all Daniel could manage. Eventually he drifted to sleep, leaving Jean Baptiste alone with the jug and his memories.

Daniel awoke to the sounds of cooking and the smell of hot grease. Jean Baptiste was occupied with cooking but had kept an eye turned to Daniel in an attempt to time the meal with his awakening. Decades of a rough life far from settlement hadn't lessened the importance he placed on eating well, a habit he considered a French birthright.

Jean Baptiste immediately noted the movement and greeted Daniel almost cheerily, promising that the buffalo liver he was frying was just the thing for a hangover.

Slowly at first, but with increasing vigor, Daniel ate a breakfast of select buffalo cuts, including the liver, and fried bread with a bone-marrow spread. For a time they limited their conversation to food. Jean Baptiste was grateful for each compliment Daniel sent his way. Near the end of the meal, Jean Baptiste praised the shaggy beast. "I have eaten the meat of every animal with a fur and some without. There is no better meat than that of the buffalo."

"I hear they're getting scarce," Daniel noted. "I didn't see any on the ride up from Maiden and there were only a few the whole time it took to come up the river."

"You are right, Daniel, they are rare in this area now. And what a pity that is." But they are still thick to the north, where even an old man like myself can hunt them. And sometimes, my Blackfoot friends bring me some from the Milk River country."

Neither man knew that even these remaining herds would soon face the same intense assault that had annihilated the once vast herds to the south.

As LaValle cleared the table, Daniel fished in his pocket for the metal shard from Shiloh and placed it on the table. Jean Baptiste immediately recognized it. "So, Limestone told you of the package I've kept for him. Did he tell you what it is?"

Daniel assumed Jean Baptiste knew what the package was. He began to wonder if Jean Baptiste would play a game with him and deny that it contained something of value. Jean Baptiste noticed Daniel's discomfort, rose quickly, and went inside the cabin. He returned with a tightly sealed wooden box and placed it on the table.

"Let's open this up and see what we've got," Daniel suggested.

Jean Baptiste refused. "No, open it later, after you leave."

After that, Jean Baptiste became less talkative. Daniel feared that he had offended the old trapper, but that wasn't it. Jean Baptiste had simply reached his tolerance for sharing the confined spaces of his cabin.

Daniel left soon after breakfast. As he prepared to depart, Jean Baptiste reached out and gripped Daniel's hand in a firm clasp. "Be careful, Daniel. There might be something valuable in that box and there are still bandits looking for easy targets." As if to make up for his earlier grumpiness, he added, "Come and see me again. I'm usually here."

Daniel worked his way out of the valley and ascended to a broad bench, which promised an easy passage across a long expanse of nearly flat grassland. With little need to guide his horse, he began to think about the contents of the box and was tempted to open it. Before he did, he was reminded of Jean Baptiste's warning. *The setting is too exposed to pause and open it here*, he thought. Daniel rode farther until the land provided an opportunity for concealment, a coulee hidden from sight and shaded by a juniper. Then he loosened the box's ties and slid off the lid.

The box held an assortment of gold nuggets, some bigger than a child's marbles, and several small bottles filled with gold flakes. It was the accumulation of most of Limestone's years of prospecting throughout Montana. Daniel was so amazed by his good fortune that his feet began to move in a little jig while his arms swept upward, his joy punctuated by an almost involuntary shout of appreciation to Limestone. After this little celebration, Daniel carefully tucked the box back into his saddlebag and slipped a few of the larger nuggets into his pockets to serve as reminders of his good fortune on the long ride to Fort Benton.

Later that afternoon, he came to a deep gulch with a cut bank and sides too steep to cross. He rode along the edge in search of a place where the banks had slumped or the entry of a side channel with gentler slopes. No such place appeared, forcing Daniel to travel well to the north of his intended path. While he reconnoitered along the edge of the gulch, the bottom remained hidden unless he looked down from its very edge. Eventually, however, he came to a bend with a view straight along the bottom of the channel. Here a chilling scene came into view. Almost immediately below him but separated by a ten-foot bank, a group of Blackfoot was busily slaughtering a cow. The men were bloody, their arms covered with it to their elbows, and their faces were streaked with a mixture of blood and sweat that glimmered in the stark light of the midday sun.

Stunned, Daniel simply stared down at the group. Before he could move away unseen, he was spotted. He offered an awkward greeting in English, but the only response he received was the sudden movement by one of the men to reach for a rifle propped against the bank. Daniel had heard enough about the Blackfoot to be alarmed. A quick calculation convinced him that his only option was to run. He turned his horse and raced across the open plains toward some badlands in the near distance, a place he hoped would offer some cover. He made several hundred yards before he looked back and saw the Blackfoot emerge from the gulch.

Daniel's horsemanship was no match for the Blackfoot, who rapidly closed the distance as they raced across the open grassland, their bodies melded to their mounts. As the riders continued to gain, Daniel flailed the reins in a panicked attempt to increase his speed. His efforts were futile. As his arms tired, his grip weakened. A dip in the land and his horse's stagger were enough to throw him from the saddle. He hit the ground hard and stayed still for a moment, groggy but unhurt, breathing in the dust raised by his fall. As he lay there, slowly regaining his wits, he felt an odd detachment from the unfolding events. Instead his mind replayed a family story, one told throughout his youth with a currency that belied its origin nearly a hundred years before Daniel's birth. His great-grandfather, another Daniel, had served in the British army and had been wounded severely in one of the skirmishes leading up to the surrender at Yorktown. As he lay immobilized, a soldier from the other side approached, bayonet fixed, ready to skewer the elder Daniel. But the soldier paused, and his grim face briefly transformed into a grin that reflected his decision to leave the wounded man to his fate.

Daniel was still in his reverie when the Blackfoot arrived and brought their horses to a jarring stop. Secure in the knowledge that they could do anything they wanted with the helpless man lying before them, they stared at Daniel with a mixture of anger and curiosity. The Blackfoot again ignored Daniel's efforts to communicate in English and spoke only among themselves. Daniel understood not a word of their language, but it was obvious that they were discussing his fate.

Looks Beyond, the youngest of the three men, was the most agitated. He urged his companions to kill the white man who had come to this land uninvited and had wasted what he didn't own. "Our people will suffer this winter without the buffalo," said Looks Beyond. "This man, and the others like him, kill without need; they kill without hunger; and for this he should be the one who suffers."

The second man nodded, but the third man, Follows Bear, responded in a more measured tone. He somehow appeared dignified even with cow blood splattered on his face. "Looks Beyond sees much that is true," he acknowledged, "but we don't know what this man did, or who killed that buffalo. Killing this man will bring no honor. His death will only bring our people more trouble."

As the conversation continued, each man speaking more loudly and forcefully, Daniel sensed that his chances were fading quickly. Despite this, he maintained a serenity that made no sense under the circumstances but it allowed him to think clearly. Finally, it occurred to him that these might be some of the "British Indians" who often crossed over from Canada. Maybe they can speak French, he thought.

"*Canada. Je suis Canadien,*" Daniel announced. A look of comprehension emerged from Follows Bear, who held up a hand to quiet the others. Daniel continued in French, "I don't give a damn about that cow. Take as many as you want. It's nothing to me, and I will say nothing of it."

These words bought Daniel more time. Follows Bear spoke enough French to understand Daniel's meaning, which prompted more discussion among the group.

Looks Beyond still urged the others to kill Daniel: "A desperate man will say anything to save his life. If we spare him, the lawmen will soon follow. Better to kill him now and leave his body where it won't be found."

As the discussion continued, Daniel thought of Jean Baptiste and remembered his Blackfoot name and that he had many friends among the tribe. Hoping he had found the words that would save his life, he called out again: "I am a friend of LaValle, who is known by your people as Raven."

The name immediately elicited a look of recognition. Continuing to speak French, Daniel explained to Follows Bear, the apparent leader of the group, how he had met up with Jean Baptiste. Their conversation continued at length, prolonged by the need to translate for Follows Bear's companions, who listened intently but remained silent.

When they seemed to be finished with the news of LaValle, Looks Beyond pointed to Daniel and assumed a fiercer expression. He spoke angrily to Follows Bear, who then translated for Daniel: "Looks Beyond hates the white man for what has happened to the buffalo. He says the white man's buffalo are puny, they will die when the winter of many deaths returns and their rotting carcasses will blacken the land." After a pause, Follows Bear added his own thoughts. "Each year we see fewer buffalo. This year there were none all the way to the Big River. How could this be?"

Follows Bear paused again, as if he expected a response. Daniel was relieved when he pointed back toward the gulch and continued. "That cow was alone and strayed far from the herd. She would have been in a wolf's stomach before the sun was down."

Looks Beyond didn't understand what Follows Bear had said to Daniel but thought it probably involved the calf. "How is it that the white men can take our buffalo and we cannot take their cattle? If they can own our buffalo, can we not also own the scrawny animals they bring into our lands?"

It was a question Follows Bear could not answer. Finally, with no indication that they were about to leave, the three men rode off abruptly. Only Looks Beyond paused to look back. It was a close brush with death and

Daniel slowly released his fear. To Looks Beyond it looked as if Daniel were grinning, and the Blackfoot man's anger deepened.

# CHAPTER 9

On a cool summer morning, Nellie and Helen boarded the stage to Fort Benton. The stage followed a well-worn road that took them almost straight north toward the Gates of the Mountains. As the distance from Helena increased, so did the two sisters' sense of freedom. They felt as if they were continuing the adventure they had begun in St. Louis. Enjoying the company of her fellow travelers, Nellie chatted almost nonstop and perhaps showed more enthusiasm among strangers than was proper for a young woman. But they all enjoyed it and Nellie's energetic conversation made the time pass quickly. By the time they reached the stage stop where they would spend the night, Nellie was exhausted.

After another long day of travel, they arrived in Fort Benton. Nellie awoke the next day in the front bedroom of her aunt's house. The room faced south toward the river and a series of steep gray bluffs. The filtered light of morning hid the rough edges of town and illuminated the cottonwoods along the river with a glow, adding their reflection to the already silvery water. Enchanted by the scene, Nellie quickly dressed to go outside and take it all in. She had hardly seen Fort Benton upon her arrival on the *Red Cloud* and was eager to immerse herself in this new setting, which offered both a chance to see Daniel again and freedom from the confines of her father's supervision.

Helen was already on the front porch and greeted her sister with a sweep of her arms. "Well, Nellie, here we are. How do you propose to find this Daniel of yours?"

"There aren't that many places to look, Helen. Let's just treat these days like a holiday and stroll the town at our leisure. Aunt Betsy said the boat traffic has already dropped off, so there's not much going on. If he's here, we'll find each other."

The two sisters strolled along the waterfront, a route that took them past the hotel where they had stayed after arriving on the *Red Cloud*. Nellie decided to enter the lobby and saw that the same clerk was on duty. He greeted them politely and with perhaps a little too much enthusiasm. "Well, hello to the Misses Sages. I didn't expect to see you here again so soon."

Nellie approached the front desk more closely. "Do you remember all the clients of this hotel?" she said with a hint of mischief in her voice.

"No, ma'am," the clerk replied, but just before blurting out that he always remembered the pretty ones, he caught himself. "I remember your family and the fact that your father was a generous tipper. We never see enough men like that."

"Oh yes," Nellie replied, "my father can be generous at times. I was also wondering, did someone pick up the note I left the day we checked out?"

"Indeed, he did, and just a few hours after you checked out. He seemed pretty put out by having missed you."

Nellie absorbed this information with much interest

and added a second question. "Do you have any idea where the man who picked up the note might be now?"

The clerk said he didn't know but thought for a moment. "That fellow looked like he might be a tradesman. He sure didn't look like a cowboy just come into town. Nearly all the men working in the trades are over at the Grand Union just down the street. You might check there."

In 1882, Fort Benton was in the midst of a building boom. On that day, workmen were putting the finishing touches on the towering façade of the town's newest hotel, the magnificent Grand Union Hotel. Nellie and Helen stopped to observe the work more closely. From the scaffolds hanging from the building, they heard a voice, or maybe a soft whistle. Helen insisted they move on. But Nellie called up in the direction of the sound, "Does anyone here know a Daniel McHarg?"

Nellie was aware that she might be pressing the boundaries of decorum that prevailed at the time, but Helen was appalled. In an instant, one of the men rappelled down the building and walked over to them. Helen suggested that they move on and started walking away, but Nellie stood her ground. "Hello, I'm Nellie Sage and this is my sister Helen." Helen looked a bit sheepish but turned back to join them.

"We haven't been introduced, but I've seen you before," said the worker. "I'm John Campbell. I was also a passenger on the *Red Cloud*, though I never made it to the upper deck. I'm pleased to finally meet you."

"Yes, you do look familiar, Mr. Campbell. Do you happen to know where Daniel is?"

"He stayed in town for a few days after we arrived. But now he's off looking for gold. He went to the mountains with an old-timer named Limestone. No one has seen him here for a few weeks."

Nellie pulled out a clipping from the *River Press* and read the article about the tragedy that had befallen Limestone. John had seen the article but had nothing new to add.

With some exasperation in her voice, Nellie continued on. "Look," she said, pointing at the article. "It also says that Daniel intended to return to Fort Benton. Shouldn't he be here by now?"

Helen and even Nellie now feared that the conversation could get awkward. Nellie didn't want to appear too eager or to answer any inquiries about why she was looking for Daniel. "When you see Daniel, please give him my condolences," she said.

John agreed to do so and Nellie turned abruptly to leave, closely followed by Helen, who quietly fumed at what she judged to be an indiscretion. She feared it might bring embarrassment to them both.

# CHAPTER 10

U pon arising early, Daniel was relieved to see that the heavy rain that had awakened him near midnight had stopped. He was cheered by the thought that he'd make it back to Fort Benton today. The country remained open prairie, broken here and there by a coulee or a low butte. With little to observe and lulled by the steady movement of his horse, Daniel's mind drifted and his thoughts turned to Nellie. In his mind she always appeared just as she had that day they'd talked on the river, her long skirt rippling from the vigor of her movement as she walked back to the boat, her white blouse tightly buttoned around her neck.

As Daniel approached the rim of a minor coulee, the sudden movement of a man standing up shattered this pleasant image. Looks Beyond had been observing Daniel from a distance for much of the morning. He was waiting for the right time to kill a man who symbolized all that had become wrong in his rapidly changing world. Daniel had a sickening recognition that this was the man he had come to fear. Before Daniel could move, Looks Beyond dropped him with a single shot to the torso. He then walked up and looked at Daniel closely, satisfied that the wound would be mortal and that without any assistance likely he would die a slow, lingering death. While telling Daniel that such a death would be his fate, Looks Beyond took Daniel's rifle and the small box in his saddlebag. He left behind the horse, which bore a prominent brand and thus brought with it the likelihood of troubling questions should he encounter anyone from the white man's government.

Daniel lay sprawled on the grass, his blood staining the ground, for most of the day. He couldn't have known for how long, for he was unconscious much of the time, but he later remembered how dried out he felt and how he had dreamed of lying in a forest with a soft mist in the air. While having this dream, Daniel felt the presence of someone. It turned out to be Jean Baptiste.

Follows Bear had visited Jean Baptiste the day after his encounter with Daniel. He had told LaValle about Looks Beyond's anger and about how he had left his fellow tribesmen the previous night. Follows Bear shared his concern that Looks Beyond would pursue Daniel. Jean Baptiste was certain of it and set out to find Daniel immediately.

The trail was easy to follow, and LaValle found Daniel lying in the coarse short grass, his location marked by the horse that remained by his side. After peeling away Daniel's bloody shirt, Jean Baptiste saw that it was a bad wound. He turned Daniel over to see if the bullet had exited, but it remained buried deep in his body.

Jean Baptiste was a surgeon of sorts. He had sewn up men and had treated the stabbings, shootings, and other mishaps that could befall a man on the frontier. He had even sewn himself up on more than one occasion. But Daniel's wound was one of the worst he'd seen, and he knew he had to remove the bullet quickly and stop the bleeding. He arranged the tools he needed for the job and began with an abundant dousing of whiskey, which caused Daniel to stir and to moan in pain. Before starting to probe, Jean Baptiste spoke: "Daniel, if you can hear me, just know this. You have to want to live. I can't help you without that."

It was a difficult process, but after an hour he was finished. Satisfied he had done his best, Jean Baptiste drank deeply from the whiskey jug and set himself up for what would likely be a long wait.

By the third day, Daniel had stirred but had developed a fever. Jean Baptiste made a yarrow tea to keep the fever in check and hoped that Daniel had the strength he'd need to survive. More days passed, and though Daniel grew more alert, he remained quiet, almost solemn, due not only to the physical toll the wound had taken, but also from a feeling that something even more important than Limestone's gold had been lost.

Eventually Daniel broke his silence. "I should have never come to this god damn place," Daniel muttered. "I'd be better off…" Daniel didn't finish the sentence before drifting back to sleep.

Jean Baptiste heard Daniel's remarks but didn't respond, thinking his patient may have become delirious. But on that day, Jean Baptiste began to worry as much about Daniel's despair as his physical wound.

During the extended periods of silence that followed, Jean Baptiste didn't mind the quiet and busied himself with Daniel's care. Nor did Daniel's silence stop him from talking. Indeed, this was the kind of conversation Jean Baptiste enjoyed most. He could talk of any subject he liked while Daniel just listened, an occasional nod providing the only acknowledgment Jean Baptiste needed to keep going. For LaValle it was certainly better than talking to himself or to his dogs, something he did with regularity when holed up in his cabin in the depths of winter.

Jean Baptiste made an occasional foray away from their camp in order to replenish their meat supply, but he usually returned empty-handed because most of the game were in the high country at that time of year and he didn't want to leave Daniel alone for long. After returning one evening, Jean Baptiste reported to Daniel that he had seen a grizzly bear not far from their camp. "It's a good sign for you, Daniel. The Blackfoot believe grizzlies have a powerful spirit." He then launched into a long story about the time a Blackfoot warrior was wounded in a battle with the Snakes. As he lay alone and slowly dying, the warrior prayed for survival and was rescued by a bear, who placed a healing mud on his wounds and carried him back to his people. Jean Baptiste concluded, "I am like the bear, Daniel. I can be cranky and sometimes need to withdraw like bears need to hibernate. But my medicine is also strong. Ha! Is it not so, my friend?"

Daniel still didn't feel like talking much—the effort brought pain to his chest. But he couldn't resist responding. "That's a good comparison, Jean Baptiste. Especially the cranky part. Maybe the hairy part as well."

Jean Baptiste was in good spirits that day and mimicked the movements of a bear, swaying from side to side and laughing heartily. He was happy to see the hint of a smile in Daniel's expression before Daniel tilted his hat down over his face to resume his rest.

After another week, Jean Baptiste declared that Daniel was ready to travel and they started toward Fort Benton. That first day they didn't go far. After a few hours of travel, they descended to the river where Jean Baptiste said there was a good place to cross over to the north side and the easier route it offered.

"Let's stop here for the night," Jean Baptiste declared. "We'll cross the river in the morning when you're fresh. You've had enough time in the saddle for one day. Get some rest."

Daniel was happy to oblige and spent the little remaining energy he had smoothing out the ground where he planned to lay out his bedroll. Jean Baptiste unsaddled the horses but held off preparing for camp. He seemed preoccupied with something, intently scanning a low palisade of white rocks that paralleled the river just above their camp site. Daniel ignored him at first, relieved to be free of the constant movement of his horse and the occasionally jarring pain it caused when his wound was stressed. He rested against his saddle in the shade of a low pine, only occasionally observing Jean Baptiste's movements.

His curiosity was piqued, however, after Jean Baptiste struck off in a hurry, declaring that he'd be nearby and within shouting range. Nevertheless, Daniel drifted off to sleep before he was aroused by Jean Baptiste's repeated shouts.

"Daniel, I found it. Come see!"

Daniel reluctantly stirred himself from the refuge of a dream. "This better be good, JB," Daniel said sourly. "I don't want to move a damned inch unless you've found some gold you cached."

"No, it's nothing like that. But it's important to me. Maybe to you too. Come on, I'll give you a hand."

Jean Baptiste retuned to where Daniel was resting and helped him to his feet, wrapping one of his burly arms around Daniel's shoulders to steady him while they slowly made their way to whatever it was that had so excited Jean Baptiste.

As they walked, Jean Baptiste began to explain. "I never thought I'd find this again. It was long ago, and I was young and just come into the country. We were at the end of our river travel and had pulled the bateau out of the water right here on this bank."

They made their way a few hundred feet farther and stopped in front of a smooth cliff that loomed before them. Jean Baptiste paused and pointed to an inscription, reveling in the sight of it while gently touching the rock face. "Here it is. I carved my name in the rock to mark our passage. I was proud to have come so far upriver and thought, well even if I get killed by the Blackfoot, someone might notice that I had been here."

Jean Baptiste looked back down toward the river and gestured. His normally placid expression revealed a torment Daniel hadn't observed before. "But, as you can see, I didn't have time to finish."

Daniel looked closely at the inscription, noticing that the depth of the inscription trailed off near the end, leaving the last few letters nearly illegible. "What happened here," Daniel finally asked.

"We were attacked by a Crow raiding party. What luck! The whole time we were worried about the Blackfoot and how we would deal with them. Instead, we were slaughtered by a tribe that wasn't even supposed to be here. Mon dieu!"

Jean Baptiste paused to collect his thoughts, obviously moved by the setting and the memories it still held. "We lost many men," he continued, "nearly half. Among them my best friend, who called for me with a fear in his voice that I'll never forget. I dropped the chisel and ran to his side. But it was too late."

Daniel listened intently but didn't probe further, not sure how much he should encourage Jean Baptiste to relive that painful day.

When he was ready, Jean Baptiste resumed. "We were able to drive off the Crows after a desperate struggle. Daniel, I'll spare you the details. But there are more things I want you to know. I was despondent after this. I wanted to leave immediately and go back to Montreal. The others wouldn't let me. So here I am forty years later. Though I'm now old and spend my time mostly alone, my life has been rich. None of the joys I've known would have been possible had I given in to my fears and the anguish I felt that day."

Jean Baptiste turned to the river again, seemingly gathering his thoughts before turning back to Daniel. "Whatever it is you want to accomplish here in Montana, it won't come easy. Daniel, you must never give up."

Those words didn't have much of an effect on Daniel that day. He was too preoccupied with the distress of his wound. Later, though, Daniel would remember Jean Baptiste's words and repeat them whenever he faced some type of adversity.

The two men traveled slowly for the remainder of the journey, taking days to complete a trip that normally would have taken much less time. Upon reaching the bluffs above the Missouri River, they paused to look down on Benton. The town seemed larger than Daniel remembered.

Despite Daniel's urging, Jean Baptiste was determined to go no farther. Thoughts of a crowded town and the barrage of questions that would follow their arrival were more than he could bear. Sensing Daniel's disappointment, Jean Baptiste responded with a quip. "The company of a woman was one of the few things that could bring me into a town. But alas, now I'm just an old bull that can't perform. A town holds few attractions for a man like me."

Daniel thanked Jean Baptiste profusely for all that he had done. Still, Daniel parted with the awkwardness a man feels when he has received a gift that can't be repaid

properly. Jean Baptiste muttered something about having
done it for Limestone, but he later regretted those words,
for he had come to like Daniel and feared his words
would diminish a bond that had become important to him.

# CHAPTER 11

Daniel was still weak, and he lay low for a few days before venturing out of his room. His first foray was to a store that also served as an assay office. The few gold nuggets he had kept in his pocket replenished his diminishing stake and left him with enough cash to get by for a while.

Word that someone had cashed in a few large nuggets moved quickly through town. The assay clerk reported that the man was a Canadian who claimed to have found the nuggets near Maiden. The small-town rumor trail led straight to Daniel, who suddenly found his boarding room filled with visitors, including John Campbell and a few other passengers from the *Red Cloud*. Daniel wasn't in the mood for company, but his friends were eager to see him.

John was especially excited because he had something to show Daniel. "I hope you found some gold, Daniel," he said, "or your admirers back in Minnesota will be disappointed." John read from a neatly folded clipping from the Montevideo Leader, which had been republished in the Fort Benton newspaper:

"'We acknowledge the receipt from Daniel McHarg, formerly of this place but now in Benton, Montana, of an interesting edition of the *River Press*, published at that place. Judging from the evidence of thrift and prosperity in the *Press*, we think Benton is bound to boom, and we hope Daniel will boom with it and come back with his pockets full of rock.'"

Daniel had forgotten that he'd sent a letter, along with a few articles from the *River Press*, to a newspaperman who had become a good friend during his time in Minnesota.

"So let's have it, Daniel," John continued. "Do you have any more rocks in those pockets of yours?"

It was good for a laugh, but they were genuine in inquiring about Daniel's health. They wanted to hear all about how he had been shot and how he had managed such a heroic escape.

"I didn't do a damn thing," Daniel said. The comment came across abruptly and without his usual humor. "If it hadn't been for an old trapper, I'd be lying there now."

John decided not to press. Remembering that he had some other news for Daniel, he changed the subject again. "I saw that Nellie of yours, she and her sister. They asked about you and seemed pretty embarrassed to be seen showing an interest in a rambler like you."

Daniel wanted to know all the details, especially whether Nellie was still in town and where he might find her.

"I don't know where she's staying," John replied, "but after we saw her at the hotel she and her sister headed toward the nice homes farther up Front Street."

Not long after receiving that information, Daniel thanked his friends for coming by and sent them on their way with the promise that he'd be better company soon enough.

The next day, after a late breakfast, Daniel tidied himself up and put on a new shirt he had hurriedly purchased at Gans & Klein, a store that sold finer goods than he typically bought. There weren't many homes on Front Street above the commercial district, so his task wasn't hopeless. He knocked on a few doors and inquired about Nellie until a woman directed him to a yellow house up the street. Before he got there, he saw Nellie and her sister sitting on the porch—a marvelous sight for a man who had begun to worry his life would unravel again. Nellie tried to exercise restraint but couldn't suppress the sweet smile Daniel remembered. She sent Helen inside to tell Aunt Betsy that the man was someone she knew.

Daniel was thinner than Nellie remembered, so that's how their conversation started. "Mr. McHarg," she quipped, "are you too busy looking for gold to take time to eat?"

Nellie followed up with an offer to serve Daniel some breakfast, but he declined, wanting nothing to interfere with such a long-awaited moment. Yet they hardly knew each other, and the intensity of their feelings was wildly disproportionate to the amount of time they had actually spent together. It wasn't easy to manage the conversation under these circumstances. They had much information to share, but neither was comfortable expressing the powerful feelings that mattered most: that they had thought of each other continuously and that something had been missing in their lives from the moment they had separated. That acknowledgement would come later.

For now, they stuck to the events. "What happened to you, Daniel? It must have been something terrible."

"It was," Daniel began. "I was shot and left for dead. But I was saved by someone I hardly knew. I owe my life to that man, Nellie."

Nellie insisted on a full account, which Daniel reluctantly provided. His account of his near-death experience was a shock, something Nellie almost couldn't bear to hear. Even though Daniel was sitting right next to her, thinner but otherwise appearing well, she felt some responsibility for his trauma. *Perhaps*, she thought, *if I hadn't left Fort Benton so abruptly, things would have been different.*

Despite Nellie's worries, they talked for almost an hour. Nellie was relieved to hear Daniel's account of his meeting with Limestone that first night in Fort Benton and how he had become determined to seek his fortune in the Judith Mountains. Daniel then left, reluctant but elated by Nellie's insistence that he return the next day for a noon meal. Though an unfortunate turn of events, Daniel's wound turned out to be an opportunity for the hopeful couple, as none of the Sage women could doubt the propriety of helping someone—even a near stranger—regain his health. Nellie would make the most of this opportunity.

As Nellie expected, Aunt Betsy agreed that Daniel would be welcome to join the family for the noon meal, thus beginning a routine that brought him to the house most days for the next few weeks. The three women shared in the cooking. The knowledge that they were helping someone recover from a serious wound made their efforts purposeful, and all three enjoyed Daniel's company. After Nellie's aunt came to know Daniel better, other possibilities for Nellie and Daniel to spend time together emerged. They took long walks through the town or just sat by the river. Helen usually joined them, but she made sure they also had time alone.

In the times they enjoyed alone, focused only on each other, they began to talk more intimately, sharing details of each other's lives—except for one thing. In those early days Daniel hesitated to tell Nellie of the tragic loss of his first wife and their unborn child. He knew he had to, but it was still something Daniel found painful to talk about. As time went on, he felt more acutely the pressure to share his burden, which revealed itself one afternoon as they walked up to an overlook above the river. Nellie noticed his discomfort.

"You don't seem to be yourself today, Daniel. Is there something wrong?"

"No, nothing's wrong. I guess I'm just disappointed that it's taking so long to recover. I feel like an old man trying to walk up this hill."

Nellie nodded, but kept her attention on Daniel, sensing he might have more to say. Daniel kept his silence until they reached the top of the hill, where a few makeshift benches had been erected by town residents eager to spot the arrival of the season's first steamboat.

"Sit down, Nellie. There's something I need to tell you." Daniel fidgeted, rubbing his palms together, hoping to find the right words. "I've been married before. Her name was Katie and she died in childbirth two years ago. I've been wanting to tell you, but I wasn't sure how to do it. It still hurts, Nellie. And I didn't want to drive you away."

Nellie was stricken by the news, but not for herself. At that moment, she cared only about Daniel's feelings and wondered how he managed to cope with such a tragedy.

"Oh, Daniel, I'm so sorry—sorry for the pain you've had to experience, but also sorry you didn't think you could tell me. I want to know everything about you." She shuddered briefly before continuing. "More importantly, I don't want you to have to carry this burden alone any longer."

She embraced Daniel, who now sat next to her on the bench, and gently rubbed the back of his neck. They held that position for several moments, remaining silent, while each of them contemplated what to say next.

"It's a relief to have told you, Nellie. Now you know just about everything there is to know about me. Except for a few things, maybe. Like my habit of howling at the moon and—"

Nellie stopped him midsentence. "No, Daniel, please don't do that. I understand now that your humor is sometimes a way to protect yourself. But you don't need to do that with me. Please let me help you."

"You already are. More than you know, you already are."

On the walk back into town, Nellie contemplated this new information about Daniel. Now she knew that his real healing would be more complicated than recovering from a gunshot wound. Far from being deterred, she vowed that day to do her best to help.

As summer waned and the days grew noticeably shorter, Daniel could feel himself recovering, not only because of the pounds he had gained, but also because of a lessening of the darkness that had crept back into his soul after he had been shot. Though he began to laugh more easily and to feel joy in Nellie's presence, sometimes a shadow would return while he was alone in the night. At those moments, Daniel couldn't help but feel a sense of futility and doubt in himself. He told himself that he was foolish to believe he could shed the burden of a tragic loss and build a new life with the stability and prosperity that a woman like Nellie should expect. With a concentrated effort, he could still push these dark thoughts away.

At the end of August, it was time for Nellie to return to Helena. Helen needed to start the school year and they had stayed in Fort Benton for as long as they could. In the times they had enjoyed alone and focused only on each other, Daniel and Nellie had begun to talk about a life beyond Nellie's remaining time in Fort Benton.

Their talk of a future life was tentative at first, but it quickly grew after they first dared to allow themselves a passionate embrace. On that day, they had walked up river, past the last houses that trickled away from the town, entering an empty landscape marked by the stumps of cottonwoods felled for their fuel. It was a warm day and the sun brought beads of sweat to their foreheads. Daniel noted that Nellie looked flushed, which made her even more radiant in his eyes, but he thought it best to return to town.

"We should turn back," Daniel offered, "before they send a posse after us."

Nellie agreed but added, "Let's find some shade and a place to sit before we do. I need to cool off or Aunt Betsy might think the worst of us."

Despite the heat, they sat closely together on a large stump, one shaded by the barren cliffs that loomed above them. They sat quietly, having sated any need for conversation, but also felt a powerful distraction from the nearness of their bodies. Before long, and without any pretense, Daniel took Nellie in his arms and held her close. Nellie offered no resistance. Instead, she brought her lips to his face, kissing his cheeks and forehead before settling on his lips. Their passions built as they explored each other's bodies with their hands. Before they could go too far, or at least farther than they intended, a horseman approached trailing a few steers. He kept a respectful distance but the interruption broke the spell. Later, Nellie realized that the rider had provided needed relief, for she still intended to save herself for her future husband and she wasn't sure what would have happened had they not been disturbed. Still, things would be different between them now. For the attraction Daniel and Nellie felt for each other was compounded by a physical passion they had only begun to imagine. Once that had been realized, if not fully released, it would emerge forcefully whenever they were together. They each began to dread the separation they knew would come soon.

After that passionate moment by the river, their talk of a future together took on greater urgency. Daniel started the conversation one afternoon with a simple question. "How would you like to be a ranch woman?"

"Well, that depends, Daniel. It depends on what you're asking me." It wasn't how she had imagined herself being proposed to, so she continued to probe in a teasing manner. "Are you asking me to be your business partner?"

"Well, you got me there. Of course not. I'm asking you to be my wife. But I don't blame you for the guff. I deserved it. Let me try again."

This time, Daniel overacted his part, getting down on his knees and making his intentions clear. But the ring would have to wait, which didn't stop Nellie from accepting his proposal. "I would be thrilled to be your wife. And ranch partner too."

They embraced, laughing, and then turned more serious. "I've got my eye on some land along the Teton River," Daniel announced, "It will be hard work to get things started, but the land is right for it. And we'll be together. That's what matters most."

Over the next few days, Daniel shared with Nellie an outline of a plan to get things started. He would begin the process of claiming the land and then go to Helena, where the government land office was located, and buy

160 acres through what was known as an exemption claim. It would take some time to perfect the claim, improvements had to be made on the land. But when the work was done he would ask Nellie's father for his approval to marry her.

When the day came for Nellie to leave, Daniel and Nellie found a quiet spot along the river to say their goodbyes. It was a place where they were comfortable, for despite the weariness they had each experienced on the long voyage upriver, they felt that the river had brought them together. Still, it was hard to face an impending separation, one they were hopeful would end well, but the reality of how little time they had spent together nurtured some doubts. Nellie tried to be strong, but her emotions prevailed. Daniel felt her tremor as they embraced, a few of her tears wetting his cheek.

"This is going to work out, Nellie. I promise."

"I think so too. But it's hard—I'll miss you, Daniel. I'll miss you every day." She then turned to walk the short distance back to Aunt Betsy's house, where a carriage was waiting to take the two sisters to the stage.

After Nellie left for Helena, Daniel got right to work. He spent a few nights camping along the Teton and walked and rode the land for several days before selecting an acreage that consisted almost entirely of bottom land, with an abundance of trees and ground that could be tilled for grain crops or hay. Although the parcel was far too small to support a cattle ranch, these 160 acres would be the home place, a haven set amid grasslands that stretched to the horizon, unfenced and still available for the taking by those with the courage and determination to turn cattle loose on a range where wolves, blizzards, and thieves were constant threats.

Later that fall, when he felt fully recovered, Daniel began the difficult work of making the needed improvements to the land, including breaking some of the ground and building fencing, corrals, and the beginnings of a house. He did much of the work himself, though he occasionally recruited John Campbell and a few other friends to help.

Before winter settled in, Daniel made a trip to the Judith River. He took along some buffalo meat for Jean Baptiste, who prepared a feast that lasted long into the night. Jean Baptiste was glad for the company, but he complained bitterly of the slow toll that age was taking on his body. "Daniel," he said, "I could once live on gristle and walk for days with a load that would make a mule balk. But now I have days when it's almost too much to do the simple things one must do to live."

Though Daniel pressed, Jean Baptiste offered no particulars on his condition. He asserted that he felt good today and that was all that mattered. Daniel told LaValle of his place on the Teton and his plans to marry and to get into the cattle business. LaValle was delighted to hear of Daniel's marriage plans but he couldn't understand his ambition to start a ranch. He believed that cattle didn't belong in Montana and that attempts to replace the buffalo made no sense. But LaValle held his tongue on the matter and instead told Daniel about a time when a Crow raiding party ambushed a group of Blackfoot very close to where Daniel was building his house. "If you hear a sound in the night like the moan of a dying man, my friend, it will be the Blackfoot," said Jean Baptiste.

Daniel grew alarmed. He was only partly reassured when Jean Baptiste told him that these Blackfoot were only lost souls and meant no harm.

# CHAPTER 12

That winter was the longest in Nellie's life. Though she and Daniel wrote often, she felt isolated from all that had become important to her, not just from him but also from some of the friends she had made in Fort Benton. Matters were made worse by an ongoing conflict with her father, who not only tried to control Nellie's activities but also seemed to disagree with her on nearly every issue she held important. Although Nellie spoke often of Daniel and their plans for the future, she thought her father didn't take the relationship seriously.

At the dinner table the conversation inevitably became argumentative, despite Mrs. Sage's gentle efforts to intercede. Mr. Sage, whose position as the owner of a major mine gave him immediate entry into Helena's emerging elite, was used to deference, particularly from the women in his own household. He found it difficult to accept any questioning of his firmly held beliefs, which nearly all his peers shared. These beliefs revolved around a sort of manifest destiny, with respect not only to Indian lands and resources but also to the relationship between labor and management, as well as men and women and their right to vote.

One evening, after Nellie and her father had an especially vehement disagreement about the treatment of miners and their families, Mr. Sage decided to try harder to modify Nellie's views. "Nellie, you really don't know anything about these people and the lives they live. Let me show you. Let me show you that the relationship between the workers and management is mutually beneficial."

Nellie remained skeptical. "I've seen the places these men and their families live. It's nothing like our home, but that's not what matters. What matters is that most of them don't have a chance to thrive. They die young, their children work before they finish their schooling, and nothing ever seems to change."

Mr. Sage was used to his daughter's objections to his world view, which he considered to be the natural order of things. *She's not only naïve*, he thought, *but she also doesn't know any of the realities of business or conditions in the places many of the miners came from.*

"Do you know, Nellie, that miners in Appalachia are dying by the score from a disease that blackens their lungs? That they die in explosions nearly every year? We have none of those things here. Our conditions are so much better than that."

Nellie remained unconvinced. She kept her silence but conveyed her skepticism with a shrug, a gesture her father knew too well.

"Very well. Let me show you things firsthand. I'm going to the mine tomorrow and I'd like you to accompany me. Will you do that, Nellie?"

Nellie reluctantly agreed. During that period in her life, she had little to occupy her time and felt she could use a diversion. Plus, she couldn't bear discussing the topic any further that evening. An agreement to accompany her father would at least relieve her of that immediate burden.

Mr. Sage had another motive driving his plan, however. He wanted to introduce Nellie to a young man who worked at his mine as a clerk, someone Mr. Sage felt had better prospects than Daniel did. Though Daniel and Mr. Sage hadn't met, Nellie's description of his circumstances provided Mr. Sage with little confidence that the young man was up to the job of supporting his eldest daughter. Mr. Sage thought that Daniel's proposed ranch would amount to nothing, and that the emerging cattle industry would be controlled by those backed with big capital behind them—such as the D-S Ranch that was building a herd of more than ten thousand head in the Judith Basin.

Before the evening ended, Mr. Sage shared some of these sentiments. "My dear, I'm afraid that without the backing of the money men, that Daniel of yours is destined for a life spent dirt-poor and an early grave. I don't want that kind of life for my daughter." He went on to imply that he might be able to offer assistance.

"I doubt Daniel would want that," Nellie replied. "And I wouldn't either. We need to make it on our own." Nellie's assertion only made Mr. Sage less supportive of the relationship.

The next day, as Nellie had reluctantly agreed, they set off for the mine, which required a long carriage ride from Helena. The distance was great enough that Mr. Sage occasionally spent a few nights at the mine site, but the prospect of living in a mining camp had little appeal compared to the elegance of Helena. Father and daughter both knew that the ride would seem even longer if the conversation became unpleasant, so they kept things light, limiting their comments to the scenery they passed through and their mutual excitement about the prospect of rail service arriving the following year.

After the carriage ascended through a narrow canyon, the mine came into view. They were greeted by the clerk Mr. Sage was eager to introduce to Nellie. The clerk was a charmer who focused his attention on Nellie immediately. "Welcome, Nellie, if you'll allow me to call you by your first name. I've heard so much about you from Mr. Sage. You're even more beautiful than your father told me!" He then offered his arm to accompany her on the tour, which Nellie declined to accept. She remained polite but found the exchange distasteful. Following this brief encounter, the usual tension between Nellie and her father returned. Mr. Sage described the clerk as a brilliant young man who would go far. "You ought to get to know him better, Nellie," he said.

Mr. Sage's comment set Nellie off. She not only found the clerk unappealing, but also resented her father's implication that she was open to meeting other men after she had told him of the seriousness of her feelings toward Daniel. "Father, you ought to know me better than to think that an obsequious clerk of yours is someone I'd find interesting." This remark set the tone for what was to come.

Mr. Sage had timed their arrival to observe the end of a shift, when the miners emerged from the depths, happy to see the light of day again. The men were accustomed to seeing Mr. Sage about the mine property; he made a habit of engaging in small talk with them and seemed to enjoy the interplay with his workers. This was what Mr. Sage had brought Nellie to see. He hoped that the good cheer he could usually elicit from the men would demonstrate that the workers didn't view him as some sort of a demon and that they maintained their dignity and a degree of joviality despite the hard work and risks their jobs demanded.

At first, all went according to Mr. Sage's plan. As the men emerged from the mine, many of them paused around Mr. Sage. He greeted many of them by name, shaking hands with each of them like a politician on election day.

"Hello, Isaac. How is your wife? Is she over her illness now?" To another man he offered a compliment. And to all in his presence, he promised a treat for the holidays. "Christmas is approaching, men. This year, I have a basketful of treats for every man. I promise it will bring good cheer to your families."

Nellie noted that the miners looked pleased in Mr. Sage's presence. However, she felt certain he had staged it all for her benefit. After several of the men had passed, her attention was drawn to a young man—a boy, really—who had been crippled by an accident in the mine and could no longer work. He supported himself with a pair of homemade crutches. Because the young man had little to do with his time, and because he knew that the miners sometimes shared leftover food from their pails, he often appeared at shift changes. On occasion the miners even slipped him a coin or two to supplement the meager settlement he had received from the company as compensation for his injury.

After seeing one of the miners hand the young man a bit of food, Nellie walked over to him. Her father observed this action as he continued greeting the workers, determined to stay until the last one had passed.

"Forgive my directness," Nellie said to the young man, "but what happened to your leg? Will it heal?"

"No, ma'am. A whole pile of rocks fell on my leg. It was a bad break, and the bone didn't get set well. I guess the doc might have been drunk." He laughed and added,

"I did get a hundred dollars from the company. It won't last long, but I guess I knew what I was getting myself into when I signed on to be a miner."

Just then Mr. Sage stepped in. He flashed a smile toward the injured miner, who now felt awkward and a little nervous in the presence of the powerful mine owner.

Looking around to see who was observing, Mr. Sage spoke loudly. "See, Nellie, the miners take care of their own. We've certainly done our part as his employer, more than what we're required to do by the law."

Nellie felt an emerging rage. "This young man's plight is tragic," she said to her father. "A hundred-dollar settlement is ridiculous. Do you not see the injustice in this?"

Mr. Sage quickly pointed out that the company had offered the standard settlement in the young man's case, and that he couldn't pay every injured man a fortune without going broke. Certain that she had already caused enough of a scene, Nellie ignored her father. Before bolting back to the carriage, however, she handed the crippled man what little money she had in her bag. Several of the miners witnessed the act.

The ride back to Helena proceeded in silence. Mr. Sage was also furious. He was uncertain as to how the men would react to the drama Nellie had created and what he should do to correct it. Just before they reached the edge of town, Mr. Sage told Nellie that he had made a decision.

"We're going back to the mine next week, Nellie. When we do, you will try to repair the damage you've done today."

Nellie was stunned by her father's declaration. An act she intended as charity had been perceived by her father as an act of betrayal. She would have none of it and cut off her father before he could continue. "I'll not re-

turn to the mine again. Not until you make some real reforms. I'll not help you sugarcoat the grim reality of how
you treat the workers."

Mr. Sage struggled to control his anger, which red-
dened his normally pale face. "I'm not going to argue
with you any further about this, Nellie. My decision has
been made. Either you return to the mine with me and
make amends, or you'll no longer be welcome in my
household."

Mr. Sage expected an immediate response, but he
didn't get one. "I'll give you my answer in the morning,"
Nellie said with some effort, working hard to maintain
her composure. The events of the day had exhausted them
both and they agreed, through their silence, to let the matter lie until the morning.

At breakfast the next day, Nellie announced her decision in the presence of both of her parents. "I've decided
to take a room here in town and will be moving out directly. I have some savings and my earnings from teaching piano that will sustain me until Daniel and I are to be
married."

Nellie's mother wasn't fully cognizant of what had
transpired between Nellie and her husband. She was
shocked and looked quizzically at her husband before
begging her daughter to reconsider. "Please don't do this,
Nellie. Your sister is already out of the house. I was so
hoping to have your company in the months leading up to
your marriage."

"Let her go," Mr. Sage said bluntly. "Perhaps she'll
learn something from this experience."

Looking back later on, Nellie viewed her months living alone in Helena as a turning point in her life. She realized then that she could make a life on her own. She
also learned more fully how rewarding it was to help others, a practice perhaps motivated by her encounter with

the crippled miner. In addition to working as a piano teacher that winter, Nellie found time to volunteer at a hospital serving the poor.

# CHAPTER 13

Looks Beyond woke early and silently left the Blackfoot camp. Follows Bear saw him leave but said nothing, having grown accustomed to Looks Beyond's habit of disappearing for a day or two with an increasing frequency. An unforeseen consequence of Looks Beyond's windfall, the gold he had taken after shooting Daniel, was his growing need for whiskey. Looks Beyond had developed a taste for whiskey as a young man when unscrupulous traders had made it readily available on Blackfoot lands. But more effective enforcement of the ban on selling liquor to the Indians had greatly diminished the availability of whiskey on the reservation. As a result, whiskey had become expensive, and Looks Beyond rarely had the funds to purchase any. Now he did.

It wasn't difficult to find places to buy whiskey and Looks Beyond soon knew them all. At first, Looks Beyond was able to exert some control over his appetite for alcohol, limiting his visits to the hell-hole places that sold whiskey to once or twice a month. But the whiskey eventually overcame him, eroding his pride as well as his long-held aversion to dealing with white men. Although

his resentment for the people who had invaded his homeland didn't diminish, the white men controlled the whiskey, and Looks Beyond began to feel that he had no
choice but to deal with them.

Looks Beyond feared no man, but he wasn't fool-
hardy. He knew that even inadvertently creating an impression that he carried a lot of gold would arouse suspicion and make him an irresistible target for the vermin
drawn to the places that sold illegal whiskey. Looks Beyond also learned that it was best to spread his business
around. His caution was justified, for he had experienced
a few close calls, even though he kept to himself and was
interested in nothing more than drinking himself into
senselessness. Without exception, however, these estab-
lishments were known for their lawlessness and penchant
for attracting misfits and miscreants of all varieties. Accordingly, Looks Beyond took only enough gold to purchase the whiskey he needed to get drunk. When he
needed more, he would seek out a place he hadn't been
previously or return to a joint he hadn't visited for several
weeks or longer.

In early spring, Looks Beyond headed off on one of
his whiskey forays. He traveled on foot, unwilling to risk
the loss of one of his prized horses, and sought out an es-
tablishment he hadn't been to previously. It was located
on a small tributary to the Missouri River and occupied a
site that was off any established travel ways. This place
was called Wolf Hole and it was well concealed by the
broken terrain that surrounded it. Wolf Hole had only two
buildings, a small cabin and a larger building that served
as a combined bar and bordello.

Looks Beyond arrived in early afternoon and approached the larger building cautiously. It was a low
slung structure with few windows. Despite its recent construction, the building looked deteriorated. A tilt to one

side proclaimed its shoddy construction. After briefly hesitating to enter the building, Looks Beyond stepped into the gloomy darkness, his need for whisky overcoming the caution he knew such a place warranted. The bright sunshine outside contrasted with the dank interior and made it difficult to see any details inside. Once inside, the building's interior reminded Looks Beyond of a bear's den. The aroma that enveloped him upon entering did nothing to dispel that impression.

After his eyes had adjusted to the darkness, Looks Beyond could see things more clearly and noted that several men and one woman were inside. The woman wore rouge and a dress, oblivious to the fact that most of her customers didn't much care what she looked like.

Once inside, Looks Beyond went straight to the bar, a primitive counter formed with rough planks. A few stools provided the only seating. He ordered a jug of whiskey, using the few words he knew in English. The proprietor, who thought he had seen him before, took a jug from the shelf behind the bar and watched Looks Beyond closely as he placed some gold on the counter. The amount proffered was the amount Looks Beyond knew was the going rate, but the proprietor immediately demanded more. Looks Beyond objected, but his eagerness for whiskey and inability to speak English overcame his concern with the price. He emptied the remaining gold he carried and laid it on the counter.

When the purchase had been completed, Looks Beyond took the jug and sat on the packed dirt floor in an unoccupied corner of the building. It was a cold day, so he preferred to stay inside. After pulling the cork with his teeth, he drank heartily from the jug, swilling it down his throat until it dribbled down his chin and forced an involuntary wretch. He was eager to lose himself in the whiskey, but the encounter with the proprietor had slightly unsettled him.

After the first gulp, Looks Beyond drank more slowly, savoring the warmth it brought to his throat and anticipating the pleasant glow he knew would follow. Between gulps, Looks Beyond observed the people inside the bar more closely. In addition to the proprietor and the woman, three other men were present. All of them were white and none of them looked as if they welcomed an Indian in their presence. They conveyed their displeasure with several comments sent in Looks Beyond's direction. Looks Beyond couldn't understand any of it, but the tone was unmistakable. Still, it was something he had become accustomed to. He drained most of the small jug before dozing off.

The white men thought they might have an easy mark and watched Looks Beyond closely. After a while, when it appeared Looks Beyond was fully asleep, one of the men spoke to the proprietor.

"Does that red devil have anything worth stealing?"

The proprietor replied that he thought Looks Beyond had given him all the gold he had, which didn't deter one of the men from walking over to where Looks Beyond slept. The man stood quietly over Looks Beyond, examining him closely to confirm that he was asleep while he scanned his body for something of value. The man's eyes settled on a small leather pouch Looks Beyond wore around his neck, a precious totem he had worn since his youth. Thinking it might contain more gold, the white man reached for the pouch. Before, he could reach it, Looks Beyond slashed the man's wrist with a knife. It was an instinctive reaction that happened so quickly that the man had little time to express his pained surprise before Looks Beyond bolted out the door.

Looks Beyond ran hard, fueled by an adrenalin rush that shook him out of his somnolence. The sudden violence and Looks Beyond's flight spurred the wounded man's companions into action. Each of them went outside, drew their revolvers, and fired shot after shot in Looks Beyond's direction as he raced into the distance. All of the shots were ineffective, partly because of Looks Beyond's speed, but also due to the amount of alcohol each of the men had consumed. Looks Beyond weaved through the terrain, hoping his sprint would take him out of pistol range and over a ridge into the next canyon.

Meanwhile, the proprietor, a former buffalo hunter, took his Sharps rifle off a rack behind the bar and searched for ammunition, knocking several items off the shelf in the process. He cussed aloud, feeling an increasing panic as he contemplated the possibility of Looks Beyond escaping. Although he knew the shells had to be nearby, he hadn't fired the Sharps in more than a year and wasn't sure where to look. He also feared that just a few more wasted seconds might allow Looks Beyond to escape.

Looks Beyond continued his sprint and was near the top of a ridge when the proprietor ran outside and prepared to take a shot. He crouched and carefully aimed. Looks Beyond slowed his pace as he neared the crest of a ridge, confident that he was out of range. He heard a boom and turned to look back when the powerful shot hit him mid stride, propelling him forward into the dirt.

# CHAPTER 14

In June, Daniel and Nellie were married in Helena in a small ceremony attended by a few close friends and part of Nellie's family. Mr. Sage did not attend. Daniel and Nellie returned to Fort Benton the next day and spent one night in the Grand Union Hotel before heading out to their home on the Teton. Their return prompted a short piece in the River Press:

*Daniel McHarg and Miss Nellie Sage were married in Helena Sunday evening, and Daniel brought his bride home last night. Mr. McHarg is well known and universally popular in Benton, and we believe his young wife will never have cause to regret the trust she reposed in him. Mrs. McHarg resided in Benton some time last year, where she made many friends who will give her a warm welcome back. The happy couple are comfortably housed in their new home on the Teton, and* River Press *joins with their friends in wishes for a happy life.*

The newlyweds rode to their place on the Teton on a glorious day when the grass retained a spring green and the river sparkled under a cloudless sky. Nellie found the setting enchanting but flinched when she saw the building that would become their home. In his letters earlier that year Daniel had tried to prepare her for the fact that the house was a simple affair and that he'd make improvements over time. But the undeniable fact remained that it was plain, small, and consisted of just two rooms. Nonetheless, Nellie was happy just to be with Daniel, and she told him it was lovely.

"Daniel, you've outdone yourself," she proclaimed with humor in her tone. "But tell me, where will the servants' quarters be?"

Daniel put on a formal manner and ushered her through the front door. "Over there," he said as he pointed to the new wing he was planning, "we'll have room for servants' quarters as well as a nursery."

Nellie's response was to push him onto a rickety bed, after which their laughter filled the small space inside the building's four rough walls.

There was still much work to do. Nellie focused on making a home of their "shanty on the prairie" while Daniel divided his time between buying and managing livestock, making improvements to their property, and occasionally working in town for a little extra income.

As evening approached one August day, when the summer was overripe and any hint of lushness had vanished from the land, Daniel and Nellie rewarded themselves with some rest. They sat in the shade by their house and gazed toward the river and the rounded bluffs just beyond. At this time of day, they often spotted deer tucked in to the folds of the land, and this was their first thought when a figure appeared at the top of a ridge.

For a moment the figure remained motionless, silhouetted against a towering sky. Then it moved, initially with only a slow wave of one arm, followed by a slow advance down the slope. It was a horseman, soon revealed to be an Indian. He seemed to be traveling alone, but they couldn't be sure. As the figure approached the house, Daniel went for his rifle and urged Nellie to go inside. She refused, stating that whatever danger they may face, they would face it together. There wasn't enough time to argue, for the horseman had picked up the pace and was within hailing distance. Daniel heard the man yell out, "Hey, Canada! Canada!"

The man was backlit by the lowering sun, making it difficult to see his features, so Daniel didn't know immediately who it was; he was only certain that it was an Indian. But the voice was familiar and brought back a painful memory. Even if the man wasn't Looks Beyond, Daniel had no reason to be comfortable with any of the Blackfoot men he had encountered that day. Once again Daniel urged Nellie to go inside, but she continued to resist, gently pushing away the hand he pressed against her hip. Daniel started to speak to the man in English but was interrupted by a request, spoken with a surprising politeness. "*Francais, s'il vous plait. Parlez francais.*"

Daniel shouted back, in French, "I think I remember you, but hold there until I can figure it out for sure."

The man stopped his advance. "Jean Baptiste sent me. There is no other reason I would be here. He asked me to do something for him. So I am here."

"Why would Jean Baptiste send you here?"

In response, the man reached for something. It was a small box with the distinctive markings that were on the gift Daniel had received from Limestone. Daniel loosened his tight grip on the rifle and urged the man to come ahead. It was Follows Bear, who reported, "Looks Beyond is dead. The whiskey got him. He was killed by this gold—the gold he took from you. I don't want the evil this brings to be among my people any longer."

Then Follows Bear threw the box to the ground near Daniel. The box opened when it hit, spilling its contents into the grass, mixing some of the fine gold dust with particles of dirt.

"First, I took this box to LaValle," Follows Bear said with an obvious sadness. "It was a gift I had given him many years ago, but LaValle said it belonged to you now." He went on to explain that Looks Beyond had left the box and the meager amount of gold it still contained with his family.

Daniel was momentarily stunned. Finally, he asked, "Who killed Looks Beyond? Where did it happen?"

Follows Bear explained that the killers had been white men—the worst kind of white men. "There's a place just off the reservation called Wolf Hole. Looks Beyond went there to buy whiskey. It's an evil place."

Daniel had heard of the place and knew that cattle thieves and other outlaws congregated there. It was a place that attracted the worst among men, a place where death was often just an argument away or merely another man's amusement. Still, Daniel wanted to know more. "Why was he killed? Did he cause any trouble?"

Follows Bear had tracked Looks Beyond to Wolf Hole after he had failed to return. Someone there, a white man, reported that Looks Beyond had tried to kill a man and was shot while trying to escape. They left his body where it lay. Follows Bear retrieved what was left of the body and would carry the painful memory of that day until his own death.

Follows Bear never answered Daniel's question directly. He simply said, "Looks Beyond was sick in his heart. His anger at the changes to our world made him sick, and the whiskey only made it worse. It was the same anger that made him shoot you."

Daniel was unsure what to do next, but Nellie quickly stepped in, thanking Follows Bear and urging him to come into the house. He refused but clearly appreciated the gesture. Then he turned his horse and trotted off.

# CHAPTER 15

**D**aniel had named their place Raven Ranch, a slightly mocking tribute to Jean Baptiste La-Valle, who had no use for cattle but had been given that name by the Blackfoot. Daniel continued to divide his time between work on the ranch and a job in town. On some days Nellie would accompany him to Fort Benton, where she visited Aunt Betsy and supplemented their income by teaching piano. By the following spring they had settled into an almost comfortable routine, but their goal of building a successful cattle business remained elusive. The coming of the northern railroad was still a few years off, and the local market remained small. Daniel found a few places to sell the beef they raised, but without the income they earned in town, they wouldn't have made it.

That summer, on a day when the work on one of the new buildings in town had been particularly hard, Daniel felt worn out. He had shrugged off prior invitations to join the boys for a drink, but his resistance wavered that day. For the remainder of that summer, a stop at the saloon became part of his routine. On some nights Daniel didn't make it back to the Teton until near dark, and he often faded into a deep sleep shortly after his return. At first Nellie accepted his behavior in the hope that it was temporary, but it became a source of conflict, which escalated after a night when Daniel failed to return at all. He arrived the following morning with his clothes dusty and adorned with bits of dried grass picked up from a night sleeping on the hard prairie ground.

That morning, Daniel felt Nellie's wrath, which she delivered quietly and without drama. "Daniel," she said, "I won't be treated this way. I can't live with a man who cares so little for his marriage, and if you don't stop it immediately, I'm going back to Helena."

She was right, he knew, and any resistance he might have felt withered in the presence of her determined stare. Daniel apologized and promised he would change.

Nellie softened a bit and continued, "Daniel, do you really know what it means to love someone? It's not about needing someone, or about feelings. It's knowing that when you're together, your life has more meaning, that together you're each a better person than you are alone. I want us to always believe that."

From that point on, whenever Daniel worked in town, he returned home promptly. John Campbell and the others understood what had to be done, but they laughed a little less when Daniel was gone.

Although he often spent more time with a hammer in his hand than working the land, Daniel remained optimistic about the future of the cattle industry in Montana and slowly built up a small herd. His optimism was challenged that winter when he went out to check on his animals and found the remains of several lying dead, their blood vividly staining the snow. One animal was still alive, its entrails hanging from a stomach that had been torn open by wolves. Daniel could barely stand the horrible sound of its pathetic cries. He dispatched the animal with a shot from his rifle, but the experience wasn't easily forgotten.

The next day, Daniel went to town and stopped at one of the saloons. It was early in the day, but he needed something to take his mind off the image of slaughter that hung hard in his memory. He hadn't been there long when an acquaintance, one of the old-timers who had been in Montana since the early days, said that he had been by Jean Baptiste's place a few days earlier and that LaValle had asked for Daniel.

"How is the old hermit?" Daniel asked, and added that Jean Baptiste had saved his life and was one of the few men he'd walk into hell to assist.

"Daniel, the man is fading. I don't think he's got much longer."

The winter had been relatively mild, and Daniel immediately determined that he had to go to Jean Baptiste's cabin on the Judith. He first went home to tell Nellie of his plans and to gather a few items he'd need to make the trip. Nellie smelled the alcohol on his breath but held her tongue.

"I need to go see Jean Baptiste," Daniel began. "I just heard he's not doing well and he might need my help. I'm leaving this afternoon."

Despite her initial intent to overlook the alcohol, Daniel's announcement changed things. "I bet I know where you picked up that news," Nellie said with some sarcasm.

"Yes, I went to the Antlers. I'll admit it. But I didn't drink much and I thought you might understand why I was there."

Nellie softened her tone, knowing that Daniel had been shocked by the wolf attack. "I don't mean to be harsh. I know what you've been through. But it's dangerous to travel alone in winter, and I don't want the whiskey to cloud your judgment. Why not sleep on it and get an early start tomorrow?"

"I can't do that Nellie. I can't rest while thinking that Jean Baptiste needs my help."

Nellie remained frightened by the prospect of Daniel traveling alone and tried to deter him. But she also knew that he could be stubborn about certain things, and this seemed to be one of them. Before he left, Nellie told him that she understood. "Come home safely, Daniel. That's all I ask."

Daniel rode off that afternoon, on a day when the sun shone only periodically but the snow cover was thin and, in many places, it had blown clear and exposed the ground. He spent the first night camped in the open.

The weather on the following day was much like the day before. Daniel made steady progress under the circumstances, but was slowed down by the need to ride around or fight his way through an occasional deep snow drift. As the afternoon faded toward darkness, the clouds began to thicken and a few snowflakes could be seen falling slowly and drifting along with a light wind. By the time Daniel was just north of Grizzly Butte, the intensity of the snowfall had increased, something he sensed more by its soft touch on his face than by what he could see in the mounting darkness. Though eager to make it as far as possible that day, he decided to spend the night at the stage stop, where he was warmly greeted by Anna, the German woman who remembered his group and the lovely sound of the violin his fellow passenger had played that day.

"That was a special day, Daniel. I remember it fondly. And how did your prospecting go? Did you find any gold?"

"Not much," Daniel replied. He began to wonder if Anna knew of Limestone's death and decided to fill her in. "The worst thing is that we lost Limestone."

Anna was shocked. "I wondered why I hadn't seen him for so long. Please tell me what happened."

Daniel told the whole story. Despite the apparent edginess in their relationship, Anna was genuinely saddened. At the end of the evening, they marked the occasion with a toast to Limestone's memory.

# CHAPTER 16

The next day Daniel awoke early. A light snow continued to fall, but little had accumulated. Anna urged Daniel to delay his trip. "Stay here for a while, Daniel," she said. "Why take a chance with the storm? You know how things can change so quickly. This can be a very cruel place."

Daniel knew that, but he was determined to make it to the Judith that day. "I'll be fine, Mutter," Daniel teased, brushing aside Anna's concerns.

In response, Anna threw a bit of bread at him. It bounced off his forehead and landed in his coffee, and they both laughed like silly children. Still, Anna was concerned when Daniel left, and she watched him until he disappeared from sight.

After crossing Arrow Creek and ascending onto the bench, Daniel left the stage road and headed to the northeast, instead following a route that would take him directly to Jean Baptiste's place. He continued to think of Jean Baptiste, hoping that the man in the bar had exaggerated his decline. He also wondered what to do if Jean Baptiste was declining rapidly. Would he bring him to Fort Benton? These thoughts occupied him, but as the snow began to fall more heavily, Daniel realized he had to focus his attention on getting there first. He still had about twenty more miles to cover. The wind had started to blow harder, pushing snow into the coulees and forming deep drifts. His horse struggled to break through the drifts, occasionally staggering as it became increasing tired. It had also become bitterly cold.

By the time LaValle's cabin first came into view, still a half mile distant, it was near dark. Daniel was now cold and exhausted. As he approached more closely, he could see that there was no light inside the cabin and no smoke emerged from the chimney. It was a dreadful sight, leaving Daniel with only the hope that Jean Baptiste had left. But it was a desperate hope, for it didn't fit with what he had come to know of how the man lived.

There was no response when Daniel pounded on the door, which opened with a lift of the latch. Jean Baptiste was at home. He sat dead in his chair by the fireplace, his body locked in a grotesque pose. Daniel looked closely at his friend, held his twisted fingers, and slumped into a chair next to him. A jug of whiskey sat nearby. The cheap liquor burned his throat, nearly choking him at first, but then it began to sooth his exhaustion. He drank heavily from the jug and started a conversation with Jean Baptiste, one that ended as Daniel slid into the frozen embrace of the long winter night.

# CHAPTER 17

Nellie had planned to wait at home until Daniel returned, but on the second day she couldn't bear to be alone on the ranch any longer. In the fading light of the afternoon, as a light snow fell, she rode to her aunt's house in town. Then, assuring her aunt that she'd be back soon, she went to learn what she could about the weather—and, hopefully, about Daniel's whereabouts, even if only a report from someone who might have passed him on the stage road.

Nellie knew that John Campbell and his friends still gathered at the Antlers almost nightly. She headed there directly and hesitated only briefly before pushing open the door. It was now full dark, and the interior of the saloon was dimly lit by a few kerosene lanterns, each casting an amber light that softened the edges of the room and the faces of the men inside. She entered the room slowly and stood there for a moment, with the hope that someone would notice her before she had to penetrate the inner sanctum of a place where women rarely ventured, certainly not alone, and not if they feared for their reputations. But she wasn't noticed immediately, and after standing still for a few awkward moments, she continued her approach toward the bar. Before she fully made her way across the room, her presence elicited a comment from one of the men.

"Boys, we have a visitor!" a man loudly exclaimed.

Nellie moved forward slowly, dreading the thought of finding herself in a room full of only strangers who would have thought her reckless or worse. She was greatly relieved when she heard John Campbell call her name, followed by a warning to his peers: "Gentlemen, this is Daniel's wife, and if any man says anything unkind, he'll have to deal with me." John ushered Nellie to a corner of the room, and his tone became more direct. "Nellie, what are you doing here? Daniel would be shocked and angry as hell to know about this."

Nellie told John of Daniel's departure for LaValle's place. "I'm worried, John," she said. "He's made this trip before, but not in winter."

John apologized for his harsh words and tried to reassure her. "Daniel knows that country, Nellie. He can take care of himself."

Nellie remained less than reassured. "Has anyone come in from the Judith country today?" she asked. "What's the weather there?" She noticed John hesitate and urged him further, "Please, John, what have you heard?"

John replied directly. "A stage driver came in from the Judith earlier today, Nellic. He claimed it was snowing hard and beginning to blow there." He regretted his honesty after seeing Nellie's worried look intensify. "If Daniel's not back tomorrow," he said, "I'll go look for him myself."

Nellie thanked him and spent a restless night at her aunt's house, waking once to a dream of Daniel alone in a vast and frozen landscape.

# CHAPTER 18

Some said the temperature reached thirty below that night; others reported minus forty. The wind blew hard throughout the night, drifting snow into impassable barriers that trapped wildlife and cattle alike, randomly coating trees and other objects with ice, and creating a deathly beauty not fully revealed until the sun rose the following day. It blew hard enough to open the door to Jean Baptiste's cabin, though perhaps Daniel hadn't latched it properly. In any event, Daniel awoke that morning covered with a light coating of snow, his eyes coated with a thin layer of ice that made them difficult to open.

His first thought that day was that he must be dead. He felt trapped in a body that didn't want to move and eyes that couldn't see. After slowly becoming aware of his surroundings, he was struck by a sudden fear that he might be frozen for good. His initial efforts to move his limbs failed, and his mind began to race, bringing thoughts of a worried Nellie, concerns about his cattle, and an appreciation of the irony of freezing to death when all his Baptist fears had been built on images of lost souls burning in hell.

He thought of trying out another body part and called over to LaValle, "Jean Baptiste, why did you have to be such a goddamn hermit and live way out here in the middle of nothing?" That his voice still worked provided some assurance, but it also reminded him that his friend was dead—and that he would be too if he couldn't get control of himself.

With great effort Daniel crawled forward. His legs dragged behind him, but he felt some strength return in his arms. A kerosene lantern and some matches sat on a log by the hearth, and he was able to start a fire, which warmed him quickly. He was surprised that he began to shiver as his body warmed. This involuntary response loosened his limbs but brought a stinging pain to places where his skin had been exposed to the cold. Gradually his ability to move was restored, but he felt too weak to travel. Still, he had to fight a strong compulsion to set off for Fort Benton and relieve Nellie of the worry he was certain she felt.

There was a little lean-to where Jean Baptiste had sheltered his animals, and Daniel's horse had shown the good sense to lie in it that frigid night. She was still there when Daniel had recovered enough to look around outside of the cabin. He fed her a few handfuls of grain and gazed upon a wintry landscape with enough snow to make the going rough. Formidable drifts were scattered randomly where the unhindered wind had been free to play. "It's hopeless to go anywhere," Daniel thought as he squinted into the dazzling light of the reflecting sun.

That afternoon, he busied himself with making a travois to haul Jean Baptiste's body into town. Even if Jean Baptiste would rather have been buried near his cabin, Daniel couldn't just leave his body there…and who knew when the ground would be soft enough to bury him properly? Later that evening, alone in the cabin with the ghostly presence of Jean Baptiste, Daniel warmed himself by the fire and fell fast asleep.

He awoke in the darkness of the winter night to the sounds of a strong wind, rattling objects outside and whistling through the chimney near where he lay. The racket was loud enough to motivate him to get up and peek out the door. The air was surprisingly warm, enough so that water had begun dripping off the roof. Daniel had heard of a warm wind called a Chinook, but he had never experienced the phenomenon. He settled back into his bedding with the hope that he'd be able to travel sooner than he had thought possible earlier that day.

By sunup, the Chinook had done its work. The warm air it brought had tamed the snow and diminished the barrier drifts that had so recently loomed around the cabin. Though only a temporary reprieve from winter, Chinooks were not unusual in Montana, where temperature increases of fifty degrees or more have been recorded, sometimes occurring within a matter of hours.

This was the window Daniel needed. He set off that morning once the sun was full up, Jean Baptist bouncing along behind him. Still, it wasn't easy going, and the ordeal of the past few days had weakened Daniel. By late afternoon, he had only made it back to the stage station, where he arrived looking worn out and a bit unsteady on his feet. Anna, who had begun to worry about Daniel after the storm had intensified, was there to greet him again.

"Thank God you made it. You had me worried, Daniel. I told you not to brave that storm and I believe I was right."

"I'm afraid you were. It was tough going and by the time I got there, Jean Baptiste was already dead."

"So all of that was for nothing. I'm sorry to hear of the loss of your friend, but at least one death wasn't the cause of another. Still, you don't look well, Daniel. You need some rest to get your strength back."

"Well, I appreciate your concern. But I don't agree it was for nothing. I was too late to help, but if I'd learned later that Jean Baptiste died over the winter and I hadn't looked in on him after hearing he wasn't doing well, I'm not sure I could have lived with that."

Anna nodded, now better understanding Daniel's motivations but still concerned about his weakened condition. In response, he turned to humor. "You needn't worry so much. I've drunk enough whiskey over the years to keep myself from freezing. I think that's probably true of most of my fellow Canadians."

In response, Anna laughed heartily. Then things quickly got serious again. "I can't stay here, Anna. I've got to get back to Fort Benton tonight and let my wife Nellie know I'm all right. I know she'll be worried, and I can't put her through another night of it."

This was the same kind of fear Anna had endured, and she knew the pain all too well. But she wasn't swayed. "Daniel, you need some rest," she said firmly. "I'll not let you risk your life again on a fool's errand."

Not long after saying these words, Anna remembered something important. "Daniel, a group of men was here earlier today that left for Fort Benton not long ago. If I leave right away, I'm certain I can catch up with them. I'll tell them you arrived here safely and have them bring the news to your wife."

Daniel objected to Anna's plan but she insisted that he stay behind. She immediately began her preparations for the ride.

# CHAPTER 19

Anna rode hard and caught up with the group several miles from the stage stop. They too worried about Anna being out alone but agreed to pass along the news of Daniel. As promised, the group went directly to the Antlers, where Anna had said they could find some of Daniel's friends. Upon their arrival at the saloon, they announced with gusto that they had news of Daniel. The buzz in the room quickly receded, and one of the travelers, a bit of a showman, stood on a chair and cleared his throat. "Daniel McHarg made it through the storm," the traveler reported. "He's still a little worse off for his night in the cold, but he's alive and resting up at the stage stop. He plans to return to Fort Benton tomorrow."

The men at the Antlers all knew Daniel, and they gleefully received the news as a better-than-usual excuse to drink too much. They competed for the right to buy the travelers their first drink, and a few celebratory toasts quickly followed. Opening the floor, John played it straight at first, with a simple appreciation for the fact that Daniel's luck had held, but soon slipped into a riff on Daniel's love of whiskey and poetry: "I'm not sure which of the two he loves most—they go hand in hand—but I do know that Nellie trumps them both. Here's to Daniel and Nellie. May they live long and raise a brood of little Daniels to help with those stinking cows!"

The toast was the reminder John needed to find Nellie and give her the news. He immediately headed for her aunt's house and saw Nellie sitting by the fireplace as he approached the front door. A light knock brought her to the door right away. She was relieved to see John's familiar grin, likely enhanced by the whiskey but not an expression he'd wear if he bore bad news.

"Daniel's all right, Nellie. He'll make it back to Fort Benton tomorrow. Hallelujah!"

Nellie didn't react as John expected. She still seemed stunned, which was perplexing. "Did you hear me? Daniel made it through the storm."

"Yes, I hear you, John. I don't know what's wrong with me. I've been so worried, my fears seem to have clouded my brain. I'd almost convinced myself he wasn't coming home."

"I understand," John said kindly. "If it helps, I'll take you to the Antlers and you can talk to the men who brought the news yourself."

"Thank you. But I can manage another night with the good news you've brought." Then they agreed to get an early start in the morning and meet Daniel on the road before he reached Fort Benton.

Nellie spent another restless night but awoke with a sense of renewal and trust in the news about Daniel. John, Nellie, and a few other friends of Daniel made up the little party that set out to greet him that morning. After reaching the high ground between Shonkin and Arrow Creeks, Nellie's sense of anticipation grew. It was flat, open country where a rider could be seen at a great distance. Nellie watched the horizon carefully and finally spotted a distant figure slowly making his way along the stage road. As the figure grew closer, Nellie could see that some kind of rig trailed behind the rider's horse.

"I think that's him!" John shouted.

Although they couldn't be sure at that distance, the group broke into a gallop. They closed the distance quickly. Well before reaching the rider, Nellie spotted the proof she needed: the rider was wearing a bright blanket coat, a cherished gift from Jean Baptiste only Daniel could be wearing.

Meanwhile, Daniel was less aware of his surroundings. He rode slowly and remained deep in thought, still replaying the events surrounding Jean Baptiste's death. Daniel had spotted a group approaching in the distance but he had no idea who they might be. The next time he took note of them, he was astonished to see that Nellie was among them. Her frantic waving drew his attention, and her shouts of "Daniel!" were the final signs he needed to realize that he was almost home.

It was a tearful but sweet reunion. When he had held Nellie long enough, Daniel turned his attention to John and the others. "What are you boys doing out here? Did the Antlers run out of whiskey?" Although his next words were to thank everyone for coming, a few of the men dismounted and pelted Daniel with snow. Daniel joined the little fray and the sound of his laughter reassured Nellie he'd be all right. John ended the little ruckus when he clamped Daniel in a bear hug and lugged him back to his horse.

# CHAPTER 20

That spring, when the ground finally thawed, Daniel and Nellie buried Jean Baptiste on their property near the river amid a stand of cottonwood. Many of the old-timers, along with some of Daniel's friends, gathered for the service. News of Jean Baptiste's death had spread to the Blackfoot community, and Follows Bear stood silently as a priest uttered a traditional remembrance, consigning Jean Baptiste's soul to God and calling for the group to join him in prayer. After the priest finished, Follows Bear asked to be heard. At first, he spoke in his native language, and then he switched to French, which Daniel translated for the group.

"Jean Baptiste was a different kind of white man," said Follows Bear. "He lived in both worlds and knew the wisdom of each. I pray the Great Spirit will be kind to his soul and bring us more of his kind."

The sky turned gloomy later that day, becoming an oppressive presence that loomed over the land. Daniel thought everyone had left after the funeral ended and was surprised to see Follows Bear in the near distance, sitting alone on small rise that overlooked the valley. He appeared to be praying. Daniel continued working in his

tool shed, repairing a bridle while looking up occasionally to see if Follows Bear was still there. By late afternoon, the heavy clouds unleased a steady rain accompanied by an occasional flash of horizontal lightning, the
sound of which grew closer with each occurrence. Still,
Follows Bear held his position on the bluff.

After the storm had subsided, Daniel looked up to
see that Follows Bear was no longer in sight. Before he
could step outside to look further, Daniel was startled to
hear Follows Bear's voice and saw him standing just outside the door.

"My soul has been cleansed," Follows Bear announced matter-of-factly.

"And so has the rest of you," Daniel replied as he
looked over the soaking man standing before him.

Follows Bear laughed vigorously, something Daniel
had not seen him do previously. They shared this laughter
for a moment before Daniel invited Follows Bear to join
them for a meal. Follows Bear declared that he was fast-
ing and declined Daniel's offer. However, it didn't stop
them from talking together and they began a conversation
that lasted well into the night.

When Daniel awoke the next day, Follows Bear was
gone. Daniel stood quietly and looked north, the direction
he knew Follows Bear would have traveled. After a moment, he was joined by Nellie. Together, they surveyed
their remaining cattle, still confined in the fenced pasture
along the river.

Nellie broke the silence. "It was a hard winter, Daniel, and such a sad sight to behold. We have so few left."

Daniel, who seemed surprisingly happy given the
state of the herd, had some news to share. "Well, that's
about to change, Nellie. I talked to a man yesterday,
someone who came to pay his respects to Jean Baptiste.
He thinks we have the best land in the whole Teton Val-

ley. He has some money to invest and wants to partner with us and build up a herd. I told him yes. Unless, of course, you object."

Nellie's response was a smile—the same smile Daniel remembered so well from that day on the *Red Cloud*.

*'Twas the dear smile when naebody did mind us,*
*'Twas the bewitching, sweet, stown glance o' kindness.*

The path before them now seemed clear.

# PART 2

The cattle business for the present year will see a boom it
has never seen before, the expressed doubts of the weak-
kneed and pessimists to the contrary notwithstanding…
~ the *River Press*, February 13, 1884

# CHAPTER 21

For many in Montana Territory, but certainly not all, the summer of 1884 was a time of growing prosperity. The railroad now connected parts of the territory to the world beyond, the grasslands were quickly filling with cattle, and more people were settling there. Over the course of the 1880s, the territory's population would more than triple, and Montana would become the forty-first state before the end of 1889.

Events moved more slowly along Daniel's stretch of the Teton River. He worked the Raven Ranch full-time now, thanks to an investment from a friend of Jean Baptiste LaValle, but the investment wasn't enough to make a big move like some of his peers. Many cattlemen—at least those with enough money backing them up—were rapidly expanding their herds in anticipation of a big payoff as the market for western beef grew. Daniel, meanwhile, still eked out a living as a small rancher and tried hard to learn how to be a cowman. It didn't come naturally. Though he now dressed the part—he had given up the garb of a tradesman and acceded to the practicality of a wide-brimmed hat and tall-heeled boots—his horsemanship and roping skills remained rudimentary. By the standards of the cowboys who worked the nearby ranches and open range, he was still a greenhorn. But he refused to let that hold him back and threw himself into the business of ranching.

On an early summer day that year, the business at hand was to bring back some cattle that had wandered off, a task that had become an all too regular occurrence. When Daniel returned to the house that afternoon, Nellie was there to greet him. She seemed distracted and agitated. After a few niceties, she began to share what was on her mind.

"Daniel, there's disturbing news in the papers. According to the reports, the Blackfoot are starving and hundreds, maybe more, are dying." Nellie spoke more rapidly than usual. "Here, let me read from this article:

"'The Indians are now on one-eighth rations, their weeks supply being scarcely more than one good meal. They are dying off by actual starvation at the rate of four to six a day, and the mortality is increasing every week, the River Press, July 9, 1884.'

"We've got to do something, Daniel," Nellie pleaded. "We can't stand by while these people die."

Daniel had heard rumors and some stories about the starvation on the reservation. But it was hard to know what was really going on and, for most people he knew, the plight of the Blackfoot was something "out there"— too far away for people focused on their own problems to deal with.

"What do you think we can do, Nellie? I know you want to help, but we don't have any livestock we can spare."

"We can spare a few head. We can always do without for those in greater need."

A part of Daniel knew Nellie was right, but he still hesitated. "It won't be an easy thing to do. There are risks involved. These people are starving and they may not be too pleased to have a white man among them, even one bearing gifts."

Nellie shared Daniel's concerns, but she couldn't let the topic go. After more discussion and a few tears, Daniel offered up the only thing he thought they could do to help. "All right, I'll take a few steers up there," Daniel said. "I'll avoid the agencies on the reservation and look for Follows Bear's band instead."

Follows Bear still spent most of his time away from the agencies. From their prior conversations, Daniel had a pretty good idea where he might be located this time of year.

He hoped that his relationship with Follows Bear would provide some margin of safety.

"Besides," Daniel added after a pause, "you can bet a few of those damned steers that keep wandering off will be among the bunch I take up there. I'm almost looking forward to getting rid of those devils!"

Happy that Daniel had agreed to help, Nellie laughed. But the next part of the conversation was more difficult.

"I want to be part of this," Nellie said softly. "I can't let you do it alone. I'm coming with you."

Daniel was upset by Nellie's declaration but held back his emotions. "I can't possibly let that happen," he responded calmly. "People are starving up there, and starving people get desperate. If there's any trouble, I'll not make it worse by having you with me."

Nellie repeated her objections about Daniel going alone. "You know I can take care of myself. I'm a better shot than you'll ever be!"

Though there was some truth to her statement, Nellie could see that Daniel was determined on the matter and wouldn't budge. After further consideration, she came up with a new proposal.

"Well, if you won't let me come with you," Nellie conceded, "we should talk to Nate. Maybe he'll agree to go."

That evening, Daniel rode over to Nate's place. Nate Tolliver was about Daniel's age and, like Daniel, had arrived in Montana Territory a few years earlier and settled on the Teton River. There the similarities stopped, for Nate was a Texan who had signed on with an outfit that drove a herd north in 1881. With little to go home for, and tired out from months in the saddle, Nate had decided to stay in Montana. Unlike most of his trail mates, he'd had the good sense to save his wages instead of squandering them on whiskey and prostitutes. This decision had made it possible for Nate to start up on some land not far from Daniel's place. Although Nate lacked the bravado of some of the other Texas cowboys Daniel had encountered, he was a match for any of them in terms of his knowledge of cattle and the skills needed on the open range. Because they were neighbors—if that term could be applied to ranchers separated by several miles—and they had a shared joy in the art of telling stories, Daniel and Nate had quickly become friends.

Unlike Daniel, Nate was a bachelor who didn't see a need to build a fancy house for himself. Living simply and alone, he focused solely on fulfilling his dream of building a ranch.

When Daniel rode up that evening, Nate greeted him with a hearty hello and an invitation to sit down on a bench by one of the outbuildings he was working on.

"You're going to work yourself to an early grave!" Daniel hollered as he dismounted.

"What else would I be doing Daniel? I get tired of talking to my horses pretty quick," Nate joked. Then he added, "I don't have a pretty wife to slow me down like you do."

Under Nellie's influence, Daniel drank less than he used to, but one of the pleasures of visiting Nate was sharing a few swigs of whiskey and the easy talk that went with it. But it was already getting late, so Daniel got to the point quickly. He told Nate about his plan to trail a few steers up to the reservation and to give them to Follows Bear's band. Nate listened closely to Daniel's plan before responding.

"I don't have any animals I can spare," Nate said, "but I can't let you risk your ass up there alone either—or, worse yet, have Nellie get involved. Knowing Nellie, I'm sure she's asked."

"You got that right," Daniel said with a laugh.

Nate was naturally curious. He wanted to know what was really going on up north on the reservation, and he had a mind to assess the country. Someday, he thought, that land might open up. Nate wasn't alone in these thoughts. Though the Montana politicians and newspaper editorialists seemed sincere in their concern about the starvation occurring on the Blackfoot Reservation, they often paired their laments with statements that everyone would be better off if the tribes were moved to the southern agencies and their vast lands opened to "the energetic stock raiser."

After further discussion, Nate agreed to accompany Daniel and help him trail a few steers to the reservation. They would meet at first light.

# CHAPTER 23

Daniel and Nate met the next day at the ford midway between their ranches and rode north. The land they passed through was raw prairie, yet it had changed. They saw no buffalo, only piles of bones scattered from the kill sites by wolves and scavengers, which had unknowingly had their last meals of buffalo meat earlier that year. The slaughter was a temporary bonanza left behind by hunters who sought only hides and thus ignored the heaps of wasted meat that soon vanished from the efforts of scavenging animals and the flies and maggots that finished the job. By the time the hide hunters were done, the once vital herds had been reduced to bone piles that littered the land. If land could get sick, Daniel thought, this is what it would look like. These sights of death didn't prepare Daniel and Nate for what they saw when they approached a Blackfoot encampment. Dotting the plains were clusters of burial platforms, many of recent construction. Their abundance testified to a time of suffering and death. Bones of prized horses, killed for their meat, provided more evidence of the desperation they were about to witness.

Partly in jest, Daniel said, "Nate, we don't have to do this. There's still time to turn around."

Nate said he almost had a mind to stop, but wanted to continue. As they cautiously approached the encampment, Daniel silently prayed that Follows Bear would be there. Upon reaching the edge of the encampment, Daniel held up his hand in a sign of friendship. He muttered to his companion, "Stay close, Nate."

They were first greeted by a few children, who moved toward them and stared curiously at the white people in their midst. An old man holding a rifle watched them closely. But most of the other adults sat idly, perhaps too weak to move or numbed by the horror of the lingering death that surrounded them. The only other activity within sight was a woman tending a pot that held water mixed with hooves of some kind, producing a weak but foul-smelling broth. The younger men had left the camp in search of pronghorn or any other meat they could find. Sometimes that meant killing cattle that grazed illegally on Blackfoot lands, or poaching from one of the ranches that were springing up around the edges of the still vast reservation.

Soon after entering the small encampment, Daniel was relieved to see Follows Bear sitting in the shade of a twisted old cottonwood and gazing into the far distance. He offered no immediate sign of recognition. Daniel broke the silence. "I heard times were hard. We brought you some meat."

Follows Bear was thinner and bore a pinched expression Daniel hadn't seen before. His first words were a command that prompted a few women into action. They quickly slaughtered one of the steers and cut off strips of meat from the carcass, some of which were eaten raw by people who had emerged from the shadows of the camp. One of the women brought over a few meat strips for Follows Bear, but he brushed her aside with words Daniel couldn't understand. Daniel assumed Follows Bear was conveying his wish that the others should eat first.

Follows Bear continued to watch in silence as his people devoured their first fresh meat in weeks. After a while, he turned to Daniel and spoke. "When Jean Baptiste died, I prayed to the Great Spirit to bring us more of his kind of white man. I need to pray more."

As he spoke, his expression softened with just a hint of amusement. The French he used with Daniel was now mixed with a few words of English. Though Follows Bear loathed the agencies, the food they sometimes provided had become increasingly essential since the demise of the buffalo. He had reluctantly led his people to an agency twice in the past year and had learned that a few words of English sometimes gave him an advantage. But after the food handouts had all but stopped earlier that year, Follows Bear had led his people back out on the prairie. If his people continued to starve, he had reasoned, it would be better to be in a place where memories of a better life remained than at an agency where he could see his people losing their very identity.

While Follows Bear watched the people's pained looks diminish as they ate, he became more expansive. "Our people are dying," he said. "The buffalo have vanished forever. And I will join them soon, for the only way I know to live has also vanished." He added that many people in his camp had died that winter, and more would be lost if they didn't find more food. "I hear that on Badger Creek, where many people have gathered near the agency, hundreds have already died."

Daniel remained silent, but his feelings were revealed by a pained expression that he couldn't suppress. Follows Bear kept his gaze on Daniel until one of the young steers made a desperate attempt to escape its fate.

Several children, better fed than the adults who had insisted the young eat first in the starving time, led a chase to grasp the rope trailing behind the anxious steer.

Amid the commotion, a woman approached. She was light skinned and about Daniel's age. She and Follows Bear spoke briefly and then turned toward Daniel.

"This woman is Jean Baptiste LaValle's daughter," Follows Bear said. "LaValle's wife was one of our people. After she died, LaValle sent her back to live among us, her original people."

Daniel was stunned by this news. He looked closely at the woman, who bore an obvious resemblance to LaValle, the man who had saved Daniel's life. There was pain in her eyes. They spoke no words, but the woman conveyed her affection for Daniel. She touched his sleeve and mustered a weak smile, briefly overcoming the despair that had seemingly become her fate.

At that moment, Daniel became determined to take LaValle's daughter home with him. Thinking it was the least he could do to repay his debt to LaValle, Daniel conveyed his wish to Follows Bear. Follows Bear didn't understand Daniel at first, so Daniel clarified his words by combining them with gestures. Then, as Daniel looked on, Follows Bear and the woman spoke at length. Their conversation became animated at times, yet Daniel had no idea what they were saying or what outcome to expect.

Finally, Follows Bear turned to Daniel. "She doesn't want to leave," he said curtly. Daniel tried to probe further, but Follows Bear cut him off. A glance at the woman, who had turned stoic, only added further to Daniel's confusion and frustration at being unable to determine what had really happened.

While Daniel pondered this interaction, Follows Bear urged Daniel to leave. "The young men will return soon, and I don't want trouble for you," he said. "Head east first. What you have done is good."

The presence of LaValle's daughter amid the suffering he witnessed that day had a profound effect on Daniel. Now the tragedy had become even more personal. Daniel left with the knowledge that his effort had been appreciated, but he also knew it was only a temporary reprieve. Soon the starvation would return. On the ride home, Daniel and Nate remained silent at first, each trying to process what he had just seen. Daniel struggled to contain the growing sense of futility that gnawed at his gut.

Nate finally broke the silence. "It's a pity," he said with a shake of his head. "These people are starving right in the middle of some of the finest grazing land I've ever seen. Don't they know that?"

Daniel thought for a moment before answering. "I don't have it figured out either. We're both pretty new to this country, and I can't claim to know much about how the Blackfoot think. But I do know this land was full of buffalo when I got here. I might not be in a hurry to raise cows if I already had so much good meat on the hoof that didn't need me to look after it."

"Well, now they've got all this land and no buffalo to go with it," Nate said. "One way or another, it's time to get some cows on this grass."

Sometimes it took something simple—a different vantage point or a change in the light—to allow a person to see a situation as it really was. Nate's comment had that impact on Daniel that day. *Whether through some grand plan hatched in Washington or the pure greed of the hordes of hide hunters, each acting on their own, the effect was the same*, Daniel thought. With the buffalo gone, it was only a matter of time before the size of the Blackfoot Reservation would be greatly diminished.

# CHAPTER 24

Nellie expected Daniel home by nightfall of the day following his departure. She kept herself busy with chores around the house, but the time dragged. As promised, when he had first brought his bride home, Daniel had expanded their "little shanty on the prairie." The house now had four rooms, including a parlor with upholstered furniture and a prized piano. Nellie tried her best to be productive that day but found it difficult not to just stare out the windows or survey the ridge to the north where she expected Daniel would first appear. Daniel and Nate had split off before reaching Daniel's house, so a lone rider on the ridge was Nellie's first glimpse of Daniel's return. Now free of the animals he had trailed, Daniel rode quickly down the ridge and across the river to the house. Nellie stood there to greet him. They embraced for a long while, saying little at first, letting their bodies communicate what needed to be said.

Once inside, Daniel gave Nellie a full account of the situation, including the encounter with Jean Baptiste's daughter. Nellie listened closely and was gratified to hear that their efforts had provided some measure of help.

Mostly, though, she was frustrated by their inability to do more.

Daniel had the same concern. He continued to brood over what he had observed. The images of starvation had become lodged in his memory, and they were especially poignant now that he knew about LaValle's daughter. Daniel was burdened by a sense that he still owed the man, even though he knew Jean Baptiste would have told him to forget it.

While Daniel and Nellie ate a late and somewhat solemn dinner that evening, Nellie announced that she had a plan. "I think I know someone who can help," she said. "Someone who has the means to have a real effect."

Daniel hesitated to say anything, knowing an obvious possibility, but also feared it might result in Nellie getting hurt again. Even after Nellie's long separation from her father, Daniel swore he could tell when Nellie was thinking of Mr. Sage by the flushed color that appeared around her cheeks. Despite the urgency Daniel felt about the situation on the reservation, he was reluctant to support Nellie's plan.

"I hope you're not thinking of meeting with your father," Daniel said. "William Sage is a damn robber baron, and he's already hurt you enough."

Indeed, that was precisely the plan Nellie was formulating. As hard as it might be to face her father, she had already vowed to go to Helena.

"It's the least I can do!" Nellie exclaimed. "If you can go up to the reservation and face the dangers I know you must have faced, I can manage to have a conversation with my father."

Daniel sat at the table with his arms folded, a sure sign that he remained unconvinced.

"I think he's changed, Daniel. My mother's letters always say that he sends his regards. I don't bother to tell you that because I know you'll just scoff."

In reality, Nellie didn't know herself what to expect from a meeting with her father. She hadn't heard directly from him and it was possible that those letters simply reflected her mother's hopes rather than a genuine change in her father's sentiments. Nevertheless, Nellie wrote a letter to her mother that night and announced that she was coming to Helena for a visit. The date she chose was likely too soon for a return letter to arrive in Fort Benton. Nellie could only hope for the best.

The next day, Nellie left for Helena. The long stage ride gave her time to think about how best to approach her father and to appeal effectively for aid. She knew that in Washington and other places people were debating how to address the tragedy on the Blackfoot Reservation, but no one seemed able to agree on a plan or to commit the necessary funding immediately. Nellie's father and his associates, on the other hand, could act quickly.

By the time the stage had reached the halfway point of the trip, Nellie had formulated a plan. Rather than directly asking her father for his financial assistance, which she knew had a low chance of success, she'd ask him to invite her to a meeting of the Helena Club.

The Helena Club was an organization made up of wealthy men who were active in civic and other affairs. They met regularly, and Mr. Sage never missed a meeting. *If given a chance to ask for their help*, Nellie thought, *I'd be able to persuade at least a few members to offer assistance*. The more difficult part, she feared, would be convincing her father to let her attend one of the club's meetings.

On the last day of the trip, Nellie was eager to make it to Helena but also keen on seeing the scenery she remembered from a prior trip. At one of the stops along the route, she approached the stage driver.

"Mister, I'm feeling a little cramped in the cabin and I'd like to see the mountains. Can I ride up front with you?"

"I don't mind the company, miss, but it gets pretty dusty up here. Can you handle that?"

Nellie assured him she could and climbed up to the front seat, assisted by the stage driver, who extended a hand to pull her up.

The last leg of the route took them through Little Prickly Pear Canyon. Nellie admired the rocky scenery and held the seat tightly as the stage moved through the narrow canyon. In places, the stage road occupied a narrow bench wedged between the river and the canyon wall. While brushing dust from her frock, Nellie shared her delight in the setting. "You must love your job. Not everyone gets to see scenery like this every day."

"What scenery, miss? All I see is rocks!" The driver chuckled, letting Nellie know he was teasing. "But I do have to keep my eyes on the road. I've come around a corner more than once to find a rock that wasn't there before. You hit one of them the wrong way and you can break a wheel or tip the whole rig over."

After they emerged from the mountains, the land opened up. "That's Helena up ahead," the driver proclaimed. It won't take long now."

Nellie saw a city that seemed huge. It had grown some since she had been there last, but more likely she was reacting to the contrast between the isolation of the Raven Ranch and the mass of buildings that loomed ahead. At first glance, Helena looked as big as the St. Louis Nellie had left behind on that memorable day when the *Red Cloud* pushed away from the levee. Helena was no match for St. Louis, but its position on a slope made it look big, presenting a traveler approaching from the north with something like a bird's-eye view. Spreading all the way to the foot of the mountains, Helena dwarfed Fort Benton, the only town Nellie had visited for over a year.

As planned, Nellie arrived the evening before the day she had told her mother to expect her. Instead of heading directly to the Sage residence, she checked in to a hotel in a different part of town. Though eager to see her mother, Nellie wanted a little more transition time before facing her father. More important, she also had to make some further preparations, such as reviewing some of the official reports on conditions on the Blackfoot Reservation and polishing the case she intended to make to the members of the Helena Club, should that opportunity materialize. Accordingly, Nellie started the next day with a visit to a library that she had gotten to know when she'd lived in Helena. She believed that one of the librarians there, Miss Prendergast, could help her gather additional information to make a case for the Blackfoot.

Nellie arrived at the library at eight a.m., just as Miss Prendergast was opening the front door. The librarian was surprised but happy to see Nellie again.

"Why, it's Miss Sage," Miss Prendergast pronounced. "I haven't seen you for a long time. Where have you been?"

Nellie quickly related the events of the past year, but she was eager to get to the point of her visit. "Miss Prendergast, I hope I'm not being abrupt, but I'm here for a particular purpose," she asserted. "I need to gather information about the conditions on the Blackfoot Reservation." Nellie added that her husband had seen the starvation firsthand and thought the situation was even worse than what had been reported in the newspapers.

Miss Prendergast nodded. "I've been following things as best as I can," she said. "I think I have some materials that may help. Let me find them for you."

The librarian disappeared among the bookshelves

and emerged a few minutes later with several reports. "Mr. Allen, the agent on the Blackfoot Reservation, has been warning for months that a tragedy was in the making," she said. "I think you'll find these reports useful, or at least informative."

Nellie spent the remainder of the morning poring over the reports from the agency as well as the newspapers from Helena and elsewhere in the territory. When she was finished, she thanked Miss Prendergast and headed up the hill to her family's house. Hoping for some time alone with her mother, she arrived in the early afternoon before her father was likely to be home. Mrs. Sage was eagerly awaiting her daughter and opened the door before Nellie could even knock. She greeted Nellie with a vigorous hug, and they both cried joyfully.

Through her tears, Mrs. Sage managed a few words: "I've missed you so much, Nellie. I never want to go so long again without seeing you."

There was so much to catch up on that it was hard to know where to begin. They spent the rest of the afternoon trying to fill the gaps. Nellie had much more to report than her mother, so she did most of the talking. After a while, Nellie alerted her mother to the purpose of her visit, which she hadn't disclosed in her letter.

Mrs. Sage didn't comment or attempt to predict how her husband might react, but she made one thing clear. "Nellie, your father is a stubborn and sometimes difficult man," she conceded. "But never doubt his love for you. I think he's missed you every bit as much as I have. He just can't seem to let his feelings show or admit a mistake. It's caused our family too much sorrow."

Mr. Sage returned home at his usual time that evening. He beamed upon seeing Nellie, yet he avoided any mention of their long separation. "I'm so happy to see you, Nellie. Your mother shares the news from your letters, but there's nothing like seeing you in person."

"I'm happy to see you too, Father."

"How was your trip? Did the blasted stage rattle your bones to the core?"

It went on like that for a while. Mr. Sage tried to act as if Nellie's presence was normal: he made the same small talk he might have made if he had just seen her yesterday. It didn't help the situation. Both father and daughter felt awkward. They didn't know how to act as a family anymore, particularly since the cause of their long separation was neither a tragedy nor an unavoidable circumstance, but was simply the result of a series of bad choices. They had allowed their differences to fester until they had become unmanageable, a chasm of emotions that couldn't be easily bridged. In such a situation, a common reaction among men is to pretend that the chasm doesn't exist, or to try to smooth it over with the lotion of good behavior in the hope that politeness alone will renew old ties. Mr. Sage's strategy didn't work that day.

Sensing the awkwardness, Nellie's mother offered a diversion. "What do you think of our ranch woman?" she asked her husband. "The life must suit her, don't you agree?"

"Yes, Nellie looks splendid. I've never seen her look healthier. I hope to hear all about her new life over dinner."

Indeed, Nellie had blossomed. She had always had a certain glow about her—the glow Daniel had first noticed on the *Red Cloud*—but now she was simply radiant. Despite her isolation on the ranch, Nellie still groomed herself carefully. More noticeable, though, was the effect of her work on the ranch. The time she spent on horseback and the other physical activities of ranch life had brought out her natural athleticism. Nellie moved gracefully and with a newly found physical confidence. Contrary to the style of the day, her complexion was slightly burnished by the time she spent outdoors and the unavoidable exposure to the winds that often scoured the plains. The effect on Nellie's appearance was stunning.

Over dinner that night, Nellie brought up the topic that had brought her to Helena. She prefaced it with a description of the suffering and desperation on the Blackfoot Reservation and her plans to raise funds for their relief.

Then she got to her main point.

"Father, I know we've had our differences," Nellie acknowledged. "But these people need our help, and I believe the best way we can accomplish that is for you to invite me to a meeting of the Helena Club and let me make a direct appeal to the membership."

Mr. Sage was stunned. He was not surprised by her desire to help the Blackfoot people, that was consistent with his understanding of the woman his kindhearted daughter had become. What shocked him was her request to meet with the Helena Club. Not wanting to jeopardize an emerging reconciliation with his daughter, Mr. Sage chose his words carefully. "Nellie, I respect your request and know your intentions are noble," he began. "But what you're asking me to do is impossible. We've never had a woman attend one of our meetings."

Mrs. Sage, no longer willing to stand by and risk losing Nellie again, carefully waded into the conversation. "Well, if Nellie can't present her proposal, William, then you could at least do it for her."

Mr. Sage had a pained expression as he contemplated his options. "No, it's not that simple. My opinions on the topic of relations with the tribes are well known to the membership. I've argued forcefully that the Blackfoot need to learn a painful lesson before they'll have the will to give up their former way of living and turn to the agricultural pursuits they need to survive. I'd be the biggest of hypocrites to change that view now."

Nellie knew that her father was being truthful. His attitude toward the Indians was what had prevented her from appealing to him directly for help in the first place. One of his virtues, if it could be called that, was consistency in his beliefs and actions. Still, his refusal stirred up in Nellie a deep sense of disappointment and an emerging anger. She determined to hold her tongue for a moment, however. She knew that a blowup now would end any chance of obtaining her father's help. Also, somewhat to her surprise, she realized that she didn't want another burst of unresolved rage to jeopardize the fragile sense of family normalcy that she dared to hope was emerging.

Once again, Mrs. Sage waded into the tension that lingered in the room. "William, why can't you make an exception this one time? That crowd of bankers and businessmen might even learn something by having a woman present now and again, especially someone as bright as your daughter."

Mr. Sage practically squirmed in his seat. But he wouldn't budge on his decision.

Seeing no way to break the deadlock gracefully, Nellie bade her parents good night and went upstairs to her bedroom. She was weary from the travel and hoped some rest would enable her to think more clearly and to contemplate her next move.

Unknown to Nellie, the conversation that had begun over dinner wasn't over for the other Sages. Mrs. Sage followed her normal routine before heading upstairs, but upon entering the bedroom, she confronted her husband.

"Your daughter came here with nothing but good intentions," Mrs. Sage asserted, "and you can't lift a finger to assist her with something that means so very much to her. Well, I won't allow it this time. If you ever want peace in this house again, you will help her, William Sage."

Mr. Sage felt manipulated and protested his treatment at the hands of the women in his own household. "Have I not provided well for my family? Does that not earn me any right to do what I think best for this family?"

For once, Mrs. Sage would not relent. "Your success as a businessman doesn't excuse you from doing what is right. You know what is right here and I expect you to do it."

Sensing no other option, Mr. Sage finally gave in and agreed to help Nellie. He promised to tell her in the morning that he had changed his mind.

At breakfast the next morning, Mr. Sage announced that he had reconsidered his position. "Nellie, you've put me in an awkward position. Nevertheless, I want to help. I'll make the necessary arrangements."

Her father's announcement came as a great relief to Nellie, for she hadn't been able to come up with another strategy for raising the funds that were needed. Nellie thanked her father and exchanged a knowing look with her mother. "But I must caution you from getting your hopes up," Mr. Sage continued. "You may not find much support from the membership."

Even with that caution, Nellie remained elated and immediately turned her thoughts to the presentation she would make to the Helena Club, which her father said would meet later in the week. That would give Nellie nearly two full days to enjoy time with her mother and to polish her presentation.

Mr. Sage now had to confront an unpleasant task. It was true that women didn't attend the business meetings of the Helena Club, not even as occasional guests. This reality presented Mr. Sage with a dilemma. Should he seek the group's permission to invite Nellie, despite knowing that they would almost certainly turn him down? Or should he just bring Nellie along and make her attendance seem like a spontaneous occurrence?

# CHAPTER 25

While Nellie was away in Helena, Daniel went about his usual ranch chores. He knew in his heart that what she was doing had to be done, but he missed her profoundly. Each day she was gone Daniel awoke to a feeling of emptiness. It wasn't so hard to get through the days, as he was accustomed to being alone and occupied by the distractions of work, but the evenings were miserable. When he returned home from his daily rounds, the house felt unbearably empty. For this was the time when he and Nellie, tired from their work and savoring a hard-earned respite, shared the news of the day and talked together leisurely. It was an important ritual in their marriage.

A few days after Nellie departed for Helena, Daniel rallied past his sadness and led the bulk of his herd out beyond the fences to Ten-Mile Bench, a plateau in the open range north of the Teton. Still struggling with limited financial resources, Daniel had devised a grazing system that differed from that of the bigger cattle outfits. Like them—and like most of the ranchers throughout Montana Territory—Daniel believed there was money to be made in the gamble of turning cattle loose on the open range. A cautious man wouldn't take such a gamble, but those with grit and some knowledge of Montana thought it worth the risk. For these men had come to realize that few other places had so much grass there for the taking, not just by men of wealth, but by any man with a determination to succeed. These men had also learned that Montana grass remained nutritious to cattle even when dried out and frozen hard by the bitter cold of the northern plains.

The lands beyond Daniel's fences, now free of competition from the buffalo that had dominated the grasslands for eternity, could be fully utilized only by mimicking the ways of these original grazers. Accordingly, Daniel set a part of his herd loose each year, betting that enough of them would thrive without protection and turn up in the annual spring roundup. Although a few head usually went missing, Daniel judged the losses to be acceptable. Unlike the bigger outfits, however, Daniel hedged his bet by keeping most of the herd close to home. He rotated his stock between the lands he had fenced along the river bottom and the open range that beckoned to the north. This system allowed him to take advantage of the free grass while minimizing his losses. But it also required him to move the bulk of the herd out and back each day between the ranch and the range.

The system worked well enough most of the time. But while out on Ten-Mile Bench that day and with little to distract him, Daniel let his mind wander to a poem he was writing. It had assumed greater poignancy while Nellie was away. He was stuck on the first verse and had jotted down only a few lines. Nellie's birthday was approaching quickly, and he was determined to finish it in time for a little celebration he was planning. For several minutes, maybe longer, he concentrated on the paper in his hand rather than on the herd. He scribbled and crossed

out several words on the two verses he was working on
before he was satisfied.

*Way out here on the high and windy plains*
*Where a vast sky hoards its thin little rains,*
*I found a love to soften my deepest pains.*

*There were days when I thought I'd lost you,*
*Nights with a blackness of the deepest hue;*
*Still you were there with a love to renew.*

When he eventually looked up and surveyed the
herd, Daniel saw that he had let them scatter too far. A
quick count revealed that a few head were missing, likely
hiding in one of the coulees that radiated from the bench,
an elevated tableland that was nearly dead flat on top but
flanked by badlands along its edges. Daniel rode along
the rim and peered down several coulees before deciding
to give up for the day. Full darkness was approaching,
and he decided that returning the next day would present
less risk than leaving the herd alone while he searched for
a few strays. Daniel was annoyed at himself for his negli-
gence, but the situation also reminded him that he needed
some help. He and Nellie still lacked the means to keep a
hired hand around day to day, so they had to handle the
work on their own, supplemented by the help of a few
neighbors when branding and other labor intensive jobs
had to be done.

Daniel barely took time to eat when he awoke the
next morning. He rode directly toward Ten-Mile Bench
but saw none of his livestock along the way. After a
quick reconnaissance on top of the bench, he decided to
follow one of the coulees down to water. Although Daniel worked hard to keep the fences tight on the several
hundred acres of bottomland the ranch had grown to in-

clude, there always seemed to be a place where a determined animal could get through. It happened often enough that Daniel began to imagine he could think like a stray. He sometimes just knew where an animal would roam. More often than not, he had determined, the strays would follow a path that led them to water and to sweet grass that flourished along the bottomlands.

With that theory in mind, Daniel followed a coulee downward and reached the Teton at a point several miles east of his ranch. The wide valley along the Teton River was mostly open but studded with thick stands of cottonwood and shrubs that could easily conceal a few strays. Daniel rode slowly downstream and followed a meandering path that took him from one tree stand to the next. By late morning, he had gone almost all the way to the confluence with the Marias River and felt himself getting more annoyed, both at himself and at a steer he had come to call Casanova. Casanova didn't seem to know he'd been castrated. Besides maintaining an interest in the ladies, he was feisty and often wandered off. Sometimes he induced a few other cattle to follow. Daniel had thought of taking him to Follows Bear's camp but later had thought better of it. Casanova was just too much trouble to trail that far.

After a slow, methodical search, Daniel finally found the strays down on the Marias, a larger river that marked the boundary of the Blackfoot Reservation. The river was still too high for the animals to be tempted to cross, so they had stopped and were grazing contentedly in the tall grass that thrived in the low spots along the river bottom. It was a relief to find the strays, which greeted Daniel's arrival calmly, almost as if they had been waiting to be found and led back to the ranch. Casanova was the one exception. He eyed Daniel warily, tensed up, and moved jerkily in a random pattern. Daniel was accustomed to this and knew that Casanova couldn't be turned with just a few yells or by outmaneuvering him on horseback. Daniel would have to use the rope and drag the steer along a ways, probably all the way back to the ranch.

Daniel approached Casanova, waved his lariat in the steer's direction, and circled the loop over his head before sending it toward the dodgy animal. His first attempt was a complete miss, due partly to the inaccuracy of Daniel's throw and partly to Casanova's ability to elude the rope. Daniel's second attempt landed around just one horn, and in the process the rope wrapped around Daniel's arm, allowing Casanova to jerk him out of the saddle. The rope left a vivid burn on Daniel's arm, tattered his shirtsleeve, and caused Daniel to land awkwardly on the ground. Daniel cussed loudly at his nemesis. Despite the pain in his arm, he was thankful no one had witnessed this fiasco.

Once he had dusted himself off and finally had Casanova under control, Daniel allowed himself a rest and paused to linger along the riverbank. The sight of an old woodpile drew his thoughts to those who had come before him, for it brought memories of a vivid story that Jean Baptiste had told him. Near where he stood, less than twenty years earlier, the Blackfoot had killed a group of woodhawks. Their only memorial was the rotting remains of the woodpile that had sealed their fate. Despite the pleasantness of the day and his need for rest, Daniel didn't stay long by the river that day, for it was a place where the suffering of men still lingered. *This land has a voice*, Daniel thought, *one more powerful than any other place I've been. But perhaps not everyone can hear it.*

# CHAPTER 26

The Helena Club met in a magnificent stone building in the heart of downtown. On the day of the meeting, Nellie met her father on the street outside the building. They greeted each other casually to avoid the appearance of having any agenda other than a social outing. After entering the building through an archway adorned with filigree and passing into a large atrium, Mr. Sage enthusiastically introduced Nellie to an assortment of club members, many of whom cast admiring looks in her direction. This part of their plan wasn't entirely unorthodox. The club's meeting format began with a social hour that was sometimes attended by a member's spouse or guest. Boisterous chatter, fueled by good whiskey and fine cigars, quickly filled the atrium's cavernous space. Nearly all the men smoked cigars and the smoke rose high into the air, making the light cast by the chandeliers appear as beacons in the fog.

When the time came to begin the meeting, the members drifted toward an adjacent room, a more intimate space where business could be conducted. The room was richly decorated and graced with a painting of Lewis and Clark greeting one of the tribes. The painting celebrated the magnificent landscape of the West but revealed no hint of the tragedies to come.

The club's business meeting always began with an opportunity for members to bring up any special matters that weren't on the agenda. This provided the opportunity Mr. Sage needed to broach Nellie's issue and summon her from the atrium. Now he was plowing new ground.

Mr. Sage raised his hand to be recognized, and the moderator invited him to address the group. "I know it's irregular, but many of you have just met my daughter Nellie. I beg your indulgence to allow her a few minutes to request our help." He smiled broadly, "If I want peace in my house, I've got no choice but to do this." Amid the awkward laughter that ensued, he said, "I present to you my daughter, Mrs. Daniel McHarg."

A loud murmur went up from the assembled members, but no one objected. Though now a respectable member of the Helena Club, Mr. Sage had a reputation as a harsh opponent, someone not to be crossed lightly.

Nellie entered the room confidently, and the chairman encouraged her to take a seat at the other end of a long table. She spoke from memory and from her heart. "Gentlemen, thank you for allowing me this time with your distinguished group. I know it's highly unusual to have a woman in attendance, but these are unusual times." She then gave an account of the continuing tragedy on the Blackfoot Reservation. She recited the grim statistics she had read in the report of Indian Agent Allen, who had repeatedly stated that the situation would get worse if help didn't arrive soon. Near the end of her presentation, she added a personal touch. "In an effort to help, my husband Daniel drove a few steers up to the reservation and saw the starvation firsthand. These people literally have nothing to eat. His account of people wasting away, including young children, drove me to tears."

Nellie ended her presentation with a poignant quotation from an editorial in the Fort Benton newspaper. "In closing," she said in a strong voice, "allow me to share with you these words:

"'A famine in Ireland or any part of the world, enlists the sympathy of all Americans, while in our midst are more than three thousand people actually starving, and not a finger raised to help them.' The River Press, 1884.

"Let it not be said that we didn't lift a finger in the face of famine," Nellie concluded. "I know we are a better people than that."

As the group began a scattered applause, the chairman politely thanked Nellie for her presentation and added that they had time for a few comments before moving on to their regular agenda. One man was eager to speak. He was coarser looking than the others, the years of hard work in a series of small mines stamped into his identity. One mine had finally paid off, which explained his presence among the members of the Helena Club. His voice revealed his beginnings in Ireland. He had learned to speak slowly to ensure he'd be understood among the American-born men who made up the club's ranks.

"You all know I'm from the old sod," he began, "and I'm old enough to remember the Great Famine. I've seen with me own eyes the emaciated bodies, the bodies of people who died with their teeth stained green and bits of grass lodged in their mouth. They had nothing else to eat before the starvation overtook them. No one lifted a finger then either. Gentlemen, we can't allow that to happen here."

Some in the room nodded in agreement, but most remained silent. Except for a few men sitting together who had begun a separate conversation among themselves. The chairman encouraged them to speak to the whole group, which prompted one of the men to share his thoughts. He had a booming voice, edged with hostility at the direction the meeting was taking.

"I commend Mrs. McHarg on her presentation today," he said. "It's a fitting sentiment for a woman to hold. But there are more practical things to consider." He went on to point out that the Blackfoot and other reservations in Montana collectively consisted of some forty-five thousand square miles—an area larger than New York State—and held only nine thousand Indians, compared to New York's population of five million. He then came to his main point. "And what do the Indians do with all this land?" the man asked. "Instead of working it, they steal cattle from their neighbors. Gentlemen, as Representative Maginnis has stated so clearly, if we want to help these people, we must begin by reducing the size of their reservation. For only then will they turn to the agrarian pursuits needed to sustain them."

The stunning irony of asserting that the best way to help the Blackfoot was to reduce the size of their reservation was lost on most of the group. Indeed, many in the room clearly shared this sentiment, which apparently trumped any sympathy they might feel for a starving people. Other members wanted to speak, but the chairman cut them off and said it was time to get to their regular agenda. He thanked Nellie again and directed one of the members to show her out. She felt her hopes for support leaking away.

Later that day, Mr. Sage had to face another unpleasant task: informing Nellie that her effort had yielded only one check, and a fairly small one at that. Only the Irishman had sought out Mr. Sage after the meeting and handed him a donation. As he walked the several blocks back to his house, Mr. Sage thought hard about how to deliver the news to Nellie in a manner that wouldn't cause another fissure in their relationship.

Like many men approaching a more advanced age, Mr. Sage had recently experienced a degree of transformation. He had shed some of the hard-edged drive of his earlier years in favor of a softer persona that placed more emphasis on the importance of family. Mr. Sage was older than most fathers when Nellie was born, having lost his first wife to one of the nameless epidemics that had swept through St. Louis with alarming regularity. Perhaps it was partly due to aging, but seeing Nellie again had affected him instantly and profoundly. He couldn't bear the thought of losing her again.

Burdened by these thoughts, he entered his home slowly, still not sure what he was going to say. Nellie and her mother were there to greet him.

"I'm sorry, Nellie, the news isn't good, and it pains me to have to tell you that." He paused briefly before adding, "I can assure you that the lack of support from the group wasn't any fault of yours. Your presentation was splendid, and I'm so very proud of you."

Nellie looked stricken, her disappointment etched into her expression. But much to Mr. Sage's surprise, she moved toward him, embraced him, and thanked him for what he had done.

The next day, Nellie prepared to leave. She was still preoccupied with devising a strategy to raise more funds, but also knew it was time to return home to Daniel and the life they had built on the Teton. These thoughts cheered her and diminished the hard edges of disappointment that lingered, and the family had a cordial breakfast together before Mr. Sage left for work. After his departure, Nellie and her mother continued a casual conversation. There was still much to catch up on, but Nellie sensed something else was on her mother's mind. Indeed there was; Mrs. Sage had some important news she wanted to share.

"Nellie, I've been thinking about the purpose of your visit, and I want to help," she began. "You see, I have a small inheritance from my dear parents, one I've kept from your father and held on to for many years. I always intended to use it for something important."

Nellie listened carefully, hoping she wasn't unintentionally conveying her concerns about her mother's decision. She wasn't sure she wanted her mother to give up the extra security her inheritance provided.

Sensing Nellie's doubts, Mrs. Sage said, "I can't think of anything more important than supporting your efforts to help the Blackfoot. Your father said he was proud of what you've done. I am too. Allow me to do this, Nellie. I'm sure your father and I will get along just fine without it."

In the end, Nellie accepted her mother's donation with gratitude. Her visit wasn't the resounding financial success she had hoped for. But the funds she had raised would help, and she looked forward to turning the donations over to a Fort Benton merchant who was planning a relief effort on the reservation.

Nellie had something else to savor on the long trip back to Fort Benton. Her visit to Helena had started a process of reconciliation in the Sage family.

# CHAPTER 27

Nellie had managed to send word ahead through the stage agent in Helena that she'd be arriving in Fort Benton on the afternoon stage in two days. The agent in Fort Benton, in turn, sent a boy to the Antlers to find John Campbell, one of Daniel's old friends from the *Red Cloud*. The boy passed on a request to get word of Nellie's planned arrival to Daniel. As a result, Daniel returned home from his chores the next afternoon to find John Campbell sitting on the Raven Ranch porch. John was wearing his right arm in a sling and had a few bruises on his face.

"Are you all right, then, John?" Daniel yelled from his horse.

"Well enough to laugh. I couldn't say that last week," John replied. "I'm on the mend now, Daniel."

Daniel was happy to see John. They rarely saw each other now that Daniel was working the ranch full-time. "It must have been a tough son of a bitch that brought this on you, John. Since when have you become a brawler?"

"No, it wasn't anything like that," John responded. "It was a damn scaffold that did me in." He went on to explain that he had been working at the new courthouse and the scaffold he was standing on had collapsed. "Thank God there was no one else with me on that scaffold. I busted up my right arm, especially my hand, and I think I'm done for as a carpenter."

John then added that he had some better news to share. "Nellie sent word from Helena. She'll be back in town tomorrow afternoon. I thought you'd like to know that."

Daniel laughed heartily. "Damn right I do! Another few days of her being gone and I'd be ready to move back into town. Nellie...well, if nothing else, these past few weeks reminded me that I need to hear another person's voice now and then."

John had even more news to share. "There's something else, Daniel. I've got an idea I want to try out on you. I'm thinking about working with you here on the ranch."

Daniel was taken aback but amused at the possibility. "You ride like a sack of potatoes, John. And with that bum arm, what good do you think you'd be to me on the ranch?"

"Kind of you to put it that way, Daniel. No, it's not my cowboy skills I'm offering." John laughed. "I'm a hay man. That's what I did on my dad's farm in Nova Scotia, and I'm thinking you and Nellie have some good hay ground here."

Daniel acknowledged that they did. "But haven't you noticed all that grass out beyond the fences?" he asked John. "The little bit of hay we grow now is all we need."

"That may be true now," John replied. "But don't you plan to expand? More important, the range out there is filling up fast. Back home, if a hard winter came, we could only keep as many cows as we could keep in hay. That day will come here too, and I'm thinking it will come sooner than we expect."

Daniel was a little skeptical, but he wanted to help his friend, who obviously needed some work. If he ended up with more hay than he needed, Daniel thought, he could probably sell it to his neighbors.

"All right, John," Daniel said with a grin. "Let's give it a try. When do you think you'll be healed up well enough to start the work?"

John replied that he'd be ready in another two weeks. "I'll mostly use my left hand to start, but I'll eventually get the strength back in my right arm. The doctor said I'd always have trouble swinging a hammer all day with this right hand, so it's time for another line of work."

Daniel nodded. "That sounds good, John," he said. "I don't have the time to plant and harvest all the hay ground here, but if we're going to do this, we'd better get started before the summer's gone too far. I'll provide the land, and you provide the seed and most of the labor. We'll work out a fair arrangement as we go."

The following day Daniel rode a buckboard into Fort Benton to meet Nellie's stage. He arrived early and sat by the river near the Grand Union Hotel to pass the time. It was too late in the season for riverboat traffic, but even so the shore was eerily quiet and the levee was less crowded with materials awaiting shipment than Daniel remembered. An old man, who was known around town as the captain, sat nearby. He had never captained anything as far as anyone knew. Instead, he had earned his nickname by lingering along the levee, seeming to know everything about the river and the boats that plied it.

"Only fifteen boats this year," the captain hollered in Daniel's direction. "We had more than double that number last year, and even more the year before. This town's future don't look too good anymore."

The old man had a reputation for latching on to people and talking too much, so Daniel kept his response low-key. "I fear you're right, friend," he said. As the captain moved closer to continue the conversation, Daniel was relieved to look up the street and see the stage coming, providing the easy excuse he needed to break things off. "That's my wife I'm waiting for, so I'm off to meet her," Daniel said as he waved the man good bye.

Daniel ran to the stage stop and arrived just as Nellie stepped out of the cabin. She was eager to return to the ranch, so they didn't linger in Fort Benton. Once seated next to Daniel on the buckboard, she began an account of her trip and talked excitedly nearly the whole way back to the Teton. Despite the less-than-resounding success she had achieved, Nellie was happy she had made the effort. Daniel was delighted to have his wife back and proud of what she had done. He was especially pleased to hear that Nellie's encounter with her father had been positive, but he was unable to resist a little teasing.

"Maybe that old scoundrel has a soft side after all," Daniel said. "He just keeps it under lock and key until a special occasion comes along!"

Nellie thumped Daniel on the shoulder but joined in with his laughter. She also wanted to know everything that had happened while she was gone. Daniel didn't have much to report, he said, and joked that Nellie must have taken all the excitement with her. But then he remembered the offer John had made the day before.

"I had an interesting visit with John Campbell," Daniel announced. "He had an accident at work and busted himself up."

Nellie expressed alarm and asked about John's injuries.

"I think he'll heal up well," Daniel said. He proceeded to explain that John had broken his arm and that his other injuries were just some nasty-looking but minor cuts and bruises. "John says he has no more work in town," Daniel reported. "The interesting part is that he wants to come work with us at the ranch. He thinks we should grow more hay. I think he may be right."

Surprised at this new development, Nellie took it all in and then offered her support. "John is a good man," she declared. "If we can help him, I'm all for that."

As planned, John returned to the ranch later that week to survey the ground more closely. Nellie and Daniel were there to greet him, and they accompanied him to some land along the river that they thought might make good hay ground.

"What do you think about this area, John?" Daniel said when they reached a low area where an abandoned oxbow had formed a shallow depression. "It stays pretty wet and might be what you're looking for."

John walked the ground intently. Although he didn't have to irrigate back in Nova Scotia, John had a carpenter's eye for judging what was level and how water could be made to spread.

"This is a good place to start," John agreed. "I'll give my arm some more time to heal up, but I'll be back next week. I'm looking forward to getting down to business."

Over the next weeks, John worked the ground carefully. He used a horse-drawn team to knock down some high spots and dug a series of small ditches that brought in water from the Teton. John planted the new areas with a mixture of hay grasses, primarily timothy and smooth brome grass, in order to determine which type would do best at each location. By the end of the growing season, John had more than doubled the ranch's hay production, which previously had been limited to the yield from a few sub-irrigated depressions close to the river.

That summer was exceptionally hot and dry. The short-grass prairie barely greened up that year and was sparse by late summer. But the Teton River still flowed, and John's irrigation efforts produced an abundance of newly emerging hay, which they could cut the following year. Come next spring, Daniel and John agreed, they'd convert even more land to hay production.

Not everything went well that year. In late fall, someone Nellie had worked with to provide aid to the Blackfoot appeared at the ranch. He had grim news to share. "I'm sorry to tell you that Follows Bear has died. I know you were acquainted and I wanted to tell you directly."

Nellie spoke first. "I thought the starvation had ended. How did he die?"

"There's finally enough food to feed the people on the reservation," the man replied. "It wasn't a lack of food. It seems that Follows Bear had simply lost the will to live. Near the end of his life, when he still had the strength, he left camp and made his way to Eagle Butte, a place where he often went to pray. His body was found there a few days later."

After the man left, Daniel let out a stinging grief. "Follows Bear saved my life and this is what he gets in return. It's happening too fast, Nellie. We're seeing the end of a way of life just flash before our eyes. And I don't see any promise that something better will replace what's been lost."

Daniel's darkening mood became apparent that evening and Nellie feared he might descend into his past grief. She had learned that an early intervention could usually make it pass. "I think it would be fitting," she suggested, "for you to recite something to commemorate Follows Bear's passing. You've got all that poetry running through your head. Something must come to mind."

At first Daniel resisted, thinking that he ought to come up with some words from the Blackfoot culture. He thought of his friend Jean Baptiste, who would have known something right to say, and regretted that not enough of Jean Baptiste's knowledge had come his way. Instead, Daniel turned to something more familiar.

> "'Under the wide and starry sky
> Dig the grave and let me lie:
> Glad did I live and gladly die,
> And I laid me down with a will.'"

Daniel struggled to remember the second verse but could only remember one of the lines:

> "'Here he lies where he long'd to be...'"

Moved, Nellie said to Daniel, "That was beautiful. Who wrote it?"

"It's called 'Requiem,'" Daniel replied, "and it was written by one of my favorite poets, Robert Louis Stevenson. I read somewhere that it's his own epitaph. So Stevenson wasn't thinking of a place like this, or a man like Follows Bear. But I think Follows Bear might agree that the words fit." After a pause Daniel said, "Truthfully, Nellie, I need a sip of whiskey to do this occasion right, but alas, there's none to be had in this house."

Nellie assumed a mischievous smile, a look Daniel always found beguiling. "Don't be so sure about that, Daniel McHarg," she said softly. "I don't want us to get accustomed to it, but I know there are occasions when a Scotsman like yourself needs a proper ceremony with the whiskey sacrament!"

Nellie disappeared for a moment and returned with a small flask of whiskey that she'd been keeping tucked away for a special occasion. To Daniel's delight and astonishment, she shared a few sips with Daniel that evening and sat by his side until they drifted off to sleep.

# CHAPTER 28

Early fall brought a letter from the Sages. Nellie picked it up on one of her trips to Fort Benton and read it immediately. She absorbed a few pages of family news before coming to the real purpose of her mother's letter. The Sages, intent on seeing Nellie again and finally meeting Daniel, were planning a visit to Fort Benton later that month. They intended to stay for several days.

Nellie was delighted by the news, but her initial elation was soon tempered by uncertainty about how Daniel would react. Daniel had moderated his views on Mr. Sage, but Nellie didn't know if he was ready to embrace a visit, particularly one that would last several days. Of more concern was the fact that the Sages planned to visit the ranch and see their daughter's new home. It was an understandable parental desire, but Nellie could sense trouble coming. Although the Sages planned to stay in town at the Grand Union Hotel, having them underfoot at a busy time on the ranch was risky. Nellie envisioned her father getting bored and Daniel becoming annoyed at the interruption to his routine. Nellie resolved to manage the visit carefully and spent the rest of the ride home strategizing about how best to do that.

Daniel was putting up hay with John when Nellie arrived home. She went to talk with Daniel immediately. After greeting both men, she let John know that she wished a moment with Daniel alone. John headed off to his cabin for a lunch break and left Nellie and Daniel alone in the field. Surrounding them were freshly cut bundles of hay that added a fecund aroma to the summer-like air that lingered in the valley.

Nellie got right to it. "Let's walk along the river, Daniel. I have some news I want to share."

Although he was tired from a long day of hard work, Daniel agreed, and they set off arm in arm on a little path that weaved through the trees along the river's edge. The cottonwood leaves, which formed a dense canopy overhead, had lost their suppleness over the dry summer and made a soft rattling sound as Daniel and Nellie passed by. Their delight in the setting created a momentary distraction that delayed Nellie's announcement as they shared the simple pleasure of being together and taking a break from the relentless demands of working the ranch.

Finally, Nellie shared her news. "I got a letter from my mother today. They plan to visit us in Fort Benton at the end of next week."

Daniel was slow to react. "I suppose your use of the term 'they' means your father too," he finally said with a slight smile.

Nellie affirmed that it did and assured Daniel that they'd work things out so that the visit went smoothly. "I know you don't think you have anything in common with my father, Daniel. But, in fact, you do. You both love Montana and the history that surrounds us. There's got to be a way to use that to some advantage."

Remaining quiet, Daniel took on an expression that

indicated he was churning things through his mind. He offered Nellie a slight nod in response.

Nellie needed more.

"Daniel," she said forcefully, "I need to know you're with me on this."

"I'm always with you, Nellie," Daniel said quickly. "I'll do whatever you need me to do. But give me a little time to get my enthusiasm up."

That was good enough for Nellie, and they let the topic rest for the remainder of the day.

When the day came for the Sages to arrive, Daniel and Nellie were there to greet them in Fort Benton. Not wanting to get in the way of a happy reunion, Daniel stood back initially, his arms folded and his expression neutral. Mr. Sage, who had been coached by Mrs. Sage on how to behave that day, quickly broke away and walked over to Daniel, who moved closer when he saw Mr. Sage coming in his direction.

Mr. Sage greeted Daniel with a firm handshake and a muted greeting. "Daniel, it's taken too long for us to meet."

*Who's responsible for that?* Daniel thought. "Right. It is about time the two of us met. I'm glad it's finally happening."

Mr. Sage looked pleasant enough, but he was clearly sizing up Daniel, who made a good initial impression that day. At Nellie's urging, Daniel had spiffed himself up for the meeting and sported a clean white shirt accented by a red bandana tied around his neck. It was rare in those days to see a man without a hat. Daniel's was a broad-brimmed felt hat with a low crown. He cut a striking figure, for he too had been transformed by ranch life. He looked the part now; his ruddy complexion and lean figure contrasted sharply with that of the pale, portly Mr. Sage, who spent most of his life indoors and thought physical labor below his station. Still, Daniel was wary of the meeting.

Mr. Sage looked as Daniel expected. By all appearances, he was the type of man Daniel would never willingly associate with. But here they were. It was a price he'd gladly pay for the opportunity to be with Nellie. Daniel was relieved when Nellie approached with her mother, who she eagerly introduced to him. In contrast to the reserve he held for Mr. Sage, Daniel was eager to meet Nellie's mother, who looked like an older and wiser version of her daughter.

Mrs. Sage smiled brightly at the opportunity to finally meet her son-in-law and eagerly embraced Daniel as if he were her own son.

Daniel's relief was short-lived, however, for Nellie quickly offered a suggestion. "Daniel," she said, "why don't you take my father for a walk along the levee while we freshen up? I'm sure he'd like to hear about all the history here."

"A splendid, idea," Mr. Sage agreed. "Would you mind showing me around, Daniel?"

Daniel agreed, and the two men set off along the idle riverfront. Both Daniel and Mr. Sage had first arrived in Montana by steamboat, and each remembered a scene very different from what he saw today: a nearly deserted levee without any working boats or piles of cargo. This provided a basis for their conversation to begin.

They hadn't walked far when they came upon the captain, who was still a nearly constant presence on the riverfront when the weather allowed. Daniel chuckled to himself when he realized that the captain, a man he had tried to avoid earlier that summer, might now provide a welcome diversion.

Daniel greeted the captain with a friendly wave and led Mr. Sage to the crude bench where the captain sat.

"Looks like not much is going on today, Captain," Daniel began.

"Well, you should have been here earlier," the captain said without much enthusiasm. "A bunch of Texans swam a good-size herd across the river today. It was a sight to see, those cowboys flailing their ropes and pushing the herd into the water. Some of those cows didn't want any part of it."

The three men talked for a while before Daniel mentioned that he had landed on this very spot just a few years earlier.

"What boat was you on?" the captain asked.

"It was the *Red Cloud*," Daniel replied. "The woman who is now my wife was on the same boat."

The captain perked up at the mention of the *Red Cloud*. "Now that was some boat. She lies on the bottom now, but how she graced this river. What year did you say it was?"

"It was 1882," Daniel answered.

"That was the year she went down. Why, it was the same trip that brought you up. The *Red Cloud* hit a snag about two hundred miles downriver from here, but you probably knew that." For a moment the captain seemed lost in thought, running through all the years and all the boat landings he had witnessed, sifting through memories that were slowly fading with age. Still, he found a story that fit the occasion. "Well," he said, "you can be glad it wasn't the year before."

Daniel was intrigued now. "What happened the year before?"

"I saw a man get shot coming off the *Red Cloud* in 1881," the captain replied. "Maybe if your bride-to-be had seen what I seen, she would have taken the next boat back to St. Louis!" The captain was amused at his comment, but his laughter brought on a wheezing fit serious enough to cause Mr. Sage to thump the old man on his back in an effort to help him clear his lungs.

When the captain's breathing returned to normal, Mr. Sage joined the conversation. "What caused the shooting? I came upriver on a different boat in 1881, but my whole family was on the *Red Cloud* in 1882. I've got more than a casual interest in your story."

The captain loved an audience, and now he had one. "You see, some of the boatmen are particular about how things are done. A man named...well, I forget his name now. Anyway, he was a mate on the *Red Cloud* that year, and he had a temper. He had started to celebrate their arrival in Fort Benton a little early that trip, and drinking whiskey only made his temper worse."

The captain had a performer's sense of timing and enjoyed an opportunity to tell a tale that had his listeners engaged. After a suitable pause, he continued the story. "One of those things the mate was particular about was the custom that no one should board a boat until all the newly arrived passengers had disembarked. That day, a man tried to board early. The mate told him to wait, but he ignored the warning and boarded anyway. He didn't get far. Without saying another word, the mate shot the man with a pistol. I was sitting just about where we are now when it happened."

After the captain finished his story, Mr. Sage and Daniel looked at each other, and Daniel gave a little wink. Before the captain could launch into another story, Daniel interjected. "I believe you are right about my wife," he said. "Had she witnessed that shooting, who knows what might have happened? But she's here now, and I believe it's time to rejoin her."

Mr. Sage nodded in agreement and they turned to leave, but not before thanking the captain and handing him a few coins for his efforts.

On the walk to the hotel, Daniel told Mr. Sage that he was familiar with the shooting incident, adding that the captain had embellished the story a bit. "The trouble did start on board the *Red Cloud*, but the shooting took place later in a saloon," Daniel said. "I suppose something like that could still happen today, but that episode tells you something about how wild a place this was. This fellow shot a man in the face point-blank and was acquitted as if he had only shot a stray dog."

In contrast to the waterfront, the hotel lobby was busy that afternoon. Nellie and her mother were seated on an ornate couch when the two men returned. Nellie was pleased to see they were still talking to each other, something she took as a good sign. Mr. Sage proposed they take an early supper, and the group retreated to the adjoining dining room, which was long and narrow with a high ceiling and windows facing the river. Oak paneling, crafted from trees a thousand miles to the east, and plush rugs from exotic places even more distant created a setting in sharp contrast to the rude streets and wild lands that surrounded the hotel. The décor was the result of a deliberate effort to fashion a place apart from its surroundings, an oasis of elegance in a remote setting.

Upon entering the dining room, they were greeted by the maître d', who immediately asked if they had a reservation, even though the dining room was half empty. The maître d's manner made Daniel uncomfortable, but Mr. Sage was in his element. Once seated, he and the maître d' studied the wine list together, their heads close, and talked as if they were old friends who hadn't seen each other for years. While the two men discussed the details of the wine selection, a process that lasted several minutes, the rest of the people at the table looked around the room aimlessly. Following much deliberation, Mr.

Sage ordered a bottle of imported burgundy, along with a dozen oysters.

After Mr. Sage had finished his little performance, the conversation among the group at the table resumed. "The railroad is going to change everything, Daniel," said Mr. Sage, "and create great opportunities for the cattleman. Are you building up your herd?"

"We're doing what we can," Daniel replied. "It's still a ways to get to the rail line from here, but the market has improved. Our biggest challenge is still the weather. That, and the wolves and cattle thieves."

"Business rewards those who take the initiative, Daniel. I think now is the time to take a gamble and bet on the future of Montana beef. If you need more capital, I'd be delighted to invest in you."

This was the last thing Daniel wanted to talk about. He glanced at Nellie, relieved that this was a topic they had previously discussed. Nellie knew how to respond. "We want to go our own way, Father. But thank you for the offer."

Mr. Sage looked surprised by Nellie's refusal of his offer but dropped the topic when the waiter returned with a tray of oysters. Mr. Sage inspected them closely, took a single taste, and sent them back to the kitchen. He declared that they weren't fresh enough for his palate and said so in a loud voice that carried through the dining room, prompting several heads to turn in his direction. Mr. Sage's behavior didn't seem remarkable at the time, but it was the start of a downward trajectory.

Acting as if nothing untoward had happened, the waiter quickly returned with the wine. He opened the heavy bottle with flair and poured the wine into crystal glasses balanced on a tray he held with his other hand. A white cloth was draped over the arm holding the tray. Daniel and the others at the table were relieved when Mr.

Sage approved of the wine. Over time he demonstrated his approval heartily by consuming most of the bottle while the others, none of whom were wine drinkers, nursed the little bits in their glasses. The hesitancy of his guests, however, didn't stop Mr. Sage from ordering another bottle when the first one was empty.

Before the waiter left the table, Daniel stopped him. "I've had about all the wine I need. Bring me a beer instead."

Mr. Sage looked slightly askance at Daniel, but the dinner remained uneventful until near the end of the evening. Mr. Sage grew less animated as the meal progressed, feeling the combined results of a long stage ride and the consumption of too much wine. He spoke less as well, perhaps because he had begun to slur his words slightly, which prompted Mrs. Sage to suggest that it was time to retire. Taking this as their cue, Daniel and Nellie declared their intention to leave while there was still light. As the plates were being cleared from the table. Mr. Sage objected. "Why don't you stay in town for the night as my guest? I'm sure they still have a room available."

Daniel declined the invitation. He thanked Mr. Sage for his kind offer but said he'd be more comfortable at the ranch and needed to get an early start in the morning.

Mr. Sage wouldn't give up easily, however. "Don't you think Nellie deserves a bit of the comfort she's accustomed to?" he asked. Hearing no response, he continued, "It would do her good to stay here for a night. You can return to your little hovel—" He corrected himself quickly. "—return to your home, I mean, tomorrow." But the damage was done.

Daniel stood up abruptly, his face flushed in anger, but he simply said good night and headed for the door. Nellie followed. As she left, she turned briefly to glare back at her father.

Nellie and Daniel didn't talk much on the way back to the Teton. Nellie apologized for her father, and Daniel remained calm. After returning home, they went straight to bed. Daniel was subdued but had one thing to say before he fell asleep. "I don't know if I can go through with this. Your father is due back here in the morning, and I'm not sure I can tolerate more of that man." Hoping to lighten the mood before drifting off, he added, "Can't we just invite your mother to come out for a visit?"

Nellie saw the humor in Daniel's remarks but she was tired too. "Sleep on it, Daniel. That's all I ask. We'll talk more in the morning."

The next day brought bright sunshine with a deep blue sky and a western clarity to the air. Despite a hangover and the awkward ending to the previous night, Mr. Sage was determined to carry through with their plans to visit the ranch. After a late morning breakfast, he arranged for a buckboard to pick them up at the hotel. Mrs. Sage was equally determined to visit the ranch and went along in silence, fearing that bringing up the unpleasantness from the previous evening would only increase the tension and make their visit more difficult.

After ascending the ridge and leaving the Missouri River Valley, the Sages drove across a long stretch of flat prairie before ascending a gentle knoll that brought the Teton River and its broad valley into view. Pausing to take in the view, they scanned the valley for a sign of the Raven Ranch, which they knew lay to the west. Near Fort Benton, the Teton Valley lacks the grandeur of much of Montana, but the dense canopy of cottonwoods and the intensely green hay meadows that spread before them were especially beautiful that day. Mr. Sage spotted a house near the river, which they concluded must be the place. They each felt some pride at the sight of what Daniel and Nellie had created in this pastoral setting, and their eagerness to see Nellie in her new surroundings ameliorated the strain between them and the awkwardness they knew likely awaited.

Nellie was there to greet them when they arrived. She remained a bit stern, even as her mother gushed about the beauty of the Teton Valley and the ranch they had fashioned from what had so recently been raw land. Nellie offered a tour of the small house, eliciting multiple compliments from Mrs. Sage "I love what you've done here, Nellie. Your house is so cute."

Mr. Sage couldn't quite bring himself to compliment Nellie on a house he thought too cramped for the likes of his daughter, so he limited his comments to the setting. "This is a fine place you've got here. I can see why Daniel chose this land to start a ranch." He then asked about Daniel's whereabouts and began to offer an apology.

Nellie cut him off before he could finish. "Daniel's cutting hay today," she said, "and you can find him downstream a ways. I accept your apology, but he's the one you should apologize to." Nellie turned to leave, escorting her mother out the door for a tour of the garden, and leaving her father alone to make things right with Daniel.

The track along the river was bumpy but easy to follow. After emerging from a stand of cottonwoods into a clearing, Mr. Sage saw Daniel, preoccupied with his effort to load hay onto a drying rack. Daniel didn't look over until Mr. Sage was nearly upon him. The two men gazed at each other for a moment before Mr. Sage stepped down from the buckboard. He didn't waste any time.

"I'm sorry for last night, Daniel," said Mr. Sage. "I can be an ass sometimes."

Daniel didn't respond immediately. Instead, he savored the admission by the man standing before him. It validated a belief Daniel had held for a long time. But Mr. Sage didn't pause for long.

"No matter what else you think of me, I want you to know how grateful I am to you for being the husband you are to my daughter. I've never seen her happier than she is with you, and that means the world to me."

Daniel had decided to play things by ear that day. If Mr. Sage tried to brush things off, Daniel figured, he'd do the same and be done with his father-in-law and a relationship that never got off the ground. But that's not what was happening. Daniel studied Mr. Sage closely and sensed sincerity in the man. *If he isn't sincere*, Daniel figured, *he must be a hell of a good poker player*. He decided to give it another shot.

"I'm glad to hear that," Daniel replied. "I'm going to admit something to you, though. When Nellie and I got married without your approval and you shut her out, you hurt her badly. I never thought I could forgive that behavior in a man, but after Nellie came back from Helena, she said you'd changed. I wanted to believe it, but now I'm not sure."

Mr. Sage was stung by Daniel's assertion but knew he deserved a reprimand. "I was wrong," said Mr. Sage. "At first I thought I was doing something right for my daughter, but eventually I realized it was just selfishness. Let's try to get past that. I may still be an ass from time to time, but it won't be because I don't love my daughter or because I question her choice of a husband."

"I can work with that," Daniel said. "Let's go eat."

# CHAPTER 29

*1885*:

The spring roundup was a major event for the cattlemen in Montana Territory. It inspired an odd combination of hope spiked with a dose of fear. Given the nature of an operation that turned cattle loose on the open range and left them generally unobserved and without any form of protection, no one could know for sure how their livestock had fared over the winter. And it wouldn't be known until a multitude of riders had finished scouring the range and brought in all the animals they could find.

Every man handled the fear a little differently. Daniel tried to put it out of his mind as much as possible, though he never fully succeeded at this. Other men dwelled on their fears. They watched the weather closely and seized on any bit of news passed on by someone who likely heard it from someone else. There simply wasn't much information available, and what passed for news was often founded on speculation. Those who obsessed about their fears tended to hold a more gloomy view of the situation, perhaps thinking that if they prepared themselves for the worst the reality would likely be at least somewhat better than the dire outcome they had imagined through the long winter.

Nate was of the pessimist persuasion. That year, he and Daniel rode to the roundup site together. Nate talked nearly constantly, expressing his worries about one thing or another. "Only a crazy man would be in this business, Daniel," one of his laments began. "I hear the wolves were thick this year. We'll be lucky to find any calves left."

Nate expected a response from this last comment, but Daniel shrugged it off. He knew they'd find out what the winter's toll had been soon enough. But Nate persisted, finally prompting a response from Daniel.

"And only a crazy man would ride out here with you," Daniel retorted. "You worry enough for the two of us."

Daniel's response didn't stop Nate from worrying, but, as Daniel had hoped, Nate kept it more to himself for the remainder of the ride. Despite Nate's overt worries and Daniel's more subdued anxiety, both men looked forward to the spring roundup. It was an event fraught with possibilities, for more often than not, it demonstrated the remarkable ability of Montana's rangeland to harbor a multitude of livestock through the winter and to produce an abundant crop of calves. Adding to the anticipation was the fact that the roundup provided an opportunity to spend time among old friends, men often isolated from each other through much of the year. For some, that opportunity was just as important as the work itself.

As Daniel and Nate grew closer to the rendezvous point, other groups began to appear, each trailing a string of horses that raised the powdery dust beneath them. The demanding work ahead of them required that each man have more than one mount.

Daniel and Nate greeted many of the men they encountered by name, and each encounter triggered cheerful banter. Some of the men had been with the same outfit as Nate on his long drive from Texas. Like Nate, they had stayed on in Montana, but unlike him, they were all hired hands working for someone else.

"Hey, Nate," one of them called out. "Or should I be calling you boss now?"

"You can knock that off, Lefty," Nate replied with more friendliness than his words implied. "I'm still a cowhand, just like you."

Another of the men wouldn't let it go at that. "Well, none of us own land or livestock. We're saddle tramps and true to the code!"

"Ha!" Nate replied. "Only difference between us is how we spend our money. I guess your code says you need to spend it all on whiskey and women."

Amid general laughter, Nate shook hands with his former trail mates. But they continued to call him boss. Ownership was an important distinction among the cowhands. Though they remained friendly, Nate had unwittingly moved on from the group.

Despite the festive atmosphere at the start of a roundup, it was not a casual affair. In a land with no fences and few natural barriers, several thousand head of cattle left out over the winter could scatter across a vast area. Often, by spring, they were many miles from where their owners had last seen them. It took a well-organized effort to find and to gather so much livestock.

Aside from the cowhands, whose numbers dominated the gathering, a few others were in attendance. These men, who stood out by virtue of their greater girth and softer hands, had instigated the formation of stock associations. They hoped to demonstrate that an association, whose members cooperated on matters of mutual interest, resulted in more profit to everyone than the near anarchy that had prevailed just a few years prior. By the mid-1880s, several of the range areas in Montana had formed stock associations. One of the earliest was the Shonkin Stock Association, which encompassed a vast area south of Fort Benton and served as a model for the fledgling association that Daniel's neighbors were working to form. In addition to organizing the spring and fall round-ups, the associations dealt with a wide range of issues, from fighting range fires to offering rewards for the capture of cattle thieves.

Still, a mass roundup was a relatively new phenomenon in Montana Territory, and strategies for organizing such an effort were still evolving. An important part of that effort was electing a captain, someone with the respect of the cowhands as well as the owners. Once elected, the captain's word was unquestioned and his authority absolute. For inevitably, a variety of decisions would have to be made.

The most important decisions were about ownership. For instance, the captain was charged with determining the ownership of livestock with brands that couldn't be read or that appeared altered in some way. An unbranded calf was assumed to belong to the same outfit as its mother, but sometimes mother-calf pairs became separated. Furthermore, there were always a few animals that somehow had managed to avoid being branded the previous year. These animals, known as mavericks, were the toughest to deal with fairly. Each stock association had a different system for resolving the ownership disputes that often arose.

The first night of the roundup was mostly a social event. A chuck wagon arrived that evening, clattering across the prairie, chock-full of pots and pans and other items that clanked against each other. These ingenious devices were ungainly but a welcome sight to the cow-hands who cheered the chuck wagon's arrival.

"Who's cooking this year?" one of the men asked. "I hope it's not that fat Mexican again. Why, even his pancakes tasted like chili powder!"

"No, it's not him," another man added. "It's Roscoe. Man, we're going to eat well on this roundup!"

Roscoe was a black man who was well known to many of the cowhands. He walked with a pronounced limp, the result of a bad fall he suffered while racing his horse at full speed in a vain attempt to turn a stampede. Roscoe loved the life of a cowhand, so when he was no longer able to ride hard, he took to cooking. Because he was one of them, Roscoe held a status among the cowhands that few cooks could attain.

The men greeted him warmly and gathered around the wagon in anticipation of a well-cooked meal. Soon, Roscoe had a grill set up and the smell of frying steaks filled the air, drawing in the remaining stragglers who lingered in little clusters at the edge of camp.

Most nights, dinner was followed by entertainment around the campfire—a combination of storytelling and singing of camp songs. After settling around the fire, one of the men pulled a battered fiddle from his kit and played a few mournful notes of a favorite tune. Nearly all the men knew the lyrics and several of them joined in, singing each verse with a slow, rhythmic cadence. The song was about the death of a cowboy out on the range, something most of them had witnessed firsthand. The sixth verse always got to Nate.

*I wish to lie where a mother's prayer*
*And a sister's tear will mingle there.*
*Where friends can come and weep o'er me.*
*O bury me not on the lone prairie.*

Daniel was sitting near Nate, who listened to the tune quietly and with an apparent sadness Daniel hadn't previously observed.

"It's just a song, Nate. Did someone you know just die?"

"No, not that I know of. But that tune always reminds me that I've still got family in southern Texas. That's a long way off. I don't know if I'll ever see them again."

Despite Nate's single-minded focus on building a ranch, the song made him realize how profoundly he missed his family.

The morning work would start early, so most of the men bedded down before the last light faded from the sky of a long evening—but not before the captain had circulated among them and made the work assignments for the next day. This year's captain, Stu Baker, worked for one of the larger outfits. Having progressed through several outfits while rising from cowhand to boss, he knew just about everyone who worked the roundup that year. An unremarkable man at first glance, Stu was of medium size like nearly all the other cowhands on the range. Yet he stood out in ways that only an experienced cowhand could really judge.

Stu greeted Daniel and Nate enthusiastically, for though he was taciturn by nature, the spring roundup was the highlight of his year, and it brought out a childlike delight in the man. Then he quickly got down to business. "I'm sending you two out to Grassy Creek tomorrow," he said directly. "There's a bunch of little draws in that area and lots of places for a cow to hide. Pick four men to go with you and pore over that ground. I'm counting on you fellas."

The morning came quickly. Daniel recruited a few men for his crew while clutching a cup of dark, steaming coffee. No one was talkative that early, so the group of six men rode off quietly and maintained their silence for most of the way to Grassy Creek. Nate was more familiar with the area, so he directed the men when they arrived at their assigned spot. The sight of several clusters of cattle shook the men from their early-morning somnolence, and each man gave a yip of excitement as he initiated the pursuit. Many of the animals they pursued had not seen a human for many months, long enough to become skittish and to run at the sight of men mounted on horses. For most of the cowhands, this only added to the excitement. They worked in a carefully coordinated manner, the fastest riders out ahead chasing down the cattle and turning them back toward the roundup point.

As planned, Daniel was in a support role. He helped to keep the gathered animals moving in the right direction while the others, including Nate, did the more challenging work. Occasionally, when he wasn't needed, Daniel watched the others work. "Yahoo!" he yelled almost involuntarily, his tone one of pure delight.

He observed the other cowhands riding at breakneck speeds, turning their horses sharply in movements synchronized with the panicked cattle that struggled to elude them. *It's a ballet of sorts*, Daniel thought, though none of the other men would have viewed it that way. They were too occupied with the demanding task at hand, yet they each felt blessed to be getting paid for doing something they loved to do.

Usually, just the coordinated movements of several horsemen were enough to turn a few cattle determined to flee, but occasionally it took more effort. So it was that day. A large steer, followed by a few cows, bolted away with Nate in hot pursuit. The steer showed no indication of stopping, which forced Nate to use his rope. He came alongside the steer and roped it in full stride. But instead of stopping in place, the steer turned toward Nate and charged, butting his horse and knocking him from the saddle. Nate attempted to scramble away, but the steer kicked him with a glancing blow, leaving Nate sprawled on the ground and helpless before the enraged steer. Determined to eliminate an unfamiliar but obvious threat, the steer lowered its head.

Daniel was the closest man to Nate and saw it all happen. Another man might have tried to stop the threatening steer with his rope, but Daniel wasn't confident in his roping abilities and did the only thing he thought might work. He pushed his horse forward, creating a collision that drove the steer to the side before it could cause further injury to Nate. This tactic saved Nate's life. It provided time for another man to rope the steer around its head, then another to rope the steer's front legs, enabling them to bring the animal down while Daniel scrambled off his horse and dragged Nate out of harm's way.

Nate wasn't badly hurt, though he sported an ugly gash on the side of his head. He was ready to get back to work once someone washed the wound and wrapped it with a bandana to stop the bleeding. At first, Nate acted as if it was just another day on the range, but he later sought Daniel out.

"I'm damned glad you're no good with a rope, Daniel," Nate said with a tone of gratitude. "I'd have tried, and it wouldn't have been enough to stop that goddamn devil steer. I never would have thought to do what you did."

In return, Daniel simply smiled and tipped his hat. That was all the acknowledgment either man expected.

When the men had gathered as many animals as they could comfortably handle, they trailed the cattle back to the corrals at the main camp, a process they repeated several times that day. Daniel couldn't help but notice that not a single animal in the groups they gathered that day bore his bird foot brand. Knowing that other crews might be working in areas where his animals had wandered, he put it out of his mind for a while.

As they approached the corrals at the main camp, Daniel's crew met up with other groups bringing in the animals they had gathered, which prompted some shouting back and forth between each group.

"That's a paltry bunch you've got there, Nate," someone shouted as they passed. Clearly this man was unaware of the nearly fatal events that had transpired in Nate's crew earlier that day. "Those cows must be scared of men as ugly as y'all." The man laughed.

"Anyone can gather cows out in the open," Nate shot back. "The captain sent the real cowhands to Grassy Creek."

The work continued for several more days. Each evening, after the crews came back and the newly wrangled cattle were sorted by brand, Daniel counted the animals that bore his bird foot brand. He mentioned the disappointing numbers to Nate while they ate supper.

"It's early yet, Daniel," Nate replied. "It looks to me like we've had a good survival rate this year. They'll turn up." Several more days passed, but only a few more of Daniel's cattle turned up that year.

Near the end of the roundup, Daniel was exhausted. The hard work had taken a toll on his body, but he was also ready for a respite from all the talk around the chuck wagon. Before supper was served one evening, Daniel sought out a quiet spot and contemplated the landscape around him. From where he sat, the land rolled away to the far horizon in nearly all directions, a vast expanse of short-grass prairie unbroken by rock outcrops or other landforms. It was the purest of landscapes, Daniel thought, a place seemingly unable to hold any secrets.

Yet many of his cattle were still out there, hidden some-how—or, more likely, he had begun to think, his missing livestock had been stolen or were already dead. That day Daniel made an important decision. He'd no longer leave his cattle alone on the range. Instead, he'd make sure the animals he grazed were tended and concentrate even more on increasing the ranch's hay production.

# CHAPTER 30

Sometimes life went slowly and uneventfully on a ranch. So it went in the first part of the summer. Daniel and Nellie continued their usual routines, modified only by the need to spend more time working alongside John in the hay fields. Over time, John had become increasingly important to the operations of the ranch. He not only ran the hay operations but also pitched in where needed, helping Daniel with the fences, and even riding with him when help was needed to move the herd around.

As John and Daniel spent more time together, John became more important to the ranch, and the men's friendship deepened. John frequently joined Daniel and Nellie for dinner. The men had thrown together a little shack for John to stay in when the work on the ranch was more intensive, and John increasingly found the arrangement to his liking. Many of his friends in town had drifted away. They could no longer find work in the building trades now that the boom had subsided.

Over dinner one night, John brought up a proposition. He pulled out a piece of paper from his pocket and carefully unfolded it before handing it to Daniel. "Take a look at this," he said. "I saw this handbill in town yesterday, and it may be the kind of opportunity to expand you've been looking for."

Despite the dry conditions, the ranch's hay production had increased to a point where Daniel had been thinking about expanding the size of his herd. He read the paper carefully. It was an announcement about a ranch that was up for sale due to the death of its owner, who had left only a widow who couldn't handle the place by herself. As Daniel continued reading, he saw that the sale could be done in part or whole, including just the livestock or the entire ranch.

"This looks interesting, John," Daniel responded. "It sounds like they want to make a quick sale. I think we ought to have a look and see what kind of bargain we can make on that livestock."

John agreed to join Daniel. "You know how I ride," John said. "It will take a little longer with me along."

"Yeah, I pity that poor horse hauling you that far," Daniel said with amusement. "I think we better take along an extra mount. You can take one of my horses." Then he got more serious. "Listen, John. That country we're going through is known to have some outlaws. Granville Stuart and the boys haven't finished hanging all the horse thieves. Are you sure you're up for this?"

John nodded. "I'm not worried, Daniel. Maybe I should be, but I'm not."

Actually, Daniel was the one who worried, probably because he knew more than John did about the dangers they might encounter in the mostly unsettled lands they'd be crossing. But he did his best to mask it. "All right, then," Daniel said. "We won't take along much cash. We can pay for anything we buy with a bank note. The widow's ranch is a fair distance off. We should leave not long after sunrise."

The next day, Daniel and John set off in the direction of the widow's ranch. Despite Daniel's urgings to the contrary, John wore his usual outfit, including a narrow-brimmed bowler that provided little relief from the unrelenting sun. John looked exactly like what he was: a tradesman and farmer who had worked with his hands all his life, endeavors that didn't require the gear or dress of a cowhand. He wasn't ready to shed that identity, even though he had embraced a ranching life. The two men were an odd pair making their way across the prairie, for Daniel dressed in full ranchman mode that day. The mismatch would bring consequences.

The terrain they crossed was gentle, and the ride was uneventful for the first few hours. Daniel called the area they crossed the Big Open. Lacking anything else to capture his attention, and lulled by the gentle swaying of his horse, Daniel slipped into a reverie. Here was a place, Daniel thought, that revealed itself to anyone who took the time to look, a place where nothing was concealed. The weather announced itself long in advance of arriving. In summer, thunderheads built to towering heights before dropping leaden drops that hit the earth with a powerful force. Winter brought low clouds that quietly slipped down the distant mountain slopes, advanced steadily across the prairie, and left a stark whiteness in their wake. All who entered this land, Daniel thought, shared a naked visibility that demanded a certain level of caution. Despite the worry he felt about their undertaking, Daniel didn't become aware of the threat they faced until it was too late. Unknown to both men, they were being watched.

Near midday, John announced that he needed a rest.

Daniel laughed. "Your horse needs one more than you do," he teased.

They switched their saddles over to the spare horses they were trailing and then sat quietly for a few minutes.

After the men resumed their ride, the setting remained much the same for another mile or so. Soon, though, they neared an area with some low hills. Unexpectedly, a lone rider approached, still at a distance when they first spotted him, but he was clearly headed toward them. The rider moved slowly and without any apparent intent, and he stopped when he was within earshot of Daniel and John. Daniel said quietly that he didn't like the feel of the situation.

John was less worried than Daniel, so he offered up a friendly greeting: "Nice to meet a fellow traveler way out here. What brings you here?"

The rider answered with equal politeness. "The pleasure is mine. I've got a ranch on the other side of those hills, and I'm looking for some strays. I guess I could ask you the same question."

John continued to do the talking, while Daniel looked around, alert to any signs of something not being right. John hesitated before answering. He thought it best to avoid mentioning their true purpose until he had a better grasp of the man they were dealing with.

"Same as you, friend," John replied. "We heard along the way that someone had spotted a few head moving in this direction."

"Well, I haven't seen nothing, but I'll let you know if I do," the man said. "Sometimes I think I spend half my damned time chasing after strays."

John found the exchange reassuring. He began to move closer so that he could continue the conversation without yelling. Daniel remained anxious and looked around carefully but saw nothing to add to his worries. Reluctantly, Daniel moved forward with John, an act the other man reciprocated by moving in himself. Now in close proximity, the three mounted men talked about the weather and other routine topics that ranch men often talk about. Even Daniel admitted to himself that the stranger was pleasant.

The men talked uneventfully for several minutes before Daniel sensed something amiss. He turned around slowly and was dismayed by the sight of three men approaching on foot, each with a rifle pointing in Daniel's direction. They had obviously concealed themselves behind the low-growing shrubs that had become abundant as they had neared the hills. The men had emerged from hiding once they were sure the distraction provided by the lone rider had served its purpose.

Daniel and John said nothing at first, each straining to come up with the right move. Despite his anxiety, Daniel remained calm. He was determined to wait and see how the situation played out before reacting. John, meanwhile, became angry and more agitated by the second. His instincts demanded that he do something quickly, more to protect Daniel than to save himself. Yet he now feared that he had hesitated too long and allowed the three men to get close enough for a sure kill shot.

Sensing John's edginess, one of the men who had emerged from hiding moved up quickly behind John's horse and stuck a rifle against his back. "Get down off that horse," the outlaw commanded. John obeyed and stood there, the fear rising in his throat and producing a bitter taste. The outlaw, a small man who was dwarfed by John, sized him up.

"Look what we have here, boys," the much smaller man sneered. "I'll bet he's a Canadian. Only a goddamned Canadian would wear a stupid hat like that out here."

Without thinking, John acknowledged that he was from Canada, a response that seemed to anger the man further.

"Well, just like I thought!" the outlaw yelled. "They pile the shit high in Canada, boys." He knocked John's hat off and gleefully stomped it into the ground with the heel of his boot.

It was too much for John to take. Before anyone could react, John grabbed the small man by the throat and held him aloft, choking the life from the despicable character in front of him and the threat he represented. A third man, who had moved behind John, quickly came to his partner's rescue by clubbing John with a rifle, toppling him immediately and drawing blood from a blow just behind John's ear.

The small outlaw said nothing at first. Instead, he rubbed his throat and twisted his head from side to side to see if John's powerful grip had caused any real damage. Satisfied he was all right and that John was no longer a threat, he spoke to the group. "I don't like Canadians. We had a good thing going, selling whiskey to the Indians. But then the goddamn redcoats showed up, and a man couldn't make an honest living anymore. I'd like to bust them all in the head!" For good measure, the man then kicked John hard in the side. This elicited a moan from John, who lay sprawled out in the dirt.

"Why don't you kill that bastard, Bill?" one of the outlaws yelled to the small man. "He's got it coming."

"Maybe he does," Bill replied as he pointed his rifle at John. He then turned to Daniel and confronted him with a chilling expression that conveyed the man's quickly mounting rage.

"What do you think?" Bill shouted to Daniel. "Don't you think it's only fair that I kill a man who tried to choke me to death with his bare hands?"

Daniel, who remained in the saddle, could feel their chances of escaping slipping away. After a brief hesitation, he replied. "Right now we're talking about a simple crime being committed. I've talked to the sheriff," Daniel lied. "He's buried with cases involving horse thefts. You leave things like they are now, and you won't be hearing from the law anytime soon."

"I reckon we won't," Bill said with a grin. "I also reckon I could kill you both without much worry. It's a big country out here."

"I'll grant you that," Daniel acknowledged. "But there's a lot of people who know we were headed here to buy some cattle. If they don't hear from us soon, I can guarantee the sheriff will take notice."

The sheriff of Chouteau County had a well-earned reputation for tracking down killers, especially when it involved a rancher or one of his men. Daniel's warning was enough to make Bill hesitate, for he knew there'd be a price to pay for a murderous rage. He contemplated this reality for a moment before responding.

"That dumb-shit lawman couldn't find his butt in broad daylight," he yelled.

It was a calculated performance intended to divert the attention of the other outlaws and give him a little more time to think the situation through. As he expected, the other outlaws laughed in unison and a few added their own observations about how inept the lawmen were. Bill continued to concentrate, fighting an urge to kill the son of a bitch who had dared to cross him.

The outlaws were all ordinary-looking men, except for Bill, who seemed to be the leader of the group. He had deep scars across both of his cheeks, and a small piece of his nose was missing. They were the kind of scars that didn't come from an accident and could make it difficult for a man to live a regular life in town. Years of experiencing children pointing him out and women turn-ing their gaze at the sight of his face had driven him away from normal society. His disfigurement had also brought out the cruelty that is hidden deep in some men but is ready to emerge under the right circumstances. Bill had long lived among outlaws and had honed his deadly craft among them. He had turned his violent tendencies and the fear they evoked into an advantage.

Daniel, shocked by the sudden violence and now fearful for his life, watched the scene unfolding before him in silence. He had been in dangerous situations before, but this was different. During his first encounter with the Blackfoot, when he was new to the territory and unfamiliar with the circumstances he faced, his ignorance had been a shield. He hadn't known what to expect then but feared he did now. *These men are simple outlaws*, Daniel thought, *the kind that flourish in a territory with vast spaces and few lawmen*. The men he now confronted, and others like them, formed loosely organized bands and hid out in the Missouri River Breaks and other remote places beyond the reach of the law. They had earned a reputation for violence, often among themselves, but on occasion it involved innocent victims, particularly those who offered resistance.

With this reputation in mind, and the threat of more violence hanging in the air, Daniel turned to Bill and spoke some carefully chosen words. "Well, it's clear you boys have the upper hand. I suggest you just take what you want and leave me to look after my friend."

Bill, now fully asserting his leadership of the group, stared at Daniel in silence before moving toward him. Daniel looked at the outlaw closely as he approached and noticed that the man's eyes conveyed no emotions. *It's like looking into the eyes of a wolf*, Daniel thought. Ignoring Daniel's reaction to his approach, the little outlaw jabbed Daniel hard in the ribs with a rifle butt and demanded that he dismount. Daniel complied, wincing in pain as he swung his leg over the saddle. The outlaws took Daniel's weapons and searched his pockets. Then they did the same to John, who still lay unconscious. After taking the reins of both horses, they turned to Daniel with a final order. "Take off your boots and those of your friend. We don't want you two getting anywhere quick."

Those words brought Daniel the first hope that they might survive. Daniel took off his boots and then John's. He was encouraged by John's moaning as he pulled off the boots that had tightened around John's feet, swollen from the heat of the day. The outlaws took the boots along with their other possessions. Before they left, Bill warned Daniel that if either of them tried to follow, or if they ever tried to look for him, he'd kill them on the spot. "It doesn't take much to make me want to kill a man," he said. "I suggest you not try to find out how little."

The outlaws rode off quickly, their boisterous laughter trailing them. Aside from killing a man when they thought it had to be done, nothing excited the outlaws more than the sense of conquest they felt after a successful heist. It was what kept them going, and any man who didn't feel that way would soon find out that he was with the wrong band. It was an expected behavior among the group to celebrate their success, which each man demonstrated with a whoop as he rode off.

When John awoke not long after the outlaws left, he was groggy but recovered his wits pretty quickly. Daniel was relieved by John's fast recovery and could see that the cut from the blow to his head would heal readily if kept clean. Daniel was probably feeling as much pain as John, for he felt a nearly constant throbbing in his ribs, and he experienced a jolting pain if he moved the wrong way or breathed too hard. Yet the absurdity of being out in the middle of nowhere, barefoot and without their horses, struck Daniel as weirdly amusing. The realization that they had survived a potentially deadly encounter, and were now likely out of danger, brought out a surge of emotion. Sometimes the line separating joy and pain is thin. Despite his pain and the property losses they had suffered, the fact that he and John had survived emerged in Daniel as a kind of joy.

"Look at us, John," he said. "We're not worth a damn to anybody. Some heroes we turned out to be."

John didn't know how to react to Daniel's statement, perhaps because he was still in the process of regaining his senses, but Daniel laughed aloud, clutching his ribs as tears of hilarity mixed with pain dripped down his cheeks.

Daniel's laughter was contagious, and John briefly overcame the pain and anger that lingered in his soul.

When their laughter died down, John said, "I still think I should have pulled my gun on them when I had a chance." Probably realizing the ridiculousness of what he was about to say, he continued, "At least I'd have tried…well, to keep some of my dignity."

Daniel responded quickly. "Is your dignity worth your life? Hell, you would have got both of us killed. There's nothing you could have done, and there's no loss of dignity in that."

John wasn't quite ready to accept Daniel's statement as truth, and darker emotions quickly overcame the laughter he had let himself share with Daniel.

As John continued his brooding, Daniel changed the subject. "Well, what do we do now? I figure it's pretty far either way we go, and I'd rather wear out my feet getting to the widow's place than accomplishing nothing at all, especially at the expense of losing our horses and gear."

Putting aside his sullenness, John agreed. "We'd better hope that widow has some horses to sell. I'm not much for walking."

"Me neither," Daniel replied, "but that's what we've got to do now. I'm hoping just as much that the widow's late husband has some boots we can fit into!"

John smiled meekly. Daniel took it as a good sign but suppressed an urge to lighten the mood further by bringing on more laughter, which he knew would be physically painful for both of them.

They set off across the prairie and dodged prickly pear and sharp rocks as they wove an unsteady path toward the widow's place. John began to tire and stumbled slightly, planting his foot squarely on a cactus. He yelped in pain before sitting down. "Goddammit, as if we didn't have enough trouble already. Now I've got a foot full of spines and we've still got miles to go."

Blood trickled from John's foot as he plucked out some of the spines, but many were beyond his reach. After a minute, he lay back in frustration, raging against all that had happened that day.

"Easy now, John. Let me help with that." Daniel grasped John's stricken foot and patiently plucked the embedded spines. The bigger spines were easy to pull, but some were finer with a texture more like human hair. These were hard to find but became irritating if left embedded. Once satisfied that he had removed most of the spines, Daniel urged that they move on. "It's not far now," he said with certainty even though he really didn't know how far they still had to go. "Before you know it, we'll be at the widow's place, soaking our feet in cold water and eating a home-cooked meal."

As John forced himself to stand, he muttered something Daniel could barely hear. "I hope you're right. That would be the first good thing to happen this whole blasted day."

Despite the slow and careful pace their bare feet demanded, gusty winds swirled the dust around them and coated their throats with a fine powder that sucked the moisture from their bodies. They had no water to drink, which remained with the stolen horses, and the parched land offered no streams or other water sources on the many miles they crossed.

Thankfully, the afternoon was fading to evening and the temperature was dropping as they moved ahead. Still, their throats were painfully dry, making it hard first to swallow and then to talk. Daniel spotted the house first and had to spit out some dust to speak clearly. "Look ahead there. See that little clump of trees? I think there's a house among them."

Another mile of trudging across the brittle grasslands brought them to the widow's ranch. She had seen them approaching and was unsure what to make of the two bedraggled men, who walked unsteadily toward her house. She greeted them with a shotgun cradled in her arms. The woman appeared to be close to middle age and was plainly dressed, yet her full figure projected an unmistakable femininity.

When they were within shouting distance, Daniel paused and tried to explain their predicament.

"Evening, ma'am," he began. "I hope you can look past our appearance. We're a couple of ranchmen who met up with some outlaws on our way to your place. They took our horses and everything else we had with us. Could you spare us some water?"

The woman remained suspicious and continued to look over the two men, searching for some sign of normalcy that would reinforce Daniel's story. Seeing none, she asked for more information. "Where are you two from, and what brings you this way?"

"We both ranch along the Teton River," Daniel replied, "not far from Fort Benton. We came to buy some cattle. Now I think we'll be needing some horses too."

The last comment lowered the woman's suspicions and brought a slight smile to her face. She knew that her handbills had been posted in Fort Benton and decided that no one would stage such a misfortune as these men had endured. They were covered with dust and obviously sore from whatever experience they'd had.

"The well is out back," the woman said in a voice still edged with wariness. "You can clean yourselves up there and drink as much water as you need. Come back to the house when you're done, and we'll talk some more."

Daniel and John thanked her and shuffled over to the well, their sore feet having reached a new threshold of pain that brought a grimace with each step. After slaking their thirst, they rinsed themselves off, splashing water on their dried-out skin and washing the blood off their tender feet. The water was cool and invigorating. When they were finished, they returned to the house, where the woman greeted them again before they knocked. She was holding some clean clothes and two pairs of shoes.

"Here, try these on," the woman directed. "My husband was about your size," she said, pointing toward Daniel. "The bigger one, well, you just might have to keep your buttons loose."

Grateful for the assistance, Daniel and John trudged off again. Because of the pain in their feet, they didn't want to go any farther than they had to while remaining hidden from sight of the house. Behind the closest shed, they stripped off their grimy clothes and tried on the clothes of the widow's dead husband. The clothes would do, though neither man felt comfortable in them. But best of all, the shoes fit well.

When Daniel and John returned to the house, the widow looked them over and commented on their improved appearance.

"You two look pretty near presentable. When you

first turned up, I didn't know whether to try and scare you off with a shot over your heads or run away myself." She laughed before adding, "I figured I could at least outrun you both with those sore feet you limped in on."

Daniel agreed that she could have outrun them. "But I'm awful glad that you didn't," he said. "You're the angel we hoped to find."

The woman laughed loudly at Daniel's comment and followed it up with an offer to come inside and join her for supper. Going directly to the kitchen, she left Daniel and John to look around the small parlor. Each man was curious to glean something about the woman and the life she had led with her husband. The tidy, carefully arranged room didn't offer many clues, except for a framed photograph depicting a man they took to be the widow's husband. The man was dressed in the uniform of a Confederate soldier and brandished the weapons common to the day, a pistol and dagger held across his chest. Both Daniel and John had the same reaction, which they kept to themselves: either they hadn't judged the widow's age very well, or the woman had married an older man. Although it was of no particular importance, both men were curious about the widow and motivated by a simple desire to enrich the conversation over the dinner they were about to begin.

Once the food preparation was complete, the woman invited them to the table. Her first words were direct: "I think it's time we were properly introduced. I'm Jenny Sprout. And who might you two men be?"

After Daniel and John introduced themselves, Jenny requested a full account of the day. When they were finished, Jenny commented that they were lucky to be alive. "I've heard of that man with the scars," she said. "He's a known killer. But I'm surprised he turned up here. I hear he usually hangs out farther east in the breaks country."

She then turned to John with a question. "Where are you from originally? You don't sound like you're from the West."

John said, "I'm from Canada. Nova Scotia, to be more specific."

"I don't know much about Canada," Jenny admitted. "I'm from Texas. Canada always seemed a long way off to me. What's it like there?"

John stumbled for words as he offered up a description. "I can only tell you what the eastern part is like. There's lots of trees, and the ocean is never far away. It's probably like trying to describe Texas—it's a big place, and each part is different."

Jenny probed more about Canada for a few minutes, and Daniel and John tried to offer some insights about how their country was different from the United States.

"Well, for one thing," Daniel offered, "we still swear allegiance to the queen. There's a lot of British customs that linger—"

Just then John broke in with a vocal burst, delivered with a bit of theatrical flair:

> "'From every latent foe
> From the assassins blow
> God save the queen!'"

Slightly puzzled by John's performance, Jenny looked on in amusement. She hesitated briefly before deciding it was all right to laugh, and the men validated her decision by joining in, even though the pain in Daniel's ribs remained. He did his best to ignore it, but the pain turned his brief smile into a grimace.

Jenny noted Daniel's discomfort, but he brushed it away and steered the conversation in a different direction:

he made a point of letting Jenny know that John was a single man.

Jenny seemed to take the news nonchalantly, but then she opened up more. "I don't think we ever lose all the ties with where we're from. I've still got family in Texas and don't have any up here. But I don't want to go back. Montana is the place for me now. Yet, I don't see how I can stay. I sure can't stay here alone on this ranch."

John couldn't resist a response, even though he feared it would be awkward. "Forgive me if I'm being too forward," he said, "but there must be men around here who could help you with the ranch. Maybe you could hold on for a while."

Jenny took John's statement in stride and answered directly. "If you mean men I could hire," Jenny said, "you're right about that. There's a lot more men in this country than there are women. But what kind of life would that be? I need more than a hired hand."

John took the bait and ventured a response. "Well, couldn't some of these men be more than a hired hand?"

Jenny smiled briefly. "Well, there's one problem. Most of the cowboys around here are just boys, and the older ones are too far gone with their wild ways to ever want to settle down." Indicating that she didn't want to pursue that line of conversation any further, she assumed a weary look and returned to the matters of the day. "Let me have a closer look at that cut on your head," she said, looking directly at John. "I think it should be cleaned off before it gets infected."

John protested briefly, pointing out that he had cleaned it off himself when they were at the well.

"I'll bet you did," Jenny said, a faint smile returning to her face. "But there's men's clean and real clean. I think we need the real clean."

Jenny and John removed to the kitchen, where Jenny

tended to the cut by tenderly cleaning it with a cloth and some soap. They left Daniel alone at the dinner table for what seemed to be a longer time than needed.

Before the night ended, Jenny looked after Daniel as well. She convinced him that a tight wrap around his torso would reduce the pain in his ribs. Not long after finishing up with Daniel, Jenny politely dismissed the two men by directing them to one of the sheds behind the house.

"We can talk about our business in the morning," she called as Daniel and John made their way across the yard.

Once they settled in for the night, Daniel asked what John and the woman had talked about in the kitchen. John was reluctant to talk at first, but he opened up under Daniel's insistent questioning.

"She's a nice woman, Daniel. I think you can see that. But she's had a hard time lately. That man in the picture was her husband, and he'd been sickly for the last few years. He finally just went and died on her, some kind of trouble with his heart." John went on to say that Jenny seemed resigned to her fate and expected that she'd have to go back to Texas, where she could at least count on her family.

Daniel had only one comment to offer John before turning over to sleep. "You keep telling me that you like being a single man," Daniel said, "but I think you don't even know what you're missing. You could do a whole lot worse than finding a woman like Jenny to be with."

John tried to brush off Daniel's words and kicked him gently in the backside before saying goodnight. But John didn't sleep well that night and thought about Jenny more than he was ready to admit.

The next morning Jenny served up breakfast in the small dining room. She appeared younger in the morning light, and her demeanor had changed. Whether it was the result of being less worried about the intentions of her guests, or of careful grooming, the effect was notable. She looked different than the day before and was clearly much younger than her late husband, the Confederate soldier in the photo. Although Jenny remained polite to both men, Daniel was pleased to see that she focused more on John.

"John, what did you do before working on the ranch with Daniel?"

"I was a carpenter until I busted up my right hand in a fall."

Jenny expressed concern and moved across the room to take John's hand. "Let me see. Do you feel any pain from it now?"

"It gets stiff now and then, but there's not much pain unless I've really worked it hard."

Jenny continued to gently rub John's hand, who felt slightly embarrassed by what seemed to him a form of intimacy that made him uncomfortable in front of Daniel. "I hope I'm not being too forward, but I'm known around here as a healer. I just can't help myself when I see someone with an injury."

Whether it was from Jenny's attentions or from a slowly dawning realization that he was lucky to have survived an encounter with a band of known killers, John's mood noticeably brightened that morning. Daniel figured it had more to do with Jenny.

When it was time to get down to business, Jenny's persona changed again, and she bluntly stated her price for the herd. Her figure was much higher than the price Daniel expected to pay. Though neither man was inclined to take advantage of Jenny, who had kindly received two strangers under duress, they had come a long way looking for a bargain and had already paid a high price on this venture. Their gratitude wasn't enough to dispose Daniel toward the price Jenny first put forward.

Daniel shook his head gently, looking for the right words. "I'm sorry, Jenny, but that's more than I can afford. Why, it's even more than what we'd pay in Fort Benton. We could have saved a whole lot of trouble by staying home and buying there."

Jenny sighed aloud while mulling over this information for a few minutes. An awkward silence hung heavily in the room. "Look at it this way," Jenny finally said. "I need to get a fair price for the herd, and I just can't bear to be taken advantage of again." She said this with a sigh of resignation. "You two have no idea what I've had to deal with these past months. I have many regrets about some of the things I've done, like selling belongings for a fraction of their value just to feel like I could move on."

Jenny managed to avoid shedding the tears that seemed to be building, but her statement had an effect nonetheless.

"Look," Daniel said, "I don't want to take advantage of your situation. I'm just a small rancher trying to get a start myself. There's got to be a way we can work something out that's fair to us both."

More bargaining ensued, and in the end, they met in the middle. Daniel purchased the entire herd for a price they agreed was fair under the circumstances.

John had remained silent through much of the bargaining, but when it was over he pointed out that they had one more item of business. "We need some horses. I've had my fill of walking for a while."

Jenny was happy to oblige. "I've sold some horses already, but there's a few left. Let me show you what I've got."

She led them out to the corral where several horses milled around. They were an odd lot. "This one's more of a work horse than a saddle horse. But he'll get you home.

John, this might be a good choice for that big frame of yours."

John nodded in agreement but took his time deciding. He looked them all over carefully and put several through their paces before selecting one, the horse Jenny had initially offered. John might have had another motive for his dallying, however. As the afternoon shadows lengthened, Jenny made them another offer.

"You won't get far this late," she said. "I don't think you should be pushing the herd in the dark. Those outlaws might still be out there, and you need to be careful."

Jenny clinched the deal by offering them another home-cooked meal. It was the opportunity John had wished for. Daniel did his best to stay out of the way but contributed to the conversation now and then, usually in a manner that put John in a positive light. As the evening wore on, Daniel was sure he could detect warmth emerging between John and Jenny, due to the simple fact that he hadn't seen either of them smile or laugh quite so much before. Despite their best efforts to be polite, John and Jenny focused their attention on each other, a slight Daniel gladly accepted.

The next day Daniel and John awoke early to leave for home. They lingered briefly in the faint light of dawn with Jenny, who emerged before they left and greeted them with freshly baked biscuits. As they prepared to leave, Jenny told them she needed time to settle her affairs, but she planned to return to Texas before winter set in. Her journey would take her through Fort Benton. After this announcement, Jenny made an innocent request. Her words were something John would savor all the way back to Fort Benton. "Would you mind if I look you two up when I'm in Fort Benton?" she asked sweetly. "It would be nice to see someone I've come to know here before leaving Montana for good."

Both men quickly said that they'd enjoy an opportunity to return Jenny's hospitality. But it was John who said, "I'll be eagerly awaiting your arrival."

John was slightly embarrassed by his comment, but Jenny's response, a warm and prolonged smile, alleviated his concern.

After gathering up the livestock they had just purchased, Daniel and John pointed the animals toward the Teton. On the way back, they were especially cautious and stayed alert for any signs of trouble. One man took point, riding ahead of the herd, while the other stayed back and kept the herd moving, breathing the dust that penetrated the cloth he used to cover his mouth and nose. Despite rotating positions along the way, they were worn out and coughing up dark spit by the time they reached the Teton.

The bitterness both men felt at the losses they had suffered and the harshness of the treatment they had endured lingered for a while after Daniel and John's return. But the bitterness quickly gave way to recognition of the reality that a lot of work lay ahead: the Raven Ranch now had a larger herd to manage.

Their bitterness was also replaced by the realization that they were lucky to be alive. As Daniel and John parted company, Daniel pointed out, "John, dead men don't have dreams."

Although his effort at humor failed, Daniel's statement lingered. Both men had a deeper realization that they had limited time available to pursue their dreams. After that night, Daniel and John rarely discussed the robbery incident. Instead, they talked about their dreams.

# CHAPTER 31

For most of the fall, John waited patiently for some word from Jenny. He refrained from talking about her because he thought it might jinx things. After hearing nothing for over two months, John began to think she had left for Texas already. Finally, he broached the subject as he and Daniel took a break from working to repair one of the ranch gates. "I didn't figure Jenny as someone who would change her plans so easily," he said to Daniel with a feigned nonchalance. "Do you think she might have left for Texas already?"

Daniel replied that he hadn't heard a thing either, so he couldn't know for sure. But he agreed with John that Jenny didn't seem fickle. "My hunch is that the business of closing out her affairs just took longer than anticipated," Daniel said. "This bad weather isn't helping either. She'll come by, John. I don't think you have to worry about her finding someone else."

Now John was a little sorry that he had asked. He didn't try to hide his interest in Jenny around Daniel and Nellie, but he didn't want to wear it like a badge. In truth, John hadn't fully come to terms with the conflict between his determination to stay unattached and his attraction to

Jenny. It seemed obvious that she was the kind of woman who didn't come around very often, and these competing priorities made him feel uncomfortable. He decided it was best not to share these emotions, not even around Daniel.

The fall roundup that year provided a much-needed diversion for John. Though they thought it unlikely that many of their cattle were still out on the range, the Raven Ranch's poor results at the spring roundup made them think that they might recover at least a few head that had been missed earlier. Either way, the prospect of getting away for a few days and recovering some of their livestock appealed to both men.

As expected, their attendance at the roundup was a pleasant diversion, which succeeded at taking John's mind off Jenny for a while. Otherwise, though, the roundup was a failure, for only a few head bearing the Raven Ranch brand turned up. But something important did occur. Near the end of the roundup, as they sat by the campfire before turning in for the night, Daniel made an offer that would change both men's lives profoundly.

"John, I don't think I can run the ranch anymore without you," Daniel began. "I've already talked to Nellie about it. We think you ought to be a partner in the ranch. What do you think?"

John was taken aback, but he quickly agreed. He added that he didn't have a lot of money to put in, but he had saved some. "I'll put every last cent I have in this ranch," he said, "and I'd consider it an honor to be your partner."

Daniel was pleased by John's response. "I think your investment would help us grow," he said. "But it's more important to me that I have your help and support." He couldn't let things get too serious, so he brought up an old memory. "Do you remember that day on the *Red*

*Cloud,* when you told me that coming west might be the biggest mistake you'd ever made?" With a laugh, Daniel said, "I think you might have had that wrong, John. We both did."

He then reached out and shook John's hand vigorously. From that day forward, the McHargs and John Campbell were equal partners in the Raven Ranch.

# CHAPTER 32

Near Thanksgiving, Jenny appeared at the Raven Ranch. She rode out alone through the snowy roads, which had begun to clear, but the melting left them muddy and an occasional drift made travel difficult. Jenny fretted about her appearance that day. She wanted to make a good impression when she showed up at the house and met Nellie for the first time. But by the time she reached the ranch, Jenny was dismayed to see that the outer layers of her clothing were heavily spotted with mud. Wondering if it would be better to return on another day, she hesitated before approaching the house. As she paused Nellie spotted her, hailed her from the porch, and urged that she come up to the house. As usual, Daniel and John were off spreading hay.

The arrival of a solitary and unknown woman at the ranch was a rare occurrence, so Nellie immediately assumed it was Jenny. Still, she was surprised that anyone would arrive that late in the day and at a time when travel conditions were difficult.

"I've got a pretty good guess that you're Jenny," Nellie said. "We've all been waiting to hear from you, and I'm so glad you made it."

Jenny tied up her horse and walked over to the house. Looking down, she inspected her clothing as if she were out on a night on the town. Hoping to allay Jenny's concerns about her appearance, Nellie invited her in. "Don't worry about that mud," Nellie assured Jenny. "You should see me after I've been out in the hayfields. That's just how it is around here."

Still, Jenny showed some reluctance. "I'm such a mess, and I don't want to soil your living room. I should just go back to town. But please tell John and Daniel that I came by."

Nellie wouldn't hear of it. She tried another tack. "Listen, Jenny, you invited my husband into your house when he needed help. Daniel tells me that he and John were a sight to give pause to anyone, but you welcomed them with kindness. I'm very grateful for that, and I'm not going to turn you away because of a little mud. Please come inside."

Jenny relented and began to feel that Nellie's welcome was genuine. She also thought, even more than before, that Nellie was someone she'd like to get to know better. Jenny took off her coat and brushed the mud off her dress.

"I can see that I've met my match in you," Jenny said happily. "I'm so glad for the opportunity to get to know you."

Once inside, Nellie made some tea and urged Jenny to sit by the fireplace. The two women took an immediate liking to each other, sharing the bond of having been married to a ranching life and the common experience of pushing against the boundaries of how women were supposed to live. After chatting for a while, Jenny said she should leave. Nellie insisted she stay the night, however, and they were having a polite standoff when Daniel returned. His arrival broke the standoff, for Daniel's additional persuasion settled the matter. He left again almost immediately and promised to return with John in time for dinner. While the men were gone, Nellie and Jenny retreated to the bedroom, where Nellie insisted Jenny try on some of her clothes as they prepared for the evening.

When he arrived at John's cabin, Daniel said nothing of Jenny's arrival but urged his friend to spiff himself up. It was a proposition John found absurd, given the weather and the time of day.

Noting John's uncertainty, Daniel added, "We've got company, John. I think it's someone you might like to see."

John was intrigued, but he didn't dare to think it could be Jenny, someone he was now sure he'd never see again.

"Don't joke with me, Daniel," John said with a smile. But his words had an edge that reflected the anxiousness he had begun to feel. "You know I've been hoping Jenny would come here on her way to Texas. I'll be more than a little put out if that's not the news you came with."

"Rest easy, my friend," Daniel said with a mischievous smile. "I wouldn't do that to you. Jenny is here, and you need to get ready to see her!" He added that Nellie was fixing dinner and Jenny would stay the night at their place.

"Well, she took her time getting here," John said. He was still slow to accept the news. "What took her so long?"

"I don't know all the details," Daniel replied. "You can ask her yourself soon enough. I only know she ran into some troubles proving up the title on the ranch."

As the reality of Jenny's arrival settled in, John tried to hide his excitement, but his expression revealed his true feelings. He quickly changed into some clean clothes and slicked down his hair with pomade. Before leaving, he asked Daniel for his advice on what he should do. Daniel had noted John's ambivalence on the matter but thought John was fooling himself and was afraid to listen to his heart. Plus, he thought John and Jenny would be a good match. The advice he offered was direct.

"That woman has her pride," Daniel said. "She won't do anything she deems rash or improper. You need to give her a reason to stay, and you need to do it soon."

That night, a real courtship began. It didn't start perfectly. Neither John nor Jenny knew the proper way to handle the situation. But their feelings became clear that night, and it took only a little encouragement from John to convince Jenny to delay her departure to Texas. She took a room in Fort Benton and remained there for the winter.

# CHAPTER 33

*I do not apprehend a hard winter on cattle. It may be cold, but it is the heavy snow storms we have to fear, and I don't think we will have them. ~ stockman interviewed in the* River Press, *September 22, 1886*

The dry conditions that had begun the previous year continued into the summer. The range greened up only briefly and was dried out and brown by early summer. Everyone had to work harder than usual, it seemed. Daniel and John had to move the cattle more often to find fresh grass, and the need to bring new areas into hay production added to the burden. It was a pleasant relief, therefore, when Helen Sage, Nellie's younger sister, sent word that she was planning a visit. Helen was a teacher in one of Montana Territory's newly organized mining districts, which was far enough away that the two sisters didn't see each other but once or twice each year.

On the day of Helen's arrival, Nellie drove a buckboard into Fort Benton to pick her up. As she closed the Raven Ranch gate and left that afternoon, Nellie noted that in contrast to the summer's dryness, dark clouds were building to the west. Helen's stage arrived on schedule. Making a racket as it rolled up the street, the stage maintained a brisk pace until it made a hard stop in front of the bank. Rather than waiting for the driver, Helen opened the door, jumped down without assistance, and ran over to embrace her sister. While the driver unloaded Helen's heavy trunk, the two sisters chatted amiably. They paused only briefly to gaze up at the increasingly darkening sky.

"It will blow over," Nellie assured Helen. "We've had these clouds lots of times this summer, and nothing ever happens. It's so dry that the rain evaporates before it hits the ground."

But not that day. The skies opened up near the half-way point on the road back to the ranch and sent down big drops that struck the two women with a stinging force. The ranch buckboard, a utilitarian vehicle built for hauling hay and heavy loads, lacked a canopy or other form of shelter. Neither did the land around them offer protection; on the treeless plain they were starkly exposed to whatever forces the weather brought. Undeterred, and laughing together at Nellie's complete failure as a weather prognosticator, the two sisters pushed ahead, struggling in vain to shelter themselves with Helen's dainty parasol. Even in summer, a short burst of rain from a Montana thunderstorm could cool the air quickly, and the women got chilled and muddy on the ride back to the ranch. Still, they laughed often. Nothing could spoil the joy they felt at each reunion.

After arriving home and briefly greeting Daniel, Nellie insisted that her sister warm up with a bath. Although the sisters were close in age, Helen remained the "baby" of the family in Nellie's eyes, and she was still a bit protective of her. Nellie set about heating water on the stove and dragged her little bathtub into the kitchen. Helen dutifully sat in the tub while Nellie poured warm water over her shoulders. They formed little animal sculptures with the soapsuds, just as they had when they were children in St. Louis. Daniel was banished from the house while this went on, but he lingered close by, as he was eager to be summoned back so he could join in on the good conversation that always flowed when the Sage girls were together.

After dinner and a few remaining chores, the group gathered in the parlor.

Nellie's small but treasured upright piano, which was usually covered to protect it from the incessant dust, was quickly put to use. Daniel watched with delight as the sisters, both talented musicians, played a series of songs, starting with solos and moving into duets as the evening progressed. They began with a few classic compositions, which were a warm-up for the popular songs that followed. Neither woman felt it appropriate to meddle with the classics, but they often supplemented their well-established routine of popular songs with improvised lyrics that fit the occasion.

One of their favorites was a song called "I Wish That I'd Been Born a Boy." They played the song straight until they finished the final verse, which they sang with contagious enthusiasm:

> "'Yes, if I had been born a boy
> All insults I'd repel,
> And there's some fellows that I know
> I'd like to thrash right well.'"

Daniel cast a mock worried look at the two sisters before they resumed the music, this time improvising:

> "Yes, if I had been born like Daniel
> I'd have a great big smile,

> And walk around in big tall boots
> Like I'd been a cowboy all the while.'"

It got sillier from there, and they all had fun. Before the night ended, Daniel joined in on the singing, even though he had a famously awful voice. As they prepared to go to bed, they heard a chorus of wolves in the far distance. Helen joked that Daniel's singing must have brought them on. Daniel laughed in response, but it masked the reality of his feelings—the unavoidable worry he felt anytime a wolf pack was close enough to be heard.

The next day, trying hard not to awake Nellie or Helen, Daniel returned to his routine and left early. He stepped carefully through the house and waited until he was outside to put on his boots—the tall boots that had inspired gleeful laughter just hours earlier. Smiling to himself at the evening's memories, he headed for the barn and gathered the tools he needed for the day. The rain from the previous day had hopscotched across the prairie in a random fashion and had missed the ranch entirely. When Daniel arrived at the hay fields, John was already busying himself with checking the flow of water and unclogging the little furrows that spread water evenly across the field. Daniel greeted him with a shake of his head and a lament:

"What are we doing wrong, John? Nellie got soaked yesterday coming back from town, and here we are still dry as a bone."

John had no answer. He just continued his work with the shovel. Daniel and John spent most of the morning moving water into the field. They got covered with mud but enjoyed the sensual feeling of working the earth and watching the precious water sink into the soil.

At midday, Daniel and John headed back to the house, where a pleasant sight greeted them. Nellie and Helen had set out a table outdoors, under the tall trees that stood just outside the house. It had become a warm day, and the shade of the cottonwoods beckoned the men to the table, which was set with a white tablecloth and a pitcher of cold water drawn from the well. The men hurriedly cleaned themselves up and slaked their thirst while the women busied themselves with bringing food from the kitchen and serving the meal. The setting felt idyllic that day. It was one of those times when the world didn't seem so harsh and the possibility of winter returning was an absurdity. Although they were already preparing for winter in earnest, summer held sway that day. Daniel and John lingered at the table and enjoyed a brief idyll before forcing themselves to return to the hard work that awaited them.

Not every day was quite so idyllic that summer, but Helen's visit enlivened the evenings and provided Nellie with an able assistant. As always, the work continued through the long days. By early July, everyone on the ranch was looking forward to a break, which would take the form of a grand celebration that Fort Benton was planning for Independence Day. The July Fourth holiday was always a big event in Fort Benton, but this year would be special.

In addition to the usual festivities, a group in town had commissioned a steamboat for a river excursion, complete with an orchestra, dancing, and all the trappings of a grand ball. Although Helen was usually discreet about it, Nellie knew that her sister was interested in meeting a man, which was difficult to do in the remote community where she lived and taught school most of the year.

As the holiday approached, the excitement in the

house became overt as Nellie and Helen planned how they were going to dress for the dance and increase Helen's chances of meeting an eligible bachelor or two. Daniel didn't know it at first, but he was part of the plan as well. His role became more apparent one evening when Nellie announced over dinner that it was time for Daniel to practice his dance steps.

"Helen needs an escort at the dance, Daniel," she said. "Lacking any other suitable candidates, you and I will need to be her escorts and join in on the dancing."

Daniel agreed that Helen needed to be accompanied, but he didn't see why that meant he had to dance. "Why can't we just be there and watch?" Daniel offered.

Nellie's ready response quickly conveyed to Daniel that such a line of argument wouldn't get him anywhere. "Daniel, you know I like to dance, and I'd like to dance with you. Wouldn't you rather be the one dancing with me?"

Daniel took Nellie's point and the mild threat it implied. If Nellie was to dance with anyone in his presence, he quickly realized, he wanted to be that person.

"All right, Nellie, let's give it a try," Daniel conceded. "But in my case, you know it's not just practice that's needed. We'll be starting from scratch."

Daniel's lessons began that evening. He was a good sport and knew it was the right thing to do, not only for Nellie's sake but also for Helen's. For Daniel had become close with Helen over the past years and would do just about anything for her—even if it meant he had to dance.

Nellie began the lesson by beckoning Daniel to come close and clasping his hand before working him across the floor. She counted off the steps of a waltz aloud as Daniel dutifully followed her lead through their little parlor. Helen played piano, looked on in amusement, and occasionally applauded when Daniel managed a dance step with a little grace—or at least avoided bumping into Nellie when he moved in the wrong direction.

After a few evenings of practice, Daniel's dancing had become passable, but it would never be a favorite activity. "I'm doing this for Nellie and Helen," Daniel said to himself repeatedly. But it wasn't all work, for the dancing lessons were brief and soon were followed by other musical activities and card games. In time, Daniel came to remember these evenings as a special time in their lives.

The day of the big celebration finally came. It dawned clear with a big ball of sun breaking the horizon, a portent of the heat that would build slowly through the day. The group left early—everyone except for John, who had his own plans that day. He and Jenny saw each other regularly, when John's work at the ranch allowed, and they had made plans to meet later in the day.

As Daniel and the group got closer to town, other groups joined them on the road and the normally quiet route into town became a procession of neighbors, many of whom greeted each other happily. The celebration had begun well before they reached town.

That day Fort Benton drew people in from far and wide, and the town was crowded by late morning when the parade was scheduled to begin. Among other things, the parade featured a twenty-piece marching band and a tableau in the form of a pyramid topped by a young woman wearing a white dress and posing as the Goddess of Liberty. The platform on which she stood was pulled by a team of four horses, their harnesses adorned with bright ribbons that reflected the patriotic theme of the day. The procession slowly worked its way through town before reaching its destination: a stage set up outside the new courthouse.

After the parade participants settled in to their places, the first of several speeches began. In those days, no Independence Day holiday was complete without some oratory on the importance of the day in American history. A few local dignitaries got the program started with brief speeches, followed by a reading of excerpts from the Declaration of Independence. The crowd sat through it all quietly and showed little enthusiasm until a town official announced the day's contests, including a horse race, shooting events, and a variety of other activities. Though not an official attraction listed on the program that day, the town's saloons did a brisk business, as men came off the streets to gather for a cold beer and a little shade. Daniel was among them; he paused at the Antlers to rest while Nellie and Helen browsed through the displays of sewing and other domestic skills that lined a portion of Front Street.

Perhaps because of all the excitement in town that day, time passed quickly. At six p.m., a band positioned on the upper deck of the excursion steamboat struck up a lively tune, signaling that it was time to board for the river cruise. Daniel and the Sage sisters made their way to the levee and found themselves in a procession of people heading that way, a well-behaved crowd of several hundred people, most of whom had dressed up for the occasion, thus masking the differences among them. Bankers, cattlemen, and store clerks all appeared the same that evening. So did the women, most of whom wore flowing skirts and loose blouses, an outfit that typically included a hat adorned with feathers or silk flowers.

Nellie held Daniel's arm as they walked toward the boat. Meanwhile, Helen scanned the crowd, keeping an eye for single men and silently assessed their potential as suitable dance partners for later that evening. Just before they boarded, two lines of passengers merged by the gangway, and a group of officers from Fort Maginnis came into view.

The uniformed men doffed their caps and nodded a greeting in Helen's direction. Helen acknowledged their greeting with a friendly smile but held her enthusiasm until the men had passed, as a young woman was expected to remain reserved in such a situation. Privately, she conveyed her excitement to Nellie with a series of small gestures that the two sisters had perfected during their childhood.

Once all were aboard, the Josephine shoved off and headed for the center of the channel. The river breezes offered relief from the heat that lingered in town, and most passengers were content, at first, to laze along the rails and enjoy the views across the water. Helen left Daniel and Nellie to themselves and strolled the deck.

Neither Daniel nor Nellie had been aboard a steamboat since their trip upriver on the *Red Cloud*. They experienced a flood of memories, which they kept to themselves for a few minutes until Nellie broke the silence.

"I first saw you, Daniel, looking down like this on a steamboat. You were with a little group of men that usually assembled around you."

Daniel smiled before replying. "Yes, and I was looking up at you, admiring you from the distance as if you were a queen up on her throne." He smiled mischievously. "I didn't know then…I didn't know that would be how things were always going to be between us."

Nellie feigned to be shocked, before laughing loudly and thumping Daniel on his shoulder. Then she grew more serious. "That day on the *Red Cloud*, I knew I had seen the man I wanted to be with. I don't know how I knew it, and it seemed almost ridiculous at the time, but I was right."

There was nothing more to say, so they just embraced in silence and watched the river swirling around the hull for a few joyful moments.

Helen returned to find them in that pose and kept her distance until Nellie looked up and nodded to her. The band had started playing again, and it was time to go below to the cabin and join in on the dancing.

The cabin had been cleared of the tables and chairs that usually filled the space, allowing an orchestra to set up in the forward area while leaving plenty of room for the dancers. Nellie had promised Helen that she wouldn't leave her until Helen had a dance partner. This suited Daniel. His relief was short-lived, though, for one of the military men approached quickly and asked Helen to dance. The officer's language and manner were formal, and he looked toward Daniel and Nellie as if seeking their permission. Daniel introduced himself, as well as Nellie and Helen, and let it be known that it was Helen's decision. Nellie paused to watch Helen and her dance partner for a while before nudging Daniel out onto the dance floor.

"Just relax, Daniel, and hold on to me," Nellie whispered. "You don't have to prove anything to me anymore."

The tension Daniel felt about dancing in public vanished with Nellie's assurance and steady but subtle guidance. They danced for several songs until the orchestra began something unfamiliar, a song that required a dance beyond Daniel's limited abilities. But he had done his duty and earned himself a spot near the door, where the river air was fresh and he and Nellie could happily watch Helen dance with a succession of partners.

Before it got too dark, the boat turned back toward Fort Benton and docked along the levee. The final activity of the day would begin shortly, but Daniel was too tired to stay. On the way back to the ranch, Helen enter-

tained them with a description of each of her dance partners. She had enjoyed one of them in particular, an officer from Fort Maginnis who had asked her for permission to write, a request she had happily granted. As the
buckboard slowly climbed the slope from the river, a py-
rotechnic display, advertised as the best in Montana Territory, lit up the sky.

# CHAPTER 34

On a late summer afternoon of that year, Nate appeared at the Raven Ranch. Nellie greeted him and invited him inside for a cool drink.

"Thank you," Nate said while still mounted. "That's a kind offer. But there's something I need to talk with Daniel about. Can you point me in his direction?"

Nellie, noticing that Nate was a bit anxious about something, shook her head slightly. "I don't know exactly where he'll be now," she said. "He left early and said he was going to check some fences and then work with John in the hay fields. I'd start looking for him down by our east fence line."

Nate found Daniel in a hay field with a shovel in his hand and mud covering his boots. "That mud is going to get the best of you," Nate yelled as he approached. "Are you going to turn into a damned farmer on me?"

"Maybe so," Daniel replied. "I may have to concede that I'm better suited for this end of ranching than for cowboying like you."

Nate wasn't himself that day. He continued to speak to Daniel in a harsh tone. "My daddy always said there were two kinds of people in this world: those who work with animals and those who work like an animal. I know which kind I want to be."

Daniel was taken aback by his friend's rancor. "What's wrong, Nate? Did something happen?"

Nate didn't answer immediately. He shook his head slowly and then launched into a tirade about a theft he had suffered the previous night. "I don't know who did it yet," he said, "but I'll find those sons of bitches."

"Now hold on, Nate," Daniel said. "What are you talking about? What happened?"

Nate calmed down a little but still wasn't himself. "They took some of my horses. I went out this morning, and they were gone."

Daniel asked Nate to tell the whole story, but Nate didn't have much more information to share. He said he saw a trail leading down to the river, but that was it.

"Let's go have a look," Daniel offered. "I'm no tracker, but maybe there's something else they left behind." He said this with the hope that his accompanying Nate back to his ranch would offer some distraction for his friend. From Nate's description, Daniel held little hope that they'd find anything, and his suspicion was confirmed when they searched the area around Nate's corrals. Whoever did this, Daniel thought, knew what they were doing. As Nate had said, the trail led straight to the river, and even though they rode upstream and then down for a considerable distance, their efforts revealed no clues to where the thieves had headed.

Daniel and Nate ended the day with a ride into town, where they reported the theft. The sheriff took down the information but offered little hope of finding the stolen animals. "I'm afraid there's a lot of possibilities here," the sheriff said. "We've had bands of Indians coming down from the Blackfoot country and even some Crow on their way north to steal horses from the Blackfoot.

There's plenty of white men at it too. But if I hear of anything about your horses, I'll let you know."

In the days and months after the robbery, Nate developed some peculiar habits. At first he brooded over the loss of his horses, but eventually his brooding turned into an obsession. He often set off alone on long rides into the open range, rationalizing his actions as an effort to survey new grazing lands. The fact that he was heavily armed, however, revealed his true purpose. He was searching for the horse thieves. Sometimes he'd sit idly on high spots while surveying the surrounding country. Other times he rode far to the east toward the breaks.

Nate never found any of the outlaws, but he paid a price for his obsession. He neglected his work on improving the ranch, particularly the small hay meadow he had started. The price he would pay wasn't immediately evident, but it would come due that winter.

Meanwhile, despite the harsh conditions that summer, Daniel remained optimistic about expanding the Raven Ranch, for his partnership with John Campbell had yielded an abundant hay crop that year and had convinced Daniel of the merits of a different approach to ranching.

One day, as Daniel and John were working together, John shared some news and made a request. "Daniel," he said earnestly, "Jenny and I have decided to be married, and I'd like you to be my best man."

Daniel was elated at the news and quickly agreed. He had thought the courtship was going well but was still somewhat surprised that John was finally putting aside any lingering determination to remain a bachelor. After clutching John in a bear hug, Daniel enthusiastically congratulated his friend. "Who would have thought that day when we limped over to Jenny's ranch that it would turn out like this? That was one of the worst days in my life.

But I'd do it all again if I knew the happiness it would bring to you and that fine woman you met."

John and Jenny were married in town later that year. After a short honeymoon in Helena, they moved out to John's little house on the ranch.

# CHAPTER 35

November brought an abrupt end to the fall that year. It turned cold early in the month, and a succession of cloudy days followed. The dry summer had left the range in poor condition, forcing Daniel to dip into his hay supply earlier than planned. After distributing hay one day, Daniel paused to survey his ranch from a low ridge. He took pleasure in the extent of the hay fields and the size of the herd that spread out before him. The wind had picked up, bringing a penetrating chill, and Daniel noted that the sky to the north was a leaden gray.

As he took in the scene, he was distracted by a flash of white that sprung from a tall cottonwood tree off in the distance. Although small in the vastness of the landscape, the whiteness of the movement stood out against the muted browns and grays that dominated the land. Daniel looked more closely and moved toward where he thought the object might be. Finally he found it perched in a tree. The snowy owl sat silently and stared at Daniel with its striking yellow eyes. This bird was not a common sight in Montana, even in territorial times, and some people interpreted its appearance as a harbinger of a severe winter.

Others, including some of the tribes, thought the white owl was an even worse omen: it always meant that something dire would occur, perhaps not immediately but with the inevitability of a god's wish. Daniel didn't consciously think of these things as he admired the impressive bird perched before him, but the image stayed in his mind, and he felt a hint of uncertainty as to what the sighting really meant.

By nighttime, a light snow had begun to fall. John and Jenny Campbell had joined the McHargs for dinner that night.

"This looks like the kind of winter we've been waiting for," John observed as he passed along a plate of potatoes.

"I wouldn't put it that way," Daniel replied. "I'm hoping for another mild winter." He then brought up his sighting of the white owl that afternoon. "I don't put much stock in superstitions like that, but a lot of people do, and they think it means we're in for a hard winter."

John agreed that the signs were pointing that way. "If it comes to that," he said, "I think we'll be ready."

The snow continued through the night, and nearly a foot had accumulated by morning. When it abated, it left behind a small measure of hope that the worst was over, for the storm had cleared out the gray skies that had persisted for weeks and brought color back to the landscape. The next day dawned with blue skies and bright sunshine. Though it cheered Daniel and John to see the sun again, they also had to confront the reality that there was a lot of snow on the ground. They were forced to continue spreading hay for the livestock, a task that would become nearly continuous that long winter. Another reality emerged that day, though neither man spoke of it yet: their hay supply wouldn't last forever. They had far more hay in storage than ever before, but how could they know how much they'd need? Both men made a silent assessment of the supply that day, and both began to worry. It was a concern they'd have to live with for several more months.

The interlude of sunshine didn't persist. It was soon replaced by a continuation of the gray and cold that had preceded it, followed by a series of smaller snowfalls that kept the ground covered. After one of the storms, Nate appeared at the ranch. "We might be headed for trouble," he began. "My animals didn't fatten up much this year, and I've heard reports from others that the range cattle aren't doing well. I'm sure hoping the winter doesn't keep up like this."

Daniel was also worried, though less so than Nate, and he knew that most of the other nearby ranchers felt anxious too. Daniel feared the worst for his neighbors, though he didn't express that sentiment to Nate. Instead, he told Nate that Montana winters were hard to predict. "You know how things can turn around in a heartbeat, Nate. We just need to hang in there for a while."

Despite Daniel's assurances, the winter would prove to be eventful in ways no one could anticipate.

The early November snows were followed by more in December—but these were mild compared to the blizzard that struck in January. Over several days, the driving snow piled up in drifts that blurred the contours of the land. From some views, the ranch looked like it did before Daniel got there—it appeared as if all of Daniel's hard work had been erased by the deep snows that covered up whole sections of his fence and masked the hay fields with wavy drifts of white.

That winter Daniel had his hands full. He and John spent much of their time spreading hay for the cattle. They switched out their heavy wagon for a sled John had crafted from a broken wagon and timbers left over from various projects. It was still difficult to break through the deep snow, but they persisted. The hay supply began to grow thin, and their worries increased. So far, though, the herd was holding up and their losses were acceptable, limited to the usual deaths from sickness and an occasional broken leg or other accident that forced Daniel to put the animal down.

Finally, Daniel and John were relieved at the arrival of a long-awaited chinook—a surge of mild air that broke the stubborn cold that had settled on the land. The warmth it provided melted some of the snow but didn't clear it all. The chinook proved to be not only short-lived but also, ultimately, harmful. For the melting was followed by a severe cold spell that froze the remaining snow into an impenetrable crust that no amount of pawing by desperate livestock could break.

After another break in the weather later that winter, Nate appeared again and told Daniel that he was worried about his herd.

"This damned weather is going to be the end of us, Daniel. My herd is out there, and I don't know how they're faring in this frozen hell we've got to deal with."

Nate went on to explain that he had tried to go out alone earlier that winter and check on the herd, but his horse had broken through the hard crust with enough frequency to make its fetlocks bloody and sore. He thought that conditions might have improved enough to try again.

"I'd appreciate it if you would come with me," Nate pleaded. "I just can't bear to wait anymore, not knowing if they're all dead, or—"

Nate broke off the sentence and sucked in his breath in an attempt to avoid the embarrassment of revealing his desperation. He said he thought most of his herd was in the country up north, where he had last seen them before the harsh winter had set in. Daniel agreed to help, but silently wondered what they could do even if they found Nate's herd alive.

As if sensing Daniel's thoughts, Nate added a final thought. "I don't have enough hay put up to feed them for long," Nate admitted. "But if we could bring them back here, I might be able to save a few and maybe lead the others to a more protected area, where they'd stand a better chance of surviving."

Daniel listened in silence. He thought Nate's plan was a product of desperation, for Daniel knew that the range was almost uniformly frozen. He was worried about Nate. Mostly, though, Daniel began to worry about how he'd deal with the consequences of the fierce winter continuing. One of his fears was that Nate would become so desperate that he'd be forced to make a plea for some of the Raven Ranch's hay supply, a request that would be hard to respond to. Daniel and John's supply was dwindling. It might not be enough, Daniel thought, to feed his own herd through this blasted winter. Yet Daniel knew that it would be hard to watch Nate's animals starve before their eyes.

Despite these worries, Daniel agreed to accompany Nate on a search for his herd. "I'll come along, Nate," he promised. "If they're still out there, we'll find them."

Daniel's words provided Nate with little comfort.

Daniel and Nate set out the next day. The thin sun that hung in the sky brought little warmth, but the punishing winds had finally abated. They noted that a few small areas were clear of snow, but most of the ground was covered, and the snow had piled up deeply in the coulees and other depressions where the winds had dumped their frozen burden. Amid some of these drifts, lifeless cattle formed a mosaic of death and ice, their legs and horns sticking up through the snow in a gruesome but sculptural display.

Nature's artistry was lost on both men, but especially on Nate, who now realized that he had lost his herd. The carcasses that he and Daniel inspected that day had a variety of brands, including some with Nate's, but what alarmed them most was that nothing seemed to be alive. The range, which had supported large numbers of cattle just a few months earlier, had become a vast wasteland. The severity of Nate's losses had become apparent. He bore the heavy burden in silence as they began the ride back to the Teton.

Daniel tried to comfort Nate. "Some of them will turn up next spring," he said to his now obviously despondent friend. "You can recover from this. A year from now, well—"

Daniel didn't finish his thoughts, for his efforts to encourage Nate were interrupted by the sight of several buffalo, including a magnificent old bull. The buffalo were upwind and unaware of the approach of the two mounted men. Daniel and Nate stopped at a distance but were close enough to see the animals well as they foraged, swinging their heavy heads from side to side in an effort to break through the crust and reach the dried but still nutritious grass below. Their efforts caused them to breathe hard and produce a billowing vapor that lingered in the cold air. *It's an impressive sight*, Daniel thought, for the buffalo appeared healthy, in stark contrast to the deathly scene they had just observed.

This caused Daniel to remember a prophecy he had heard during his fearful encounter with the Blackfoot, a day that remained vivid in Daniel's memory. Looks Beyond had warned that the winter of many deaths would return and the carcasses of the white man's puny "buffalo" would be scattered across the prairie. Looks Beyond had seen this future, Daniel now realized, but most of the cattlemen had refused to see it until it was too late.

Nate had a different reaction to the sight of the buffalo. Their survival seemed to mock him and brought out his frustration with an intensity that bordered on rage. "I'm going to shoot them!" he yelled. "I always wanted to kill some buffalo, and this might be my last chance."

Daniel tried hard to stop him. "You know there's so few of them left. Leave this bunch alone," he pleaded. But his words had no effect on Nate's intentions.

"Goddamn you, Daniel," Nate cursed. "You think because you're sitting pretty now, you can tell me what to do? Well, you can go to hell!"

As Nate pulled his rifle from its scabbard, Daniel rode off. He cringed as shot after shot broke the profound silence that had surrounded them. After that day, things were never the same between Daniel and Nate.

# CHAPTER 36

William Sage, Nellie's father, had his own challenges that winter. The mine had experienced a series of mishaps, including a major cave-in, which resulted in extended periods of lost production. Though the men worked tirelessly to repair the damage, Mr. Sage was forced to take on more debt than he was comfortable with. Now some of his creditors were demanding payment.

After a particularly difficult meeting with one of his bankers—a meeting that produced satisfaction for neither party—Mr. Sage slowly trudged back up the hill to his house. Knowing that one of his favorite meals would be served that evening, he tried to put aside the nasty business of the day and focus on the comfort that awaited him. Nevertheless, he continued to fret about how to get out of the untenable financial situation he found himself facing.

Earlier that day, Mr. Sage had noted that his breathing had become more strained, but he had chalked it up to the unusual stress of his present situation. He had remained convinced that the fresh air and exercise of a walk home would do him good. So, despite experiencing a shortness of breath again that evening, he pushed ahead until he nearly reached his house. Pausing for a rest near the front stairs, he felt oddly detached from his surroundings and noted an unusual pain in his left arm. He also realized that he was sweating even though it was a cold day. As he loosened the buttons on his coat in the hope that the cold air would revive him, Mr. Sage blacked out, just as an ungodly pain emerged in his chest. Unable to control his movements or to call out for help, he crumpled to the ground. In his remaining moments of consciousness, as he lay on the sidewalk, he thought of his family.

Later that evening, the doctor presented a grim prognosis. Mr. Sage had been moved to his bed at home, where his distraught wife and the family doctor watched over him. The doctor examined Mr. Sage in silence, not allowing his expression to reveal his thoughts. After a few moments, he spoke.

"His heart is weak. I can barely detect a pulse. I'm sorry, Mrs. Sage. I don't think he'll recover."

# CHAPTER 37

Unaware of the events in Helena, Nellie took advantage of a rare break in the weather to ride into town. She awoke to a bright day and lingered for a while to see if the sun would warm up the heavy, cold air that blanketed the Teton Valley. After a few weeks of isolation, the prospect of visiting with others, shopping for supplies, and picking up the mail cheered her. Nellie saved the post office for last because she knew the letters likely awaiting her would distract her from her other chores. Furthermore, reading the mail on the ride home was a treat, something to break the monotony of the slow ride home along a route that she and the horses knew by heart.

It had been several weeks since Nellie had been to the post office, so a pile of mail greeted her that day. She commented to the clerk, "Oh, my, by the looks of this stack you'd think I'd been gone for a year!"

"I haven't seen most of the ranch families much this winter," the clerk replied. "When I do see them, they seem worried. How are you and Daniel holding up?"

Nellie wanted to get home before the light faded, so her response was polite but intended to discourage more conversation. "As long as our hay supplies hold up, we'll be fine," Nellie replied. "But no one seems to have much experience with a winter like this or a sense of how much hay is enough. So, we do worry."

With that, Nellie headed for the door while shuffling through the stack of mail. She noted with pleasure that among the stack was a letter from her mother, which she'd savor on the ride home.

Eager for the family news that her mother's letters usually contained, Nellie opened the letter as soon as she was outside of town. The greeting was familiar: "*My dearest Nellie.*" But instead of offering cheery news, it began grimly:

*I'm so sorry to have to tell you this. Your father has died.*

Nellie clutched the letter tightly, removing it from her sight, hoping a second reading might change the reality she had just been presented. Then, with a shudder, she turned her gaze back to the letter.

*He had an attack walking up the hill to our home and died less than a day later. I'm sorry there was no time for you to see him again, for he called for you repeatedly in his delirium.*

The news now sank in and struck Nellie like a heavy blow. She pulled the team to a halt, sat by the side of the road, and cried, her body convulsing from the strain of her emotions. Despite the difficulties she and her father had experienced, Nellie immediately felt a deep sense of loss. The loss of a parent, even when in adulthood, was something that changed a person's view of the world, often bringing a different sense of one's own mortality and leaving a void that couldn't be replaced. Nellie struggled with these feelings for what seemed like a long while. She was a lone figure amid a stark landscape that seemed to draw out the raw emotions that followed the news of her father's death. After she allowed herself some time to feel her grief and to embrace the pain, Nellie's thoughts turned to her mother. She needed to be with her mother now, she realized, and she immediately began planning her travel to Helena.

After sharing the news with Daniel, who comforted her as best he could, Nellie began packing. It was to be a long and frigid journey.

# CHAPTER 38

On the day of Mr. Sage's burial, a long procession left the church and wound its way through the streets of Helena. Whether motivated by respect for Mr. Sage or just wanting to be among the other luminaries, many of Helena's leading citizens turned out for the event. Mrs. Sage and her daughters, each dressed in black from head to toe, rode together in a carriage. When the service was over, the women returned home. Finally done with the tedious planning for the funeral and the frequent interruptions of well-wishers, the family could now turn to planning for the future.

Although Mrs. Sage appeared strong throughout the ordeal of losing her husband so abruptly, her daughters still worried about her living alone, or at least without any family nearby. Nellie quickly proposed that her mother come to live with her and Daniel on the ranch, an offer that Mrs. Sage politely rejected as impractical given the smallness of their house and the remoteness of the ranch.

"Besides," Mrs. Sage said, "I'd be underfoot, and I don't want to interfere with your lovely marriage."

While Nellie's offer was being discussed, Helen re-mained quiet and looked pensive and almost worried. She hesitated before offering her own proposal. "Mother," Helen finally announced, "I'll return to Helena and live here with you. My teaching contract expires at the end of the year, and I'm ready for a change. I want to be here with you."

Nellie and Mrs. Sage agreed that it was a sensible proposal that would have the desired effect of filling the sudden void in Mrs. Sage's life. But neither Nellie nor Mrs. Sage knew then that Helen was involved with a se-rious romance that had begun the prior summer, when Helen had danced with several young men from Fort Maginnis. One of them, an intense but sensible captain from southern Maine, had followed up on his request to correspond with Helen. They had kept this up for several months and had even met discreetly on two subsequent occasions. It was enough to convince the young man that Helen should be his bride. In a letter, he promised to pro-pose the next time they were together.

Helen was flattered but unsure how to respond to her suitor, for she knew that the young officer was planning to return to Maine the following month. His tour of duty was up, and he was determined to return to the family farm and his extended family. Helen hesitated to accept. She dreaded the thought of leaving her family behind in Montana for a place so very far away. Yet she was in-trigued by a new lifestyle and sure that her love for the man would grow with time. When news of her father's death arrived, Helen had just received the officer's in-formal proposal and was still wrestling with the conflict it presented. She had felt it improper to bring the matter up at a time when the family was preparing to bury her fa-ther.

Because Helen had kept the details of the officer's

marriage proposal from her family, her offer to move back to Helena didn't seem to be a great sacrifice. Still, Nellie probed: "And what about that young man you met last summer? What will become of that?"

"We'll continue to write," Helen assured Nellie, "and there's really no hurry. We're both still young, and there will be plenty of time for things to develop."

Thus assured, Nellie and Mrs. Sage were delighted with Helen's offer. But Helen's decision had long-lasting and unforeseen consequences. Her relationship with the officer didn't end abruptly, there were several more letters exchanged, yet it wasn't enough to overcome the inevitability of the relationship's fading away from the corrosive forces of time and distance. Helen would remain unmarried and live with her mother until Mrs. Sage died many years later.

# CHAPTER 39

The hard winter of 1886-1887 took its toll on Daniel. He began having trouble sleeping. He would often wake up in the slack hours well before dawn and lie awkwardly still to avoid awaking Nellie with his movements. During a particularly long and sleepless night, Daniel was unable to put aside his fears of recurring blizzards and the images of starving cattle that repeatedly surged through his mind. In this worried state, he thought he heard a sound coming from outside. The sound was muted by the rustle of the wind as it moved through the tangle of cottonwood branches that sheltered the house. His efforts to make out the sound only made it harder to return to sleep. Time seemed to pass more slowly in the nether night, but after a while, the wind subsided and the source of the sound became alarmingly clear. Daniel's body tensed at the realization that several wolves were somewhere in the distance and likely not far from the ranch. Now faced with a potential threat to his livelihood and no chance of returning to sleep, Daniel rose quickly and stood still in the darkness as he strained to see if Nellie was awake. She turned under his gaze, mumbled something unintelligible, and returned to sleep as Daniel said softly that he'd be back shortly.

Daniel emerged from the house into a night full of darkness and quickly saddled his horse, intending to probe his pastures for any sign of the wolves and the devastation they sometimes left in their wake. His lantern provided a faint light but illuminated his frozen breath, which drifted slowly before vanishing into the dry, frigid air. He rode methodically along the river, following an irregular path that led to places where he knew his cattle tended to bed down. A survey of the pasture closest to the house revealed nothing amiss. He was relieved to see most of the herd bedded down or standing quietly in small clusters. The same was true of the middle pasture. As he approached the far pasture, however, Daniel could see immediately that something was wrong. The cattle were all standing, and they exhibited their anxiety with jerky movements and a few shrill cries. As he rode among his livestock, the source of their displeasure soon became clear: three carcasses lay at the far end of the pasture, each surrounded by an unmistakable pattern of wolf tracks etched in the snow.

Daniel followed the tracks for a while before concluding that there wasn't much he could do that night. He was all stirred up as he returned to the house, his thoughts focused on crafting a plan to prevent any further depredation. Determined to hasten into town, Daniel left his horse saddled. It was barely dawn but Nellie had risen and offered him coffee as he entered the house. "Here, Daniel, this will warm you up. What did you find?"

"They've been here all right. I counted three dead and there will be more to come if we don't do something. This wasn't the work of a lone wolf. There were tracks all over."

Nellie rubbed the sleep from her eyes and nodded in

agreement. "But there's nothing to be done now. Daniel, you need to get some rest."

Daniel was weary but determined to get ahead of the problem. "I'm going to town to buy some traps. I've only got a couple on hand and we need more than that. I need to get those traps set out as soon as possible."

Nellie wanted to talk through the situation more and was concerned that Daniel was pushing himself too hard. "If you won't go to bed, you need to at least sit here by the fire for a few minutes and warm yourself up."

Daniel left after only a brief rest. By the time he reached Fort Benton, he deeply felt the toll a frigid day can take on a man's energy. His lack of sleep didn't help matters. Still determined to buy some steel traps and set them out before darkness settled in again, he headed straight for the mercantile. The store was quiet that day and apparently empty, except for a man Daniel didn't notice as he first entered the store. The man sat quietly in the corner of the room. Partially obscured in the dim light of the winter day, he idly basked in the warmth of an ornate potbellied stove. The warmth drew Daniel in as well; it was an almost involuntary response to the cold that had settled somewhere deep in his body. Daniel didn't recognize the man and took little notice of him as they both focused on the stove and enjoyed the alluring heat. The man offered a muted greeting, which Daniel acknowledged with a slight nod.

A clerk soon emerged from a back room and greeted Daniel with a friendly hello. "What brings you to town, Daniel? Getting a little stir-crazy out there on the ranch?"

"No, I got plenty to do, all right," Daniel replied. "More than I care for. I'm here because some damned wolves have taken an interest in my cattle."

After commiserating with Daniel, the clerk asked, "What can I do for you, Daniel? I've got some traps in the back room that will stop a wolf in his tracks."

"I reckon I need some," Daniel replied. "A dozen or so ought to do the job."

The clerk disappeared into the back of the store. While the clerk was gone, the man sitting by the stove stirred.

"Don't waste your time with traps," he said softly, looking past Daniel to the street.

Daniel expected the man to continue, but he remained silent, forcing Daniel to probe further. He now took a good look at the man, who was rough looking, wore a scraggly beard, and didn't seem comfortable looking someone in the eyes. Instead, the man seemed to be looking far beyond the person he was talking to. Yet he had a manner that reminded Daniel of someone else. Putting aside an urge to place the stranger, Daniel responded. "Very well, my friend. If traps are no use, what would you have me do?

The man remained taciturn. "Put out some poison."

Daniel felt his annoyance rising. He was tired and still upset about the loss of his livestock. "Mister, talking to you is not an easy task. Do you ever speak with more than a single sentence?"

The man made a strange sound. It struck Daniel as an effort to clear his throat, but his countenance suggested that the sound may have been a form of laughter. The man responded more fully this time. "I know a little about wolves. I spent most of the past ten years earning a living by killing them. I figure I've killed as many wolves as any man in Montana."

Daniel now placed him. He didn't know the man, but he knew the type. Men of his ilk were known as wolfers, and though they performed a service many of the cattlemen believed necessary, they weren't much admired. Most wolfers were former buffalo hunters, and they tended to be outcasts, men with blood on their hands who didn't give a damn what others thought of them.

"I've heard what happens when you wolfers put out poison," Daniel said. "It kills more than just the wolves."

"You've got that right, friend," the wolfer replied. "I've seen it too. You put out an antelope or a deer carcass laced with strychnine and it'll kill just about anything that walks, crawls, or flies nearby. But it works, and isn't that all you cowmen give a damn about?"

Daniel thought about this for a moment before replying. "That may be right. But there's more to it."

Just then, the clerk returned with a wooden box full of traps, one so large that he had to drag it across the floor, which produced a scraping sound that preceded him into the showroom. Despite the noise, the clerk had heard the wolfer's comments.

Determined to make a sale, he interjected. "Daniel's right. There's a lot more to it. Especially when you've got a wife like Nellie. I know Nellie, and I know she wouldn't be part of that kind of slaughter. Take these traps, Daniel. It's the best thing you can do."

The wolfer thought further before responding. "It's not a pretty thing. I understand that. But if you don't know what you're doing with a trap, you'll fail. Those wolves are too smart. They won't come near your traps, and they'll keep killing your cows. Killing is what they do, and with all the buffalo gone they're going to kill beef."

Daniel found himself wondering how to deal with the man who now stood before him, someone who obviously knew much about killing wolves. Yet Daniel was reluctant to ask him for advice, partly because he feared the wolfer would pressure Daniel to let him help with the wolf problem. Daniel did need help, but he didn't trust the wolfer and didn't want to bring such a man anywhere near Nellie. After a brief pause, Daniel overcame his hesitation to engage the man further. "I don't want to spread poison around my own ranch," Daniel said with obvious determination. "You say traps are no good. What's left?"

Daniel was relieved by the man's response. "Can you shoot straight?" asked the wolfer. Without waiting for a response, he told Daniel to stake out the pasture where the wolves had last struck and wait for them on a high spot. "Near dawn is the best time. Keep upwind from where you think they'll come in and rub some dirt or cow shit on your face and clothes. What you use is your choice, but if they pick up a man's scent, they won't come near."

*Fine option that is*, Daniel thought. But he had to do something. The wolfer overcame Daniel's remaining doubts by handing him a piece of wood he pulled from his pocket.

"Here, take this," the wolfer said. "Practice with it for a while before you go out. When you can make a fair approximation of a wolf howl, it's time to try. This should bring them in."

Daniel was taken aback by the man's unexpected generosity. He thanked the wolfer and accepted the gift.

As Daniel headed for the door, the wolfer gave him one more bit of advice. "Go for the lead wolf," he said. "If you kill him, the others will scatter and take their time about coming back again."

After Daniel left, the clerk told the wolfer to get out. The wolfer had known he'd get the boot after spoiling a sale, and the clerk's words didn't faze him. "I'll be back," he said to the clerk as he headed toward the door. "You'll get bored soon enough and realize that an occasional thing like that is a small price to pay for the entertainment I offer."

The clerk wasn't in the mood to agree, but he did enjoy the wolfer's stories, which a little coaxing always brought out. "Get out," he said again, this time less forcefully. The wolfer left, knowing that another cold day would likely find him by the stove that heated the mercantile showroom.

By the time Daniel made it back to the Teton, he was truly exhausted. Nellie insisted that he eat and went about preparing him a meal. While she cooked, Daniel gathered up some shells and explained his new plan of rising well before dawn and taking a position on the high ground facing the far pasture. Despite his weariness, Daniel couldn't resist an opportunity to tease Nellie. "Do you know how keen an ability wolves have to pick up a scent?" He recounted how the wolfer had told him to mask his scent with manure or something else earthy. "Will I still have a place in your bed when I get back?"

Nellie laughed. "I'll make sure there's a pan of clean water by the stove and a clean rag. Mr. McHarg, if I were you, I'd be sure to use them before getting in bed."

It was a short night, and Daniel had a hard time getting up after just a few hours' sleep. He had to force himself out of the warm covers to face the cold that awaited him. He quickly gathered his gear and rode toward the far pasture, practicing a wolf call along the way. The next hours brought something close to misery. It was frigid, and nothing was moving. The wolfer had told Daniel to keep as still as he could, and this made the cold even more unbearable, for the stiffness in his joints grew and spread into parts of his body that he didn't think could get stiff. Finally, not long after the sun had risen, Daniel gave up and decided to return home. He nearly fell as he struggled to make his stiff limbs carry him back to his horse.

For the next few nights, Daniel carried on the same routine, each time with the same results. Despite the difficulty of the effort, his determination only increased after John reported that two more cows had been lost to wolves. On the fifth night, Nellie attempted to convince Daniel to take a break. He was looking haggard and had been neglecting his other duties. John had picked up the slack and continued to spread hay alone each day. John wasn't complaining, for he knew Daniel was doing what had to be done. Yet Nellie noticed that both men were showing the strain.

"It's time for you to give it a rest, Daniel," Nellie insisted after he returned that morning. Empty-handed again, Daniel moved like an old man, with joints so stiff that he might topple over after a slight misstep.

Daniel promised he would rest soon, but not that night. "I think it's going to be a clear night, Nellie, and the moon is near full," he said. "I can't miss this opportunity."

As Daniel had hoped, he awoke before dawn to a bright sky illuminated by a nearly full moon. He took up his usual position and waited. He kept still except for the slight movement he made from time to time to sound the wolf call, a skill he had honed well, he thought, despite the lack of success so far. At last, he heard a response. First, it was a faint howling sound in the distance. Daniel called again and then waited. He remained completely still and strained his eyes to see any movement. The next howl was closer. Daniel's rifle, cocked and ready, was propped on a rock cairn that gave him a clear shot to the open ground just beyond the cottonwoods that lined the river.

One wolf appeared, followed by several more. The first wolf to emerge, no doubt the leader, was light colored—a distinct disadvantage to the animal in this situation, for Daniel could see him clearly. Daniel waited until he was sure he had a shot and then pulled the trigger. The

rifle shot produced a booming sound that seemed ampli-
fied by the frigid air. Several of the wolves retreated into
the trees, but not the light-colored one. He lay where he
fell. Daniel exulted briefly before gathering his horse and
riding down to the river bottom. When Daniel arrived, the
wolf was still there, but he was not alone. Another wolf
stood near, tenderly licking her mate's wound until Daniel approached too closely. She left before Daniel could
get off another shot.

Daniel dismounted near the downed animal and, eager to confirm his death, ran to his body. But the wolf
wasn't dead. Though he lay still on his stomach, his eyes
remained open, shining brightly in the moonlit night.
Daniel shouldered his rifle but hesitated to pull the trigger. He had expected to be enraged, but the sight of the
dying animal's mate and the intelligence he saw in its
eyes gave him pause. He watched for a few moments until the wolf's body made a slight movement and the life
faded from the intense eyes that seemed to have been observing Daniel until the final moment. Dragging the wolf
on a crudely fashioned travois, Daniel returned home.
Nellie expected him to be exuberant when she heard of
his success, but he only wanted to sleep.

# CHAPTER 40

The wolves stayed away for the remainder of the winter, but Daniel remained worried. The hay supply was all but gone by the end of February, and nearly all the livestock were painfully thin. Some relief arrived in mid-March when the air finally warmed up enough to soften the crust of ice that covered the range. Some of the herd still had the energy to scrape away the snow and graze on the dried grasses below. But this took effort, and many of the animals were too weak to sustain themselves in this manner. These animals stood around listlessly, their ribs protruding, a few pathetically bawling now and again in an expression of their anguish. It was painful to observe.

Even without much hay to distribute, Daniel and John continued their daily rounds. "It breaks my heart, John. I wouldn't have gone into this business if I thought we'd have to endure this."

John remained silent, his face a grim caricature of his normally gentle expression. After riding a little farther, he replied, "Well, it's out of our hands now. Only God can bring on a winter like this. We did our best."

"No, we didn't, and it's my fault we didn't. Last

spring you wanted to convert that area on the other side of the river into hay. I'm the one who said we should hold off."

"Let it go, Daniel. If things keep going like this, we'll need all the hay in Montana to keep our stock alive."

By mid-March, their daily rounds had become a grim deathwatch. With the hay supply exhausted, they were unable to do anything but drag away the new carcasses that appeared each day. A profound sense of helplessness set in. They began to think that the herd would be decimated unless the weather warmed dramatically.

When things seemed to be at their lowest, Daniel and Nellie talked at the kitchen table one morning, each of them holding their coffee mug with both hands, clinging to the warmth it brought. It was another frigid morning, a day Daniel dreaded to face head-on, knowing that the freezing temperatures had likely brought more death to their struggling herd. Nellie sensed his sadness acutely that morning. Though they talked often about the challenges they faced, Nellie felt she had allowed too much of the burden to fall on Daniel.

"I'd like to go with you this morning. I've not been out there with you enough."

"There isn't much we can do, Nellie. There's nothing to be gained by having you see the suffering too. John and I can take care of things."

"That's not fair to you. I know what's happening. I know the hay is gone, yet you go out there every day. You can't help them now. I'm as responsible for their suffering as you. Let me share that burden."

"I know you care as much as I do, Nellie. But you don't need to see what I see every day. The sight of a mother cow trying to protect her dead calf. When we drag them away, the mothers bawl, and I swear they feel guilty because they didn't have enough milk to give. These things stay with you."

Nellie insisted she go with him that morning. It was just as Daniel had described. She forced herself to keep her composure, knowing that he needed her strength that day. In one of the pastures where a newly dead cow lay, they dismounted and walked over to the carcass. As Daniel prepared to loop a rope around the body, Nellie saw his hands tremble.

"Even if we lose the herd, I know we can come back. We'll rebuild, Daniel."

"I don't know if I can do that." He shook his head before adding, "Anyway, we can talk about that later. For now, I'm going to focus on the present."

"No, you can't dwell in this misery. When the present is too much to bear, we need to think of the future. Hope lies in the future, and hope is what brought us together in the first place. We can't let that go."

Nellie feared Daniel had reached the limits of his endurance. She didn't know it at the time, but her words gave him the strength he needed to last another few days, which proved to be enough.

After a few false starts, spring finally arrived in earnest that April. The warmer weather made it easier for the remaining cattle to hold on, and in just a short time the new grass would emerge. There were only a few more deaths that winter. Nearly three-quarters of the herd had survived. The losses the ranch suffered that winter were considerable, but they were mild compared to the losses of many other ranches in the region. For some, the winter had resulted in a nearly total loss of their herd.

When the ground had dried enough, Daniel and John began working another area that they planned to convert to hay. It was hard work, but they shared in the satisfaction of improving the ranch and increasing their readiness for another winter. On occasion they paused to observe the migrating waterfowl soaring overhead and to bask in the sunshine that renewed their spirits and stirred new life in the meadows and marshes that surrounded them. Daniel couldn't resist looking toward the sun and bellowing, "Where the hell were you when we needed you?"

John laughed at Daniel's antics before joining in. Raising his arms in praise, he echoed Daniel's question to the sun and danced a jig. Then it was Daniel's turn to follow. The two men continued an energetic dance until they became breathless. Finally they slumped to the ground and simply laughed. Reveling in the softness and fragrance of the fresh grass that had begun to cover the land again, Daniel and John lay still for a moment. The land was renewing itself, and in its renewal Daniel and John were finally freed of a long winter's worth of struggle.

The terrible winter wouldn't leave gently, however. It had one final surprise to offer. The surprise appeared in late spring, when the air was unmistakably warm and the winds rolled over the landscape, seemingly determined to force out any remnants of a winter that had persisted past its time. Along with the warmth, the spring brought rising waters. The rivers swelled, overtopped their banks in low-lying areas, and swept across the landscape. Along the way, they picked up an assortment of debris, including tree trunks and the usual detritus of the spring surge. Daniel kept an eye on the river, for much of his land was in the floodplain and he needed to keep track of which areas would dry out first and move his livestock accordingly. For that purpose, one afternoon, Daniel and John ascended one of the higher bluffs near the house and surveyed the valley below. The river carried an unusual burden. John was the first to see it.

"Daniel, look through that gap in the trees!" he shouted over the wind. "There's something bobbing in the current, and I don't think it's just a bunch of logs."

Daniel studied the river more closely and was ready to tell John he was seeing things, when one of the dark masses in the river turned over and revealed itself more fully. It wasn't a log, he could now determine, for what he had first taken to be tree trunks with some broken branches still attached was something else entirely. The branches were horns. The river was carrying along dead cattle that spun around in the currents as the carcasses worked their way down river, where they would eventually reach the Missouri River.

Daniel and John watched in morbid fascination. "That kind of sums things up, don't it?" Daniel finally said. "Each one of those carcasses belonged to someone who's probably had dreams just like us. Now it's over."

After a few more minutes of watching the bizarre spectacle, the two men returned to their chores. But the images lingered in each man's memory.

In June of that year, Nate showed up at Raven Ranch. He drove up on a buckboard loaded with a few household possessions.

"Come on in the house," Nellie urged as Nate approached. "I've got a cherry pie I just made, and we can't eat it all."

"I can't stay," Nate replied. "I'm headed back to Texas."

The news was a shock for both Daniel and Nellie, who urged him to reconsider, or at least to come in and tell them more about what was going on.

Nate declined. "I appreciate your concern," he said. "I got word that my mother is sick and I need to see her again before she passes. And the fact is, I just don't have the heart to start over again anyway. Not in a place like this where another winter could wipe me out again."

After they said their good-byes, Nate started the wagon moving. Before going far, Nate turned to Daniel. "I'm sorry, Daniel. I'm sorry this didn't work out, and I'm sorry for the way I acted that day out there in the snow."

Daniel nodded, and he and Nellie stood to watch until Nate disappeared from sight. "He didn't have someone like you to get him through, Nellie. That might be the only difference between him and me."

It was a sad occasion, which prompted Nellie to ask Daniel to recite the last verse of the poem he had given her on her birthday a few years earlier. She always found the words reassuring:

> "'There were days when I thought I'd lost you,
>   Nights with a blackness of the deepest hue;
>   Still you were there with a love to renew.'"

# EPILOGUE

In the summer of 1929, John Campbell received a letter addressed to him at the Raven Ranch. The letter bore a postmark from Boston, Massachusetts, and the address was written in a script he judged to be that of a woman. Not knowing anyone from Boston, he was curious about the author and opened the letter immediately.

*My Dearest John:*

*I hope that you have done well this past year and that everything is going well on the ranch. I think of you often and miss the ranch and the life I led there so very much. I'm now living in Boston, where we moved a few months ago to be closer to some of Sarah's fellow performers. It is a joy to see one's daughter rise to the highest ranks of the musical world, performing in major venues before large crowds. Sarah is a star in every sense of the word and a source of great pride for her mother. The small contribution I made as her first music teacher is the capstone of my musical career, which was mostly characterized by futile attempts to train people who were tone-deaf!*

*I must admit it is overwhelming here at times. The streets are crowded and the air often oppressive. Some days I yearn for the quiet of the ranch and the views across a landscape that stretches to the far horizons. But most of all I miss Daniel.*

*John, I want you to know that I'm so pleased to know that Daniel's legacy is in your capable hands.*

*Please send my regards to our friends in Montana. Tell them I miss them all and hope one day to return.*

*With my warmest regards,*

*Nellie McHarg*

John was moved by Nellie's letter, which inspired him to visit Daniel's grave. Daniel was buried on a bluff overlooking the Teton River Valley. He died in 1928, at the age of seventy-five, with the satisfaction of having built a thriving ranch that prospered through the Big Die-Up and the other lean years that followed on an unpredictable but inevitable cycle. After Daniel's death, Nellie had lingered on the ranch for a while, but she eventually moved away. She'd said she wanted to be near her daughter, but the reality was that she couldn't bear to stay on the ranch any longer. There were too many reminders of Daniel at the Raven Ranch, and though she cherished his memory, it didn't feel right to be there without him.

Despite the fact that the ranch had grown and several full-time hands lived there, John still spent a lot of time alone. Jenny had passed away a few years earlier, and John was the last of the original partners. He was now in his seventies, and he often shared his thoughts with Daniel. Sometimes, when he had something especially important to share, he went to Daniel's grave. That day, he walked to the grave with Nellie's letter clutched in his hand and read it aloud to Daniel.

## Author's Notes

The winter of 1883-84 is sometimes referred to as the *Starvation Winter*. The annihilation of the buffalo herds and the government's ineffective relief efforts resulted in the deaths of hundreds of Blackfoot. It wasn't until January 1885 that Congress enacted a special appropriation that effectively ended the widespread starvation on the Blackfoot Reservation.

W.T. Hornaday, chief taxidermist at the National Zoo, led expeditions to eastern Montana in 1886 that killed and collected twenty-five buffalo. At the time, it was estimated that no more than three hundred buffalo remained on the Montana plains. Hornaday was concerned that the rapid disappearance of the buffalo would prevent his institution from acquiring quality specimens for display. Several of the buffalo he collected, including a magnificent bull, are now displayed in Fort Benton at the Museum of the Northern Great Plains.

The winter of 1886-1887 resulted in the deaths of hundreds of thousands of cattle. An exact number will never be known. Following that winter, sometimes called the Great Die-Up, Granville Stuart famously stated, "A business that had been fascinating to me before, suddenly became distasteful. I wanted no more of it. I never wanted to own again an animal that I could not feed and shelter." Some historians consider that winter to be the end of the open-range era. It was an event that led to many reforms in the cattle industry.

In 1887, the railroad arrived in Fort Benton and effectively ended the era of steamboat transportation, which had already begun a steep decline in 1883.

In 1888, the great Blackfoot Reservation was reduced to a small fraction of its original size. In return for ceding their land, the Blackfoot received $150,000 annually for ten years to "promote their civilization, comfort and improvement."

In 1890, the U.S. Census Bureau announced the end of the frontier, meaning there was no longer a discernible frontier line in the West, nor any large tracts of land yet unbroken by settlement.

This is a work of fiction. My interest in the time and place depicted in this book was inspired by events in the life of Mell Keith, my great-grandfather. Mell left New Brunswick, Canada, in 1879 and arrived in Fort Benton, Montana Territory, in 1881. Mell and several other Keiths from the same small area in New Brunswick settled in Montana in the 1880s. Some of them prospered there, while others, including Mell, never found their stride. Mell left Montana around 1890 and continued west to Spokane, where he lived for most of the remainder of his life. Unable to do physical work in his later years, he moved east to Boston, where he had a brother, sometime before 1920. He died there in 1929.

Although the story in these pages is fictional, Mell did own a ranch on the Teton River, spent some time in the mining camp at Maiden, and married a woman named Nellie Sage, who arrived in Montana with her mother and sister aboard the *Red Cloud*. Mell also had a deep interest in poetry.

Most of the newspaper quotes I have included are authentic. Only the announcement of Limestone's death is completely fictional. Two others, including the congratulatory piece on Daniel and Nellie's wedding, were slightly altered.

Tom Keith

*Mell Keith, probably a few years before he went west*

*The author with Mell's second wife, Josetta Patwell Keith*

# ACKNOWLEDGMENTS

I have several people to thank for their assistance with this book. Nikki Bruno Clapper edited most of the book and did the heavy lifting on early drafts. Caroline Kaiser reviewed a later draft and provided valuable suggestions for improvement. I'm grateful to both for their support and excellence in improving this novel.

The Montana Historical Society maintains a great library in Helena, where I conducted some early research for this book. The library has a collection of newspapers from the territorial era, including the *River Press* in Fort Benton and *Mineral Argus* in Maiden, that were the source for many of the quotes included in the book. In addition to tracing events in the life of my great grandfather, Mell Keith, I read numerous accounts of issues and attitudes of the time that informed this book.

Another important source of information was the Overholser Historical Research Center in Fort Benton. Here, with assistance from Ken Robison, I learned of the work of people such as Joel Overholser and John Lepley, whose books are a treasure trove of information on the early days of Fort Benton. Collectively, they helped me understand the importance of Fort Benton to the history of Montana and the West in general.

Finally, thanks to my wife Ann who tolerated my absences. Even though I was often just in the next room, she learned to tell when my mind was somewhere else, usually in Montana Territory. Her support was vital to completing this book.

# About the Author

Tom Keith has long had an interest in history and is the author of *A Few Days in August: A Story of Death and Survival in the Patwell Family during the Dakota Conflict of 1862*, an account of the tragic events in which several members of his family were participants. He has also published several essays, including one set in the Missouri River Breaks and the discovery of a rock inscription made by J. B. LaValle, which inspired the character of the same name in this book. *Beneath a Towering Sky* is his first work of fiction. Keith is a principal in a planning and design firm and lives in Fort Collins, Colorado.

CPSIA information can be obtained
at www.ICGtesting.com
Printed in the USA
LVHW080039090919
630372LV00005B/114/P

9 781644 371176